CAT SLOAN IS SWIRLING

JAMEY MOODY

Cat Sloan is Swirling

©2023 by Jamey Moody. All rights reserved

Edited: Kat Jackson

Cover: Cath Grace Designs Instagram: @cathgracedesigns

This is a work of fiction. Names, characters, places, and incidents are the product of the author's imagination or are used fictitiously. Any resemblance to an actual person, living or dead, business establishments, events, or locales is entirely coincidental. This book, or part thereof, may not be reproduced in any form without permission.

Visit my website or sign up for my mailing list here: www.jameymoodyauthor.com.

I'd love to hear from you! Email me at jameymoodyauthor@gmail.com.

As an independent author, reviews are greatly appreciated.

❦ Created with Vellum

CONTENTS

Also by Jamey Moody   v

Prologue   1
1. Three Months Later   7
Chapter 2   15
Chapter 3   23
Chapter 4   32
Chapter 5   41
Chapter 6   49
Chapter 7   57
Chapter 8   66
Chapter 9   74
Chapter 10   82
Chapter 11   91
Chapter 12   100
Chapter 13   108
Chapter 14   116
Chapter 15   125
Chapter 16   134
Chapter 17   142
Chapter 18   151
Chapter 19   159
Chapter 20   168
Chapter 21   177
Chapter 22   186
Chapter 23   196
Chapter 24   205
Chapter 25   213
Chapter 26   221
Chapter 27   229
Chapter 28   238
Chapter 29   247

Chapter 30	256
Chapter 31	265
Chapter 32	273
Chapter 33	281
Two Months Later	289
About the Author	295
Also by Jamey Moody	297
Chapter 1	299

ALSO BY JAMEY MOODY

Stand Alones

Live This Love

One Little Yes

Who I Believe

* What Now

The Your Way Series:

* Finding Home

*Finding Family

*Finding Forever

The Lovers Landing Series

*Where Secrets Are Safe

*No More Secrets

*And The Truth Is ...

*Instead Of Happy

The Second Chance Series

*The Woman at the Top of the Stairs

*The Woman Who Climbed A Mountain

*The Woman I Found In Me

Sloan Sisters' Romance Series

CeCe Sloan is Swooning

Cory Sloan is Swearing

Cat Sloan is Swirling

Christmas Novellas

*It Takes A Miracle

The Great Christmas Tree Mystery

With One Look

PROLOGUE

"What are we looking at?"

"It looks like a shopping center to me."

"Oh, it's not just any shopping center," Cory replied. "It's ours. You are gazing upon the Sloan Sisters' Shopping Extravaganza."

At forty-four years old, Corrine Sloan was the oldest sister. She had thick blond hair and clear blue eyes that saw a vision of what this property could be.

"What are you talking about? I think I would remember buying a shopping center," CeCe remarked.

Cecilia was the quintessential middle sister of the Sloan siblings. Her fiery red hair and crystal blue eyes matched her personality. She was a forty-two-year-old good time ready to happen and was usually responsible for the fun.

"We didn't buy it," Cat Sloan said. "Explain yourself, Cory."

The youngest and therefore the baby sister, Catarina was thirty-seven. Her rich dark chocolate hair set off her blue eyes that matched her big sisters'. She was the quiet, reserved one, but not to be overlooked.

"Do you remember when Dad's rich uncle died and gave us all that money?"

"Of course I remember," CeCe scoffed. "He took us out to dinner and told us not to get any ideas about spending it."

"Yeah, as far as I can remember that's the only time he spent any of it," Cat added.

"Well, Daddy set aside part of that money for us," Cory said. "He left explicit instructions for us to do something with it together. This shopping center includes three stores, one for each of us."

"Why are we just now finding out about this?" CeCe asked, giving her sister a measured look. "And why isn't Mom telling us about it?"

"You know since Dad died Mom gave over all the financial stuff to me," Cory said.

"Yeah, Dad's been gone a year, Cory. What took so long for us to find out about this?" CeCe demanded.

"Dad had this in an investment that didn't mature until now. Mom told me about it last month," Cory replied.

"Why didn't you tell us!" Cat exclaimed.

"Because I had to be sure there was plenty of money for Mom to live comfortably going forward," Cory said defensively.

"I thought Dad made sure of that with his life insurance," CeCe said.

Cory nodded. "He did, but there were other things we had to do to get the money. It was all documentation bullshit and as you've both told me numerous times, neither one of you cared to be bothered with that. Right?"

CeCe and Cat looked at each other and smirked. "So, tell us what happened," CeCe said with a dramatic sigh.

"Mom told me about the investment. I contacted the company and they gave us an option of monthly disbursements or a lump sum." Cory took an envelope out of her pocket and handed it to CeCe. "This is what Dad wanted."

CeCe opened the envelope and held it so Cat could read over her shoulder. Tears welled in both their eyes as they scanned the handwritten letter.

CeCe looked up at her sisters with fire in her eyes. "I don't know why he couldn't have enjoyed this money instead of saving it for us! He kept working at that damn factory, building planes, when he could've retired and spent time with Mom or us!"

Cat put her arm around her sister. "He loved building those airplanes. Can you imagine him sitting around? No, that wasn't who he was. The man was always building something. And did you ever hear Mom complain? Did any of us ever really want for anything growing up?"

CeCe sighed loudly. "We weren't poor, but we damn sure weren't well-off either!"

"This is what Dad wanted," Cory said, taking the letter from CeCe's hands. "Can you imagine how proud he would be if we owned our own stores, side by side? This is the place!"

"It's not even finished yet," CeCe observed.

"That's the beauty of it. CeCe, you have always wanted to open your own salon. You can customize this space and make it yours. How many chairs do you want?" Cory asked.

"Hmm." A smile grew on CeCe's face. "I can see three on each side as you walk in and then two or three stations in the back to do nails and facials."

"Okay, so CeCe gets her salon. What kind of store are you going to open, Cory?" Cat asked.

"There's not a liquor store within ten miles of this area. Look at the storefront at the end. That's about to become The Liquor Box," Cory said proudly.

"What!" Cat laughed.

"That's right," Cory replied with a laugh. "I'm a lesbian and that's what we do. We lick—"

"Stop!" CeCe and Cat yelled in unison.

"We know what you do. You've told us over and over," CeCe said.

"We get it. The Liquor Box," Cat added.

"I've already lined up my first big customer."

"Who?" CeCe asked.

"You know that sapphic resort at the lake where the Hollywood gays go?"

"Yeah, Krista Kyle owns it with Julia Lansing. I've done their hair and they've brought several of their clients in over the last couple of years," CeCe said.

"Didn't you go out there for a party last summer?" Cat asked.

CeCe wiggled her eyebrows. "I certainly did. Those Hollywood folks know how to have a good time."

Cory and Cat both chuckled.

"So CeCe opens a salon and you're opening a liquor store. What do you have in mind for me?" Cat asked.

"Well, little sister. I have an idea, but if you could open any store you wanted, what would it be?"

"Hmm," Cat murmured as she stared at the building.

"Oh, I know!" CeCe exclaimed. "It has to have something to do with books. You love to read!"

"That's what I was thinking." Cory nodded.

Cat glanced at her sisters with a sly smile on her face. "I'd love to open a bookstore, and in the back I'd have an exclusive toy store."

Cory and CeCe gazed at their little sister with confused looks on their faces.

"A private, clandestine adult toy store," Cat stated.

"Oh!" CeCe exclaimed as her eyes widened.

Laughter bubbled from Cory as she said, "Oh my God, Cat. That's perfect!"

The three sisters gazed at the building as ideas flowed through their heads.

"What do you think? Will you join The Liquor Box?" Cory asked.

"I can see it now," CeCe said, holding her arms out wide. "Salon 411. You'll not only get the perfect hairstyle, but you'll know everything that's going on in town."

"Oh, I like it," Cory said. She turned to Cat. "Your turn."

"Hmm, let's see. How about Your Next Great Read?"

"Yes!" CeCe exclaimed.

"Do you have a name for the room in the back?" Cory asked Cat.

"Yeah, I think I'll call it The Bottom Shelf." Cat grinned. "But let's not tell Mom about that part."

Cory chuckled. "You have to watch out for the quiet ones."

"So, little sister. Do we get a discount?" CeCe asked.

Cat laughed. "Do you think this is what Dad had in mind?"

"I can see it now!" Cory exclaimed. "Our clients can stop by and get a drink, a book, and get their hair done."

CeCe held out her hand. "I'm in."

"I'm in," Cat said, placing her hand on top of CeCe's.

"Watch out," Cory said, placing her hand on top. "Here come the Sloan Sisters!"

1

THREE MONTHS LATER

Cat Sloan quickly glanced at her watch and couldn't believe that just a few short hours ago she'd been with her sisters, toasting to the success of their new businesses as they opened the doors for the first time.

As she walked back through the opening between her store and CeCe's, she'd taken a moment to gaze around her brand new bookstore. Your Next Great Read filled her with pride and anxiety in equal measures. Cat had never owned her own business; neither had her sisters. But in a twist of fate—or was it a lucky break? Either way, she, Cory, and CeCe had the money to make this happen.

Cat chuckled as she remembered Cory telling all their friends and family that they were opening the Sloan Sisters' Shopping Extravaganza. In spite of the silly name, this wasn't your typical shopping center, though. It was more eclectic.

Cory opened The Liquor Box on one end of the building and Cat's bookstore was the anchor on the other end with CeCe's beauty salon nestled between them. While finishing the building, Cory had made sure there was a large opening between each store so people could browse all three locations without walking outside.

It proved to be a smart addition as people walked from store to store during their open house.

Cat overheard CeCe explaining to her clients that they could get their hair done while enjoying a good book or a drink. Several customers had stopped by the bookstore after buying their favorite bottles of wine from Cory and mentioned making an appointment at CeCe's salon.

So many thoughts swirled in and out of Cat's head as she waited on customers or straightened the shelves. She loved to read and after discovering sapphic fiction and romance, she wanted others to know about this genre. Cat loved these books because she often saw herself in the characters.

She may have been a quiet tax accountant by day, but when she escaped into the world of sapphic literature she became the ice queen having a secret affair with her assistant. Or the girl-next-door with a crush on her high school best friend. Sometimes she wondered what it would be like to be the domme or a submissive in some of the spicier books.

Cat walked along and let her fingers lazily roam across the titles in one particular section: second chance romance. An unintentional sigh escaped from deep inside her. *Fucking Hattie Tucker.*

"Are you all right?" Jessica asked from behind the register.

"Sure. Why wouldn't I be?" Cat replied, walking towards her.

"I know that sigh. You're thinking about Hattie, aren't you?" Jessica said.

Cat narrowed her eyes. "I knew it was a bad idea having you come work here."

Jessica smiled. "What's so bad about having one of your best friends working with you?"

"Because, evidently, you know my sighs. I'm not sure that's a good thing," Cat said with a soft smile.

"I only know your Hattie sighs. And that's because your sisters made it my job to make sure you don't waste another minute thinking about that good-for-nothing ex of yours," Jessica explained.

Cat furrowed her brow. "If they made that part of your job, are they paying you as well?"

Jessica chuckled. "What do you think?"

Cat nodded. "Just as I expected."

"Seriously, Cat. I know you can't help but think about her sometimes."

"If it were up to Cory she would erase the woman from my memory," Cat said.

Jessica laughed. "You've got that right."

"Now, CeCe is a little more reasonable. She simply wants her banned from the metroplex."

They both laughed.

"I wasn't really thinking of her in the way you might imagine. I was looking at second chance romances and thought there was no way that would ever happen to me."

"Really?" Jessica said, tilting her head. "You mean to tell me if Hattie walked in here right now and told you what a fool she'd been, you wouldn't reconsider?"

Before Cat could reply, a bell echoed through the store, indicating a customer had come in the front door.

Cat smiled. "I've got this." She winked at Jessica and walked towards the front of the store.

Cat put on her best smile and was silently grateful to this

customer who just helped her avoid answering a question she didn't even want to think about, much less believe would happen.

"Hi, welcome to Your Next Great Read. I would be happy to help you find a book or point you in the direction of your favorite genre," Cat said.

The woman who'd walked into the store returned Cat's smile and paused. "Are you the owner?"

Cat nodded. "Yes ma'am. I'm Cat Sloan." She held out her hand and the woman gently held it then released it. Cat could feel the warmth from this woman's hand and once again smiled at her.

"I've been watching this place during construction and couldn't wait for you to open. I'm Elena Burkett."

"It's nice to meet you, Elena. You must love books since you were waiting for us," Cat said.

"I do love to read and honestly it's too easy to download a book these days, but there's something about walking among the titles and seeing what draws you in," Elena said.

The smile on Cat's face grew. "That is exactly how I feel. You never know what you'll discover from simply browsing around the store."

"That's what I'd like to do, but I wanted to ask about a specific genre, if I may," Elena said.

"Please do. I'm here to guide you on this adventure or step away when you want to explore on your own."

Elena chuckled and raised an eyebrow. "Do you mean that or are you trying to sell me a book?"

"Oh, I mean it, but ..." Cat let her voice trail off as she grinned.

"I think you may love books as much as I do," Elena stated.

"I did quit my job to open a bookstore, so yes, I love

books. You'll find a wide variety of genres in the store, but I have a love of sapphic fiction and romance so there is an extensive inventory of those titles," Cat explained.

"Show me," Elena said as her eyes widened.

Cat grinned and guided Elena past the displays at the front of the store and into her favorite section.

"There are labels at the top of each shelf so you'll know what books those shelves hold. For example, this first section is romance. But it is further broken down into more specific tropes."

"Oh, I see," Elena said, scanning the shelves. "There's age gap and friends to lovers. Oh, and second chance. How about ice queens? The chillier the better."

Cat chuckled. "Oh, Elena. I have ice queens on top of ice queens." Cat showed her the section and then pointed out a few favorites.

"I'll let you look through the titles without me looking over your shoulder, but I wanted to point out the reading nook at the end of these shelves."

Elena gasped. "Isn't that cute!"

"Feel free to have a seat and read a little before you decide what to buy," Cat said. She looked into Elena's soft brown eyes and for a moment she felt like she'd made a new friend. Cat didn't make friends easily. She was quiet and stayed to herself. It took her a while to warm up to new people, so this was definitely an unusual feeling.

"Thank you, Cat. I have a feeling I'm going to be spending a lot of time here," Elena said.

"You're welcome to stay as long as you'd like," Cat said. She walked down to the reading nook and put a few magazines back into the rack. This was Cat's favorite part of the store. She wanted her customers to have a place to unwind, even if it was just for a few minutes.

She glanced over and noticed Elena had several books in her arms as she inched her way towards the reading nook. Cat's attention was drawn to the opening between her store and CeCe's.

"Hey, CeCe," Cat said as her sister came into the store with a client. They both were drinking a glass of champagne and Cat was reminded of their sisters' toast before their stores opened that morning. They had champagne and all kinds of complimentary snacks for the open house as well as sales and discounts in each store.

"Hi, sis. I'd like you to meet...probably my favorite client." CeCe smiled at Alexis. "This is Dr. Alexis Reed."

"Oh, CeCe," Alexis scoffed. "Hi, it's nice to meet you," she said, holding out her hand.

Cat took it and smiled.

"Listen, Doc, you've worked hard and earned your title. Everybody would be calling me doctor if I'd gone to school that long and accomplished the things you have. You're a big deal," CeCe said.

Alexis shook her head and smirked.

"This is Cat, my little sister," CeCe said, finishing the introduction.

"Hi, Alexis. It's nice to meet you," Cat said. "I've heard CeCe mention you."

"Uh oh. Am I one of her problem clients?" Alexis asked.

"Not at all. She's always happy after your appointments," Cat explained.

CeCe looked over at Alexis and shrugged. "What can I say, I'm glad I'm your stylist."

Alexis smiled at CeCe and sipped her champagne.

"I gave Alexis a tour of the salon, but I saved the best for last. Do you mind?" CeCe asked, nodding towards the back of the store.

Cat Sloan is Swirling

"It's all yours." Cat winked. "Mom has already been by so you don't have to worry about her seeing you come and go."

"Thanks for the warning. I haven't seen her yet," CeCe said as she and Alexis walked to the back of the store.

Each store had been customized for their specific businesses. At the back of Cat's store was a hallway with restrooms like her sisters' stores, but there was also a room that Cat had made into her clandestine den of sex toys called The Bottom Shelf. She had always wanted to have a secret room if she ever owned her own business and attributed it to her love of mysteries.

But her imagination didn't stop there. She wanted to make it fun and just a tad bit scandalous. Cat would never consider herself sexually ambitious or even overly curious, however, she had experimented with a vibrator and a dildo at one time or another. If you couldn't love yourself, how could anyone else?

Her sisters were surprised when she'd suggested the sex toy shop. Cat may be the quiet little sister, but that didn't mean she didn't have desires. She was a woman who was used to taking care of her own needs. As the little sister she was oftentimes forgotten when her older sisters were involved in all sorts of school activities. She'd learned to take care of herself and even though she could count on her sisters to always be in her corner, she knew she had to rely on herself first.

The Bottom Shelf was a way to take the embarrassment or bashfulness away from women who wanted discretion, but also wanted to explore themselves or open up to their partners. She didn't advertise her little shop in the back, but a few well placed yet discreet suggestions were all it took to get the word out.

She watched CeCe and Alexis disappear into the back of

the store and walked over to the reading nook where she found Elena with a stack of books.

"I love the welcoming vibe of your store," Elena said as Cat sat down in the chair next to her.

"Thank you. I want people to be able to walk in here and ask for whatever kind of book they're looking for, without hesitation."

"I had no idea there were so many titles in the sapphic genre," Elena said.

Cat smiled. "It's a niche that opened up a new world for me when I discovered it after I graduated from college."

Elena gave Cat a long look. "I'm older than you, but I can remember reading a few books like these under the covers when I was in college."

Cat furrowed her brow. "You're not that much older than me."

Elena nodded. "Oh, yes I am." She stared at Cat again then said, "I'm forty-seven and I'm guessing that's at least ten to fifteen years older than you."

"Does it matter?"

Elena chuckled. "Not one bit. I don't even know why I'm telling you this."

Cat grinned. "I'm thirty-seven, so I'd say your guess was pretty accurate."

Elena leaned in. "Can I ask you something?" she said quietly.

"Of course."

"Those two women walked rather stealthily to the back of your store then disappeared. I couldn't help but overhear them as they asked about The Bottom Shelf."

2

Cat nodded and smiled. "The redhead is my sister, CeCe. She owns the beauty salon next door. That was her favorite client, also known as her crush."

Elena gasped and giggled.

Cat couldn't believe she'd shared that, but there was something about Elena that made her feel safe. "I'm sorry. I really shouldn't have said that. CeCe would kill me, but it's true."

"I could tell from over here that they are both quite smitten," Elena said.

"I know!" Cat laughed. "My oldest sister, Cory, owns the liquor store at the end of the shopping center. It was her idea to build these openings between all three stores."

"I planned to go there and look at their wine selection." Elena paused, then asked, "Is The Bottom Shelf a secret?"

"I wouldn't say that. It's more discreet than secretive."

A slow smile crept onto Elena's face. "I'm the definition of discretion, my new friend."

Cat chuckled. Yep, she and Elena Burkett were going to

be friends. "It's a secluded room full of..." Cat leaned in closer. "Sex toys," she said quietly.

Elena nodded and Cat didn't see the surprise on her face that she'd expected.

"I love it," Elena said softly.

"Yeah?"

"Do you think I could go back there sometime?"

"Of course."

"Okay, but not today, since your sister and her friend are back there. I want these two books today." Elena handed the books to Cat.

"Good choices," Cat said, looking at the titles.

"I'll put these back and meet you at the register."

"I'll do that for you. Follow me," Cat said, walking towards the register.

Cat was ringing up Elena's purchases when she noticed Cory coming into the bookstore.

"Hey, Cory," Cat said.

"Hi," Cory said, smiling at them both.

"Cory, this is Elena Burkett. I was explaining to her that we're all in this together," Cat said.

"It's nice to meet you. I'm the oldest sister and The Liquor Box is my store," Cory said with a friendly smile.

"I love the name and logo." Elena grinned. "Cat was just telling me about the openings between the stores. That's a genius idea," she said.

"Thanks," Cory replied.

"I love the reading nook and plan to be here often." Elena smiled at Cat.

"That's why I created it," Cat said.

"Hey, I'm going to get something from the back," Cory said, giving Cat a knowing look.

"It's okay, Elena knows all about The Bottom Shelf," Cat said.

"Oh, okay." Cory chuckled.

"CeCe is in there with Alexis Reed," Cat said, raising her eyebrows.

"I'll be right back," Cory said.

"Don't embarrass CeCe," Cat warned as Cory walked away.

"I can imagine the fun the three of you have," Elena commented.

"Most of the time," Cat replied.

"I was serious about spending time here," Elena said. "I'm a homebody and this would be the perfect place to get me out of the house."

Cat tilted her head and smiled at Elena. "I hope to see you tomorrow then."

"I think CeCe and Alexis are slipping away."

Cat turned to see CeCe wave at her as she and Alexis went back into the beauty salon.

"It appears Alexis may have found something at The Bottom Shelf," Cat said.

"I thought she was holding a sack in her hand." Elena chuckled.

"Maybe you'll have to see The Bottom Shelf for yourself tomorrow."

"Maybe. Hey, I need someone to talk about these books with and to recommend more," Elena said.

"Be careful, Elena. I'm usually quiet, but I love to talk about books."

"Me, too. I'll see you tomorrow."

Cat smiled and watched Elena leave the bookstore.

"She seems nice," Cory said, walking up behind Cat.

"Yeah, she does." Cat turned to her older sister. "You

didn't embarrass CeCe, did you?"

"Not on purpose." Cory shrugged.

Cat smirked and shook her head as Cory walked out of the store. She was about to take the other books Elena didn't purchase back to their shelves when she noticed CeCe walking Alexis out of the salon's front door. These openings between the stores were a great idea. Cat could keep an eye on the other stores and her sisters.

She stopped and watched them for a moment and was reminded of earlier that day when they'd met in CeCe's salon before they opened the doors for the first time. They each had a glass of champagne and CeCe suggested a toast before they unlocked the doors. Each of them offered a few words, but it was CeCe that quipped: "May we live happily-ever-after."

"Hmm, maybe CeCe was making her toast a reality," she muttered to herself.

Cat was through with the idea of happily-ever-after, but she wanted it for her sisters. At one time she thought she had hers, but once again she'd learned there was only one person she could count on: herself.

* * *

Elena walked into her kitchen from the garage and heard banging. She set her purse and the bag from the bookstore down on the island and walked into the living room.

"Hi, Nicolas. I didn't think you'd be working this late," Elena said, gazing at the large bookshelf he was hammering a small nail into.

"Hi, Ms. E. I'm just finishing up."

"Are you never going to call me Elena?"

"I just can't do it," Nicolas said. "At least I don't call you

Ms. Burkett any more."

"Okay, okay. You're doing such good work," Elena said with amazement in her voice.

"Thank you. This is going to hold more books than I'll ever read."

"No, it won't." Elena chuckled.

"If it wasn't for you I wouldn't be reading anything," he said, putting his tools away.

"You give me too much credit. All you needed was a little help getting started."

Nicolas smiled at her and stood to his full height. "You've been gone for a while and that makes me happy."

"Why?"

"Because you don't leave this house often enough."

"You'll be happy to know that I've found a place to 'hang out' as you like to say," Elena said.

"Yay! Tell me about it," Nicolas replied.

"You'll never believe it, Nicolas. I've been to a bookstore."

He threw his head back and laughed. "Of course you have. Is it the new place with the liquor store and the beauty salon?"

Elena nodded. "The Sloan Sisters' Shopping Center or something like that."

"The Sloan Sisters' Shopping Extravaganza," Nicolas corrected her and chuckled. "CeCe cuts my hair and her sister named the place. I think it's kind of a joke."

"I only went into the bookstore today, but I'm going back tomorrow and may stop by the liquor store."

His brows rose and he smiled once again. "You're going back tomorrow?"

"The bookstore has a place to sit and read, and the owner, Cat, has agreed to talk about books with me," Elena explained.

"That must be a little piece of heaven for you." He smirked.

"Don't tease me. Besides, you never know, I may find a book or two for you."

"Hmm, I'm not sure they'd have the kind of books I like to read."

"If Cat doesn't have it, she'll get it for you. What are you looking for? Let me guess… Cabinetry."

Nicolas scoffed. "I know all about building things. I learned everything from my Pops. You know that."

Elena chuckled. "You and your father are the best. That's why I wanted you to build this bookcase. Now, back to the books. What can I bring you from the bookstore tomorrow?"

Nicolas lowered his head and shuffled his feet. "Are you serious?" he asked, looking up into her eyes.

"Yes," Elena said softly. "How about a gay romance?"

A smile played across Nicolas's face. "She'd have that?"

Elena nodded. "Yep. I saw a few. One had a very hot man on the cover and he wasn't wearing a shirt."

"Ms. E!"

"What? There's nothing wrong with reading romance novels, Nicolas. I've told you that over and over."

"I know, but I only talk about those books with you."

"Your dad wouldn't care if you read those books. He's happy you're reading."

Nicolas nodded. "I thought he'd kick me out of the house when I told him I was gay, but instead he and my mom both hugged me."

Elena smiled, remembering Nicolas sharing that story with her. He had been relieved and surprised.

"I'm proud of who I am, but I'm not sure many of my friends read gay romance."

Elena chuckled. "You might be surprised. Anyway, I'll

bring you something tomorrow."

"Thanks." Nicolas gathered his tools and put them out of the way. He looked up at his work and smiled. "It's coming along."

"It looks great," Elena said.

"I'm happy to help you put your books in it when I'm finished."

"I don't have very many books left. I donated most of them when I moved into this smaller house."

Nicolas furrowed his brow. "Then why am I building this huge bookcase?"

Elena's smile lit her face. "Because I'm going to fill it with books I'm going to read. I have a new genre that I'm rediscovering and there are so many books."

"Do you miss it, Ms. E? Teaching kids to read?"

"Things just aren't the same since my husband died," Elena said quietly.

"That's why you moved out of your big house and into this one, huh?"

"Yep. This one is more my size. But it's missing something. Maybe the bookcase is what it needs."

"You never know, Ms. E. Someone else may come along," Nicolas said with a kind smile.

Elena chuckled. "Oh, the optimism of a twenty-five-year-old. I hope you always have it."

"You'll get your spark back. It won't always be like this."

Elena studied him for a moment. "Such wisdom from one so young."

"I'm not that young and you know it."

Elena chuckled. "You are compared to me."

"Nah, you always told me books can take you anywhere in the world and you can become whoever you want to be in those pages. It doesn't matter if you're young or old. Maybe you'll find the person you're meant to be in these new books you bring in from the bookstore. You're discovering your next chapter."

"That's a great way to look at it, Nicolas. Thank you."

"Anytime," he said, walking towards the front door. "I'll see you tomorrow."

"Bye." Elena smiled and locked the front door after he closed it.

It had been almost twenty years since Nicolas Navarro had shyly walked into her classroom. She had tutored him from first grade all through elementary school. After that she followed his progress through middle school then on to high school. There were times he needed her help when he was struggling, but he worked hard and was a good student. After graduation, all he wanted to do was work with his father and build things. They had a small construction company and did all sorts of renovation jobs.

Whenever she needed something repaired around the house, she called Nicolas. They had become friends more so than teacher and student as the years passed. Elena and her husband, Dean, didn't have children, but if they'd had a son she would have wanted him to be like Nicolas. He had a big heart and such a positive outlook on life. She needed his optimism right now.

After Dean had died suddenly, their roles had reversed and it was Nicolas checking on her rather than the other way around. He called or came by and it always lifted her spirits. Maybe she'd come up with another project around the house when he finished the bookcase.

Elena went back into the kitchen and took her new book purchases out of the sack. She planned to eat a light dinner and start on one of these books. It was time to escape her sadness and a sapphic romance was a great place to start.

3

Cat was at the register ringing up a customer when she saw Elena walk through the front door. "Hey," she said with a big smile. "You came back."

"I told you I would. I'm sure you can guess where I'm going."

"I'll meet you in the reading nook."

Elena smiled and kept walking towards the comfortable chairs.

Cat finished with her customer and walked over to where Elena was already settled into one of the chairs. "I've added something to this little oasis. How about a cup of coffee?"

"Oh, how nice," Elena said.

"It's nothing fancy, but there are a variety of creamers," Cat said.

"I'm not fancy," Elena said. "Let me see what you have."

After Cat showed Elena the options, Elena prepared a cup of coffee. She inhaled the familiar scent and said, "I almost finished one of the books I bought yesterday."

"I have plenty more waiting for you."

Elena went back to her chair with her cup of coffee and sipped. "This is just right."

Cat smiled and looked at Elena.. "You mentioned yesterday that this was a good reason to get out of the house," she said tentatively.

Elena nodded. "My husband died not too long ago and I decided to move from our way too large house into one that felt more my size."

"Oh, I'm so sorry," Cat said. Her heart lurched in her chest and she felt such sadness for her new friend.

"Don't look so sad," Elena said, reaching over and patting Cat's arm. "I'm glad I moved and now I have a place to go that makes me happy."

Cat smiled. "I'm glad you're here."

"So am I. Now, you mentioned yesterday that you quit your job to open the bookstore," Elena started. "What did you do before?"

Cat sighed. "I was a tax accountant. I know. What a boring job."

"Not at all. My husband was a lawyer with one of the big firms in Dallas and worked a lot of long hours. I have a feeling you did, too."

"You would be right." Cat tilted her head. "Several of my clients were law firms. Who knows, I may have worked for him at one time."

"Wouldn't that be interesting? His name is Dean Burkett."

"Hmm, was he with Jennings, Turner, and Allen?"

"Yes, he was a partner there. Did you know him?"

Cat shook her head. "I didn't know him personally, but I did some work for one of his clients. It's a small world."

"It really is."

"Do you have kids?"

Elena chuckled. "Yeah, about two hundred of them."

"What!"

"I was a teacher. After Dean and I got married, he rose up the proverbial ladder rather quickly. I had been teaching for about five years and saw a need in my elementary school. With Dean's success we didn't need my income, so I quit my teaching job, but then I started a reading program. I could concentrate on a few students at a time and it made a big difference not only in my life, but also in the lives of my students."

"That's amazing," Cat said in awe.

"These kids were slipping through the cracks and needed a more one-on-one approach. It worked out well."

"Are you still teaching?"

Elena shook her head. "When Dean died I felt lost, so I turned the program over to a group of volunteers."

Before she could even think about it, Cat reached over and squeezed Elena's hand.

Elena smiled at her. "I haven't talked about this with very many people and here I am telling you all about it and we just met."

"We may have just met, but I know we're going to be friends," Cat said.

"Me, too!" Elena exclaimed. "We are friends."

"I have a feeling you'll figure out what you want to do next and in the meantime you have a place right here at Your Next Great Read."

Elena smiled. "I told you this place had a welcoming vibe. I hope you don't get tired of me."

"Never." Cat paused and leaned in a little closer. "Maybe it's time for us to visit The Bottom Shelf." She watched as Elena's eyes widened.

"Oh, that sounds like a great idea."

"Yeah?"

Elena nodded.

Cat stood and got Jessica's attention, indicating she'd be in the back. "Let's go."

Elena got up and followed Cat to the back of the store. Before going inside, Cat stopped and turned to Elena. "Do you want to go in alone? I don't have to go with you."

Elena grinned. "No, I want you with me. I may need your expertise."

Cat could feel her cheeks begin to warm. "I'm not sure that would be me." She opened the door and they walked inside. "Honestly, Elena. I learned about sex toys from CeCe's customers."

"What?" Elena asked as she gazed around the room.

"You'd be surprised what people share with their stylists." Cat chuckled.

"Or new friends that are easy to talk to," Elena added.

Cat stopped and met Elena's soft brown eyes. "Yeah, I wonder why that is."

Elena shrugged. "I don't know. Maybe it's easier because new friends don't know all about you. However, you have your sisters. I'm sure you can tell them most anything."

"Some things, but not everything," Cat said. "CeCe was telling a story about a vibrator one of her customers mentioned. It got me thinking, but I certainly didn't tell my sisters. I would've never heard the end of it."

"What did you do?"

"Well... I went online and bought a small vibrator similar to this one," Cat said, pointing to a palm-sized vibrator.

"It comes in three colors," Elena quipped.

Cat chuckled. "It does."

"I guess you're glad you bought it because you have quite a selection in this room."

"That little vibrator taught me a lot," Cat said.

Elena turned and looked at Cat.

"I bought it because sex had become almost non-existent with my girlfriend. I thought it could be a way for us to talk about things and maybe find our passion once again."

"Did it help?" Elena asked quietly.

Cat shook her head. "She said she didn't need a toy, all she needed was me."

"Aww," Elena said.

"Un-huh," Cat replied. "That wasn't exactly true because it didn't make things better for us and she found someone else to have sex with."

"Oh, Cat!"

"She didn't exactly cheat on me, but she broke up with me and moved on rather quickly," Cat said. "After that, the little purple vibrator and I became friends." Cat chuckled. "I've known all along the one person I can count on in my life is me. Hattie showed me that once again."

"Can I ask you a question about the vibrator?" Elena said, narrowing her gaze.

"Sure."

"Did you find out new things about your body that you didn't know before?"

Cat nodded. "That's why I wanted this little shop in the back. You'd be surprised what you can learn about yourself and I wanted to create a place where you'd have the opportunity to find out."

Elena nodded.

"Now, don't get me wrong. I'm not saying vibrators will change your life, but sometimes you need to try new things. Maybe you'll discover something you didn't know."

Elena smiled. "Dean and I didn't have the greatest sex life. We were the best of friends and I loved him dearly. I mean, it was fine, but it made me wonder…"

"If the sex these characters have in the books we read is real or just fiction?"

"Yes! Is it fiction?"

Cat shrugged. "I think it's real. But I also think you have to not be afraid to say what you like. That can be hard. I know it is for me."

"Maybe the vibrator will help you speak up with your next girlfriend."

"Oh, no. I'm not planning to do that ever again," Cat said adamantly.

"I know what you mean, although for different reasons. However, a wise young man told me yesterday that you never know when someone will come along," Elena said.

Cat smiled and met Elena's gaze. "Have you seen anything that looks interesting?" she asked Elena, changing the subject.

Elena scoffed. "Interesting is one way to put it."

Cat waited as Elena walked around the small room looking at the choices. There were small vibrators and larger wand styles as well.

"You know, Elena, you don't have to buy one," Cat said.

"Oh, I know, but I want to." She turned to Cat. "When Dean knew he was going to die, he told me to go find the person I'm meant to be without him."

"Oh, wow," Cat said.

"Yeah, I wasn't sure what he meant at the time, but I think he wanted me to explore and see what there is to discover about Elena Burkett."

"What have you found so far?"

Elena chuckled. "I'm a little like you. I quit my job, even

though I was a volunteer. I bought a smaller house. I never liked our larger house, but Dean thought we needed it when he occasionally entertained clients."

"What else?"

"I'm working on a project at my new home, and I think a vibrator is next."

Cat smiled. "All right, then."

"I want the one you showed me at the beginning. Instead of purple, I like the blue," Elena said.

Cat reached in a drawer and took out the vibrator Elena selected in its box. She put it in a bag and handed it to her. "If you have any questions…"

Elena laughed. "I may."

"I hope coming by here and spending time in the reading nook is part of your exploration," Cat said.

"Oh, it is, but it's not just because of that cute little reading nook," Elena replied.

"I'm going to like you being a regular around here," Cat said, opening the door.

"Do I need to pay back here or at the front?" Elena asked.

"This is on me," Cat said. "I want to be part of your journey."

"Thank you, Cat," Elena said as they walked back to the front of the store.

"Let's talk about the book you read last night," Cat said, sitting in one of the comfy chairs in the reading nook.

"Do you have time?"

"I've always got time to talk about books with you, my friend."

After a lively conversation about the book Elena was reading, she hopped out of her chair. "I almost forgot, I want to buy a book I saw yesterday."

"Do you need any help?"

"Nope, I'll meet you at the register," Elena said.

Cat watched her walk away and chuckled. "Okay, then." She walked over to the register and waited.

Elena plopped the book down on the counter and Cat scanned it. "Aren't you going to say anything?"

Cat looked at the cover. "That's a very handsome bare chested man on the cover." She looked up at Elena and grinned. "There's no judgment at Your Next Great Read."

Elena chuckled. "I have not dipped into the gay romance genre yet, but the friend I'm giving this book to loves it."

"Dipped?"

Cat giggled as Elena's eyes widened. "Really?"

"You're the one who said it."

"Nicolas, the man I'm buying this for, is working on a project at my house. He was one of my first students."

"How cool is that?" Cat said.

"I can assure you I did not foresee him reading gay romance when I helped him all those years ago, but hey, he's reading."

"Are you renovating?" Cat asked.

"No, I'm adding—" Elena tilted her head. "You know, he'll be finished with it soon. How would you like to come over and see it?"

Cat raised her eyebrows. "See what?"

"Oh, I think I'll keep it a surprise. Are you interested?"

Cat narrowed her eyes. "Hmm, can I bring wine?"

"Absolutely!"

Cat laughed. "Okay, I'd love to."

"That reminds me. I need to go to Cory's and buy wine."

"She's got a wide selection."

"Thanks, Cat. I'll see you tomorrow."

Cat grinned and watched Elena walk through CeCe's

salon then into The Liquor Box. She was surprised about the things she shared with Elena today, but then again, she was so easy to talk to. Cat hadn't even told her sisters about the vibrator and trying to reignite her and Hattie's sex life. It felt too personal. But with Elena, it felt like the most natural thing to share. Of course, they were surrounded by sex toys so that may have had something to do with it.

Cat chuckled. Opening this bookstore had brought her a new friend. At least she hoped so, because there was something about Elena Burkett that made Cat want to know more. How do you talk to someone about your sex life when you've known them for two days? Why did she feel like she could tell Elena anything and not be judged? Cat was not the nosy type, yet she wondered about this project in Elena's new house. She knew Elena must be caring because the guy working in her house was a former student from years ago. That means she must have kept up with him.

Yep, she wondered all sorts of things about Elena Burkett.

4

Elena walked into the bookstore and found Cat in the sapphic romance section.

"Well, I see you've been cheating on me." Cat smirked.

"What?" Elena gasped in surprise.

Cat grinned. "Your hair looks great. CeCe told me you came in yesterday afternoon."

Elena felt relief wash through her body. She knew Cat was kidding, but the idea of cheating on Cat threw her.

"I've had long hair for years and decided it was time for a change," Elena explained. Her straight dark brown hair fell just above her shoulders.

"You have such beautiful hair," Cat said, reaching out and then stopping herself.

Elena's eyes met Cat's but she couldn't read her expression. "CeCe is so talented. I wasn't sure what I wanted and she knew what style would look best on me."

"It looks really great. Do you like it?"

"I think so. I can still pull it back into a ponytail which I often do in the summer."

"It'll be here before you know it."

"Hey," Elena said, giving Cat a playful smack on the arm. "I didn't cheat on you. I came by here before my appointment with CeCe."

Cat chuckled. "I know you did. It wouldn't be the same if you didn't come in every day. What would I do?"

"Uh, sell books to your other customers."

"But I wouldn't get to talk about them with you."

"Coming here is the best part of my day," Elena said with a smile, "and it's not just because of the books."

Cat smiled and Elena followed her gaze as she kept looking at her hair. "What is it? Do you not like my hair?"

"No, no. I love it," Cat said, meeting Elena's eyes. "I didn't mean to stare."

"I came by this morning to see if you have to close tonight," Elena said.

"I do not. It's Jessica's night."

"When you get off, would you like to walk over to Cory's happy hour bar with me? I've wanted to try it out."

"Yeah, that would be fun," Cat replied.

"Okay, I'll be back around 5:00," Elena said.

"You're not going to have a cup of coffee now?" Cat asked.

"I know I'm not your only customer and you have things to do," Elena said, putting one hand on her hip.

"I have all day to get things done. Besides, I wanted to talk to you for a minute."

"All right. Let's have that cup of coffee." Elena followed Cat to the reading nook and began preparing her cup. "Aren't you having any?"

"Maybe in a minute," Cat said, sitting in one of the comfy chairs.

Elena sat down next to her and furrowed her brow. "Are you all right?"

Cat nodded and smiled. "I'm a little..." She hesitated, seeming to search for the right words.

Elena sipped her coffee and waited. She knew that Cat was thoughtful and sometimes paused before she spoke.

"The other day when we were in the back room, I hope I didn't make you uncomfortable talking about sex. I'm not usually like that," Cat explained.

Elena smiled. "You didn't make me uncomfortable."

"I got to thinking about it and..." Cat rolled her eyes, shook her head, and sighed. "You must think I'm some kind of—"

"Do you believe in fate?" Elena asked, interrupting Cat's obvious distress.

"I'm not sure. Maybe."

"You said I was easy to talk to, right?"

Cat nodded. "You are."

"So are you. I've never told a soul anything about my sex life with Dean. But there I was talking to you about it. I think we were put into each other's lives so we have someone to talk to. Someone to say those things we can't say to anyone else."

A slow smile grew on Cat's face.

"Honestly, it made me feel better to say it aloud to someone who'd been through it. Well, we may not have experienced the same thing, but you knew what I meant." Elena paused and took a breath. "I hope you know that you can tell me anything, especially the things you don't want to tell your sisters, but need to say. Don't ever feel embarrassed around me, Cat. I'm your friend."

Cat sighed then smiled. "Thank God. I'm your friend, too. I'm the person you can talk to about anything."

"I know how it feels to want to talk about something, but not know how. That happened to me with Dean."

"I wanted to talk with Hattie, but she didn't. For something that can make you feel so friggin' good, sex can also be so hard. That's one reason I wanted to open The Bottom Shelf. We all have options and sex toys are nothing to be embarrassed about."

Elena smiled. "I have to tell you, Cat. There's no way I would've gone into a sex store without you."

"But you've only known me for a minute," Cat said.

"It's been longer than a minute and you know it. I don't know what it is we have, but there's something," Elena said, pointing her finger between her and Cat. "Whatever it is, we both must need it and I'm not questioning it."

Cat grinned. "I think I'll have that cup of coffee now."

Elena sipped from her cup and watched Cat prepare her own coffee. She was looking forward to their happy hour date.

Date? Was that what this was? Interesting, Elena thought.

They drank their coffee and had their usual conversation about books. Elena promised to be back at five to walk over to Cory's and have a glass of wine.

In the meantime she ran a few errands and got back home just as Nicolas was finishing the bookcase.

"Oh, my! That looks beautiful!" Elena exclaimed as she walked in from the kitchen.

"It really is," Nicolas said.

"You sound surprised." Elena chuckled.

"It was your vision and design. I knew I could build it, but I didn't think it would look this good after I painted it."

"It's better than I imagined."

"Now what?"

"I have a few books to put in it."

"You'd better get to reading then. You have a lot of shelves to fill," Nicolas said.

"Are you ready for another book?"

"Ms. E, you don't have to keep buying me books," Nicolas protested.

"But I like to. Hey, why don't you come to the bookstore with me and you can meet my friend Cat and pick out a couple of books," Elena said.

"Your friend Cat? Is she the owner who you talk about books with every day?"

Elena smiled. "Yep. When can I put books on the shelves?"

Nicolas peered at the shelves. "It should be dry by tonight."

"Thank you. This house is feeling more like home," Elena said.

"I'm ready for another project when you are," Nicolas said.

"I have other ideas, but for now let me work on filling this bookcase."

"Sounds good. Have a nice evening," Nicolas said, throwing his tool bag over his shoulder.

"Oh, I will. Have you heard about the happy hour bar at The Liquor Box?"

"I have," he replied.

"Cat and I are going after she gets off work."

"I'll get out of here so you can get ready. Call me if you need a ride home," he said, walking out the front door.

Elena laughed. "I'm just having a glass of wine with my friend," she muttered to herself. Then she walked into her bedroom and decided to change clothes. She touched up her makeup and ran her fingers through her hair. *Yeah, this new look feels right.*

Cat Sloan is Swirling

A little later Elena walked back into the bookstore and found Cat at the register waiting for her.

"There she is," Cat said with a smile.

"Are you ready?"

"Let's go."

They walked through CeCe's salon and then into The Liquor Box. Cory was in the back at the bar when they each slid onto a stool.

"Hey there, welcome," Cory said. "What can I get you ladies?"

Cat giggled. "How about a glass of wine?"

"That sounds perfect," Elena said.

"I have a nice white with a crisp bite to it," Cory said as she poured them each a glass.

They both took a sip and nodded.

"How are things going with that liquor rep you've been complaining about?" Cat asked.

"You won't believe it!" Cory exclaimed. "She's playing volleyball at my gym."

"Oh my God. She isn't on your team, is she?"

"No, but I've seen her practice and she's good."

"This is going to be fun," Cat said under her breath.

Elena chuckled and sipped her wine.

"I may need you both to come support me and CeCe when we play her team," Cory said seriously.

"We can do that," Elena said. "Let me know when and where."

"Thanks, Elena. I appreciate it," Cory said. "I'd better go back up front and see if Randi needs any help."

"Thanks, sis. See you later," Cat said as Cory walked away.

"Cory and CeCe play volleyball?"

Cat nodded as she sipped her wine. "Cory is the athlete

in the family and CeCe fills in when someone on her team can't make it."

"Where do they play?"

"Your Way. It's a fitness center not far from here. They have a league," Cat explained.

"I once did yoga there," Elena commented.

Elena felt Cat's eyes travel up and down her body. "I can see that," Cat said.

"Are you checking me out?"

Cat chuckled. "I'm admiring your lithe body. I can imagine you practicing yoga, not so much this unathletic frame I have been blessed with." Cat gestured with her hand up and down her body.

"Who cares if you're athletic? I think you look just right," Elena said with a smile.

"I was not fishing for a compliment, but thank you. I do try to make Cory's games as her cheerleader from the bleachers. Were you serious about going sometime?"

"Yeah, I think it would be fun."

"Okay, I'll let you know when she plays."

Elena sipped her wine and furrowed her brow. She knew she could ask Cat anything and she'd been wondering. "Let me get this straight," Elena said, then giggled.

"Did you just giggle?" Cat asked, chuckling. "I don't think I've ever heard you giggle."

Elena knocked her shoulder into Cat's and snorted.

"What is so funny?"

"Nothing. I want to ask you a question and now maybe I shouldn't," Elena said.

Cat chuckled. "Come on. You have to now."

"Well, I was wondering if you and your sisters are all gay?"

Cat smiled. "Oh! Now I see why you're giggling. Um, not

exactly, but we're not *straight* either," Cat said, emphasizing the word. "Cory is a lesbian and knew from a young age. CeCe is bisexual, and I can see her and Alexis together for a long time."

"Really?"

"Yes, they are falling in love right before our eyes, and I'm happy for them."

"What about you?"

"Hmm, as I learn more and more about myself—wait, I know that sounds funny."

"No, it doesn't," Elena said, resting her hand on Cat's forearm. "I'm learning new things about myself every day."

Cat smiled. "I'm finding that I'm attracted to the person. It doesn't matter their gender. My relationships have been with women, but I've also dated men. I have a friend who is nonbinary and through discussions with them I've come to the conclusion that I'm more pansexual." She shrugged. "I'm queer, Elena. I'm the odd Sloan sister."

"There is nothing odd about you," Elena assured her.

"Honestly, after Hattie walked out, I knew it would be a very long time, if ever, that I would trust or give my heart to someone. Right now, I simply want to appreciate other people's beauty." She turned to Elena. "And everyone has beauty. My heart became so dark and I don't want to be that person. I'm trying to find the light that was once inside me."

Elena felt a mixture of anger and compassion. She wanted to knock this Hattie woman into tomorrow for hurting her sweet friend. She also wanted to hug Cat, but knew that wasn't a good idea in this moment. "I see light in you, Cat. Why else would I come into the bookstore every day? Yes, I enjoy the books, but you brighten my day. So, I'd say your light is coming back."

"Thanks," Cat said, bumping her shoulder into Elena's.

"There I go again. You didn't ask for all of that." Cat finished off her wine and looked over at Elena. "But it's kind of your fault. If you weren't so easy to talk to..."

Elena laughed. "I'm not the only one who's easy to talk to. I'm glad you shared that with me."

Cat nodded. "It's your turn. What things are you learning about yourself?"

"Well, have I told you that I kissed a girl?"

5

Cat was surprised by Elena's admission. She got up and went around the bar, reached into the refrigerator under the counter, and took out the bottle of wine. She topped off both their glasses then returned to her seat.

"Here's to learning new things," Cat said, holding up her glass.

Elena grinned. "And to making new friends."

They clinked their glasses together and both took generous drinks.

"Now, what is this about kissing girls?" Cat asked.

"Do you remember when I first came into the bookstore?"

"Sure I do."

"We went straight to the sapphic literature shelves," Elena said.

"Straight? There's that word again."

Elena chuckled. "My last year in college, I met a woman —in the library of all places."

"Come on, Elena. In the library?"

"I kid you not. She was working on her graduate degree and was researching lesbians in literature. I can't remember the time period she was studying, but I found both her and her research fascinating."

Cat took a sip of her wine to let Elena gather her thoughts. She could tell by the faraway look in her eyes that Elena was back in that library.

"We became friends and I helped with her research. She was a lesbian and would tell me about the bar she and her friends went to and the parties they had. I was mesmerized. I couldn't get enough of her or her stories."

Cat smiled as Elena continued her story. She could remember how it felt when she and her first girlfriend were getting to know each other. The excitement of finding someone who thought you were as special as you thought they were. Come to think of it, that's how she felt every time Elena walked into the bookstore. She'd have to think about that later, but right now she wanted to focus on Elena.

Elena took another sip of wine and continued. "She kept asking me to meet her at the bar and one Saturday night I said yes. It was eye-opening since the only lesbian I knew at the time was her. I tried not to stare and at the same time take it all in."

Cat smiled. "Oh my God, I can imagine."

"We danced and danced," Elena said. "We drank beer and she introduced me to a few of her friends. I recognized a couple of women who had been in my classes."

"Were they surprised to see you?"

"Not really. I'm sure it was obvious that it was my first time there. Anyway, a slow song started to play and she put her hands on my hips. She pulled me close and we swayed to the music. I can remember the soft lights glowing, the music, and the smell."

Cat chuckled. "There's nothing like the aroma of stale beer and heated bodies."

Elena nodded. "So true. The song was winding down and she pulled back to look into my eyes. I remember feeling like my heart was about to beat out of my chest."

Cat leaned in a little closer as Elena's voice dropped. "She looked at my lips and then softly pressed hers against mine." Elena's eyes widened and she stared at Cat. "I thought I was going to die!"

"But you didn't!" Cat exclaimed.

"That was the best kiss," Elena said. "Do you remember some of the great kisses you've had?"

Cat nodded.

"That was some kiss. So gentle, so sweet, yet so hot all at the same time," Elena said.

"What happened next?"

Elena took a big drink and sighed. "I graduated."

"What? Didn't you see her again?"

"We met one more time at the library." Elena leaned a little closer. "And we made out in the stacks in the women's lit section." Elena laughed. "Can you imagine? I would've died if we'd been caught."

Cat chuckled. "No you wouldn't have. There's no telling how many people have made out or even had sex in the stacks at a library."

Elena laughed again. "Let me have my moment."

"By all means. You were a wild one."

"When Dean told me to find out who I was without him, my first thought was of that kiss."

"Really?"

"Yes, I met Dean soon after that and the rest, as they say, is history."

"Do you know what happened to the woman?"

Elena shook her head.

"Do you want to find her?"

"No! Not at all."

"But that kiss..."

Elena smiled. "That kiss tells me that maybe I'm not straight."

Cat stared at Elena, but before she could say anything, Cory came around the bar.

"Sorry about that," Cory said. "We had a little run of customers."

"It's okay," Elena said. "Cat knows where the wine is."

Cory chuckled. "I see she took care of y'all."

"I didn't mind," Cat said. She went to take a sip from her glass and realized it was empty.

"Would you like another splash of wine?' Cory asked, holding the bottle.

Cat covered the top of her glass. "I have to drive home."

"Me too," Elena said, taking her last sip. "That was excellent wine, Cory."

Cat saw Elena reach in her purse and take out her wallet. "Oh, no," Cat said, covering Elena's hand with hers. "I've got this."

"But I invited you," Elena protested.

"*I've* got this," Cory said. "I'm happy you both came by although I didn't get to visit with you."

"Thank you, Cory. Next time is on me," Elena said, smiling at her.

"Thanks, sis. I'll see you tomorrow."

Cat and Elena walked out of The Liquor Box through CeCe's salon and back to the bookstore.

"That was fun. We should do it again," Elena commented.

"I'd like that," Cat said with a smile. "Let me get my purse and I'll walk out with you."

"You were going to pay, but you didn't take your money with you?" Elena asked.

Cat chuckled. "My credit is good at that bar." She began to walk to the front door with Elena in step beside her.

"Um, Nicolas completed my project this evening. Would you like to see it tomorrow?"

Cat gasped. "Yes!"

Elena grinned. "Okay, would you like to come over when you get off?"

"Yes. Are you going to give me a hint about what this project is?"

"Nope. You'll see," Elena said. "I'll provide the wine tomorrow."

"Okay, but I don't know where you live."

"I'll text you my address. But I'll see you tomorrow right here. I need to get Nicolas another book."

They walked out the front door and Cat followed Elena to her car.

"I'm really glad you suggested this. Thanks for trusting me with your story from college."

Elena smiled as she opened her door. "I know I can trust you, Cat. You'll find out you can trust me too."

She got in the car, but before she could shut the door Cat said, "What I don't understand is how you get me to talk about things I usually don't share."

Elena shrugged and smiled. Cat shut her door and backed away. She gave Elena a little wave as she backed out of the parking space.

Cat got in her car and on the short drive home she

thought back on her conversation with Elena at the bar. She didn't usually share personal things with other people. Since Hattie left, her sisters were always asking how she was doing and it got to be annoying. So much so that Cat told them what they wanted to hear, but that didn't stop them. She finally proclaimed she was never falling in love again, and she would never trust someone with her heart. Her directness seemed to startle them enough that they stopped asking.

But with Elena, it was easy to open up and tell her things that she knew her sisters would want to discuss further. Cat thought back to her statement on attraction. What was she attracted to in a person? The fact that she was even thinking about it was a step forward for her because she was so over love. Or was she? Watching CeCe and Alexis fall in love had softened her heart just a little.

She pulled into her garage and went into her house. Snippets from her past began to filter through her brain. What had attracted her to Hattie?

"Duh," she muttered. Hattie was beautiful and when she smiled at Cat and looked into her eyes, Cat felt special. She had a way of making Cat believe she was the most important person in the world. But as time went on, Cat began to feel like she was an afterthought. Hattie didn't listen to her and when Cat tried to talk to her about it, Hattie got defensive or told Cat she was making problems that weren't there.

Sex had always been good for them, but their lovemaking became less frequent and Cat could feel Hattie getting farther and farther away. She tried to talk to her and then bought the vibrator in hopes of trying to bring the spark back to their relationship.

Cat sighed. She didn't want to think back to those times. She had moved past them and now found herself with a new friend. A friend who was easy to talk to and openly shared parts of her life with Cat. Was she attracted to Elena? Or was she simply happy to have someone to talk to who didn't push for more or question her outlook on love?

What made them connect that day Elena walked into the bookstore? Was it a shared sadness over loss? Or simply the desire to talk about books? And now Elena had told her she wasn't so sure she was straight?

"Hmm." Was Elena attracted to her? Is that why she told her the college story?

"No," Cat said, shaking her head. "She told me that story because she needed to share it with someone who would understand."

Cat sighed as she walked to her bedroom and began to undress.

"Fuck you, Hattie. You've made me scared to trust people," she said as tears began to burn the back of her eyes. She took a deep breath, willing the tears not to spill over her cheeks.

"Elena doesn't want to hurt me. She's curious about herself and I happen to be her queer new friend."

Cat walked into the bathroom and looked into the mirror. "There you go talking to yourself out loud again, Catarina. What would Cory and CeCe think?" She chuckled.

Cat stared into the familiar blue eyes. She shared this vibrant blue color with her mom and her sisters and she had received compliments on them all her life. She wondered if people could see the pain behind the pretty blue orbs, but as she looked closer she noticed a little sparkle.

But why did Elena's admission that she'd kissed another woman give Cat such pause?

"I'm through letting you hurt me, Hattie," she said to her reflection.

Elena told her tonight that she trusted her and Cat knew she could trust Elena, but still. In the short time they'd known each other Elena hadn't asked Cat for anything.

"Maybe it's time to trust yourself," Cat said.

6

The next day Elena texted Cat and told her she wouldn't be by the bookstore, but to please come to her house after work. She had the wine chilled and waiting.

She realized when she got home that Cat might have gotten the wrong idea from their conversation the previous night at Cory's bar. She'd asked Cat several rather personal questions then told her about her experience in college. Elena knew Cat was a private person and wasn't sure why she'd been so intrusive. Was it eagerness to know more about her friend or about herself? Whatever it was, she owed Cat an apology and didn't want to have that discussion at the bookstore.

She peeked out the front window several times and felt her heart speed up in her chest when she saw Cat pull into her driveway.

Elena opened the front door before Cat could knock and smiled shyly. "Hey, you found me."

Cat grinned and tilted her head. "Of course I did. You gave me your address, remember?"

Elena nodded.

"Is something wrong?"

"No, come in. I'm happy you're here," Elena said, stepping out of the doorway so Cat could come inside.

"I love your home. It's so welcoming. The flowers are beautiful. Do you garden?"

"Thanks. I thought it needed a pop of color and decided to give it a try."

"I think you have a green thumb."

Elena shrugged. "Maybe."

Cat walked into the open living area and Elena noticed the bag in her hand. "What do you have there?"

"Oh," Cat said, opening the bag and pulling out a book. "You were going to get your friend a book today and when you didn't come in…"

Elena smiled but didn't say anything.

"Anyway, I got this in today and thought he might like it." Cat handed her the book.

Elena looked at it and smiled. How thoughtful. Maybe Cat wasn't upset with her. "He will love this. It's by one of his favorite authors."

"Oh, good. I took a chance." Cat leaned in and added, "I don't read gay romance."

Elena chuckled. "I haven't yet either."

"Yet? Does that mean maybe someday?"

Elena shrugged. "We'll see. How about a glass of wine?"

"I'd love one."

"How was your day?" Elena asked as she walked around the island that separated the kitchen from the living area.

"It was busy. I realized on the way over here that I'm looking forward to this glass of wine."

Elena handed her a glass. "I hope you like it."

Cat took a sip and nodded. "Mmm, just right."

Elena chuckled. "Let's have a seat before the big reveal. I owe you an apology."

Cat sat down on the couch and furrowed her brow. "An apology?"

"Yes," Elena replied, sitting next to Cat but leaving plenty of room between them. "I want to apologize for asking you such personal questions last night and then telling you about my..." Elena hesitated.

"About your library fling," Cat said with a smile.

"I'm not sure it was a fling, but yes. I wasn't coming on to you. I know your ex hurt you and you must have thought—well, I don't know what you thought," Elena said, waving her hand. "I don't want to ruin our friendship just as it's getting started."

Cat smiled and took a sip of her wine. "I didn't think you were coming on to me. I thought you were sharing part of your past with someone you hoped would understand." Cat shrugged. "You can talk to me about anything, Elena. That's the kind of friends we are. Please don't hold back because of my ex. If anything, I should be thanking you."

"Thanking me?"

"Yes. Hattie left me doubting myself. I decided last night that I was not going to let her keep hurting me. I have to trust myself. I know you're my friend and we're getting to know each other. That means I have to open up and let you know me, which is what you did last night."

"It wasn't too much?"

"No. I'm glad you could talk to me about this woman."

"I've never told anyone about her. I pushed that memory so far down because I had Dean and we were so good together."

Cat reached over and took Elena's hand. "Some memories have a way of resurfacing no matter how deep you bury them. Maybe you felt safe to share that with me because I, too, have kissed a girl," Cat said with a grin.

Elena squeezed Cat's hand. "We're okay?"

"Yes, we're more than okay," Cat said with a wink.

Elena's hand went to her chest and she let out a deep breath. "Thank goodness."

Cat furrowed her brow. "Is this why you didn't come to the bookstore today?"

Elena could feel her cheeks warming and she nodded slightly.

"Oh, Elena."

"I didn't want to have this conversation at your store."

Cat nodded. "I can understand that. But I missed you."

They both smiled and took a sip from their glasses.

"Now, what is this big project I'm here to see?" Cat asked.

Elena got up and smiled. "I hope I haven't made this out to be more than it really is." She winced.

"Elena!"

"Okay, okay. Right this way."

Elena walked back towards the kitchen and past the small dining area. She stopped and put her hand on the wall that separated the dining area from the rest of the house. "On the other side of this wall is the project Nicolas has been building."

"Okay," Cat said, raising her eyebrows. "Are you going to let me see?"

Elena stepped out of the way so Cat could come around the corner and into the open space.

Cat gasped. "I think I'm in love," she mumbled in awe.

Elena chuckled. This was the reaction she was hoping for.

The bookcase took up the entire wall, but she'd had the ceiling raised so the top of the bookcase followed the angle of the roof. On the wall that faced the back of the house, Nicolas had installed transom windows that flooded the space with natural light. There were two doors that opened onto a patio, letting in even more light. The other side of the room had a matching bookcase complete with a sliding ladder that could be moved to the other bookcase.

On one side of the room there were two chairs, similar to the ones in Cat's reading nook, that begged to be sat in. There was a small loveseat on the other side of the room that looked just as comfortable. When Elena walked into this room, she felt peace and exhilaration at the same time.

"This is amazing," Cat said, almost reverently.

"Do you like it?"

"Like it?" Cat whipped her head around to stare at Elena. "I want to live in it!"

Elena laughed. "It was originally a bedroom. I explained to Nicolas what I had in mind and he suggested tearing out this wall and making it open to the living area and raising the ceiling."

"You don't know it's here when you walk in the front door, but when you come around the corner—wow!" Cat exclaimed. "Except..."

"Except what?"

"The shelves are empty. Can I help you put your books in it?"

"That's the fun part." Elena grinned. "I donated most of my books. You'll notice there are a few on this shelf." Elena walked over to one shelf that contained several books.

"I'm confused," Cat said, furrowing her brow.

Elena chuckled. "What an adorable look on your face."

Cat dropped her chin and eyed Elena.

"The fun part is that I get to fill it with books I'm reading now. Once I've read a book, I'll put it on a shelf." She walked across the room and pointed to a few books on another shelf. "These are the books I've read so far from Your Next Great Read. I intend to fill this bookcase with books I love. I have a feeling sapphic literature may fill these shelves."

Cat had an amazed look on her face and then smiled. "You want to fill these shelves with sapphic books?"

Elena nodded. "There are so many sapphic books to read and I know I won't want to part with any of them."

"You know, there are books in other genres," Cat said.

"Yes, I know that. But these are the books I've been wanting to read since college."

"Then why are you just now reading them?"

"Let me top off our wine. Please, sit," Elena said as she hurried to the kitchen to get the bottle. When she walked back into the room, Cat was sitting on the couch staring at the bookcase across from her.

"It's so beautiful," Cat said.

"Thank you. Nicolas did such a good job," Elena said as she filled their glasses.

"He did. I want to meet him."

Elena sat down next to Cat and smiled. "I would love for you to meet him."

"Okay, you were about to tell me why you haven't read sapphic books since college."

"Fear. I worried about what other people would think if they saw me buying a sapphic book."

Cat scoffed. "You can get them delivered to your doorstep. You know this."

Elena laughed. "Yes I know that." She ran her finger around the rim of her glass then looked at Cat. "Honestly, I was afraid if I started reading those kinds of books again I might find out some things about myself that I wasn't prepared for."

The compassionate look on Cat's face went straight to Elena's heart. "I get that," Cat said. "Are you ready now?" Before Elena could answer, Cat added, "I guess you are or you wouldn't be in my bookstore every day."

"When I found out there was going to be a bookstore in that shopping center, I went to Your Next Great Read's website and saw you wanted to make it sapphic-centered. I can't tell you what that did to me," Elena said. "It felt like a sign from wherever signs come from, that it was time for me to do exactly what Dean asked of me."

"To find out who you are without him," Cat said softly.

Elena nodded. "These books have opened up a world that I knew was there, but I was afraid to step into. Your bookstore and *you* have given me the courage I needed. It's also given me so many questions and you're my queer friend with all the answers."

Cat threw her head back and laughed. "Oh yeah, I'm such a success in the relationship game."

"You know what I mean," Elena said, reaching over and squeezing Cat's hand.

"I'm happy to answer any of your questions, my friend."

Elena took a deep breath and sighed. "Hattie really hurt you, didn't she?"

Cat nodded and sipped her wine. "What hurt the most was that I tried to fix it, but Hattie wouldn't."

Elena took Cat's hand while she sipped her wine with the other.

"I knew things weren't right and I tried to talk to her about it which was a big deal for me," Cat said with a sad smile. "But she would assure me we were fine and it was just a rough patch, as they say. Those rough patches seemed to last longer and longer. I blamed myself because I worked such long hours."

Cat looked over at Elena and smiled. "Hattie was in corporate sales and she was always around people. She was, or is, a people person. I'm rather reserved and was never sure how we got together. But I think she loved being the loud fun one and knew I'd be right by her side, meekly laughing at her antics. The perfect partner who would let her shine."

Elena smiled and squeezed Cat's hand.

"I felt like a failure. How could I not save this relationship that we'd built over the years?" Cat said.

"You're not a failure, Cat."

"Kind of," Cat said, raising her eyebrows.

"Not if Hattie wouldn't do her part."

Cat shrugged. "Jessica asked me the other day what I would do if Hattie walked into the bookstore."

"What did you say?"

"Nothing." Cat turned so she could look into Elena's eyes. "The bell rang over the door and a customer walked in. You."

"Me!" Elena exclaimed.

"Yep. That's the day we opened and you walked through those doors."

7

Cat grinned at the look on Elena's face. It was somewhere between shock and disbelief. "It's okay, Elena. You're the best thing that's happened to me in a long time."

She watched as Elena took a big drink of her wine then reached for the bottle.

"Are you okay?" Cat asked.

"Yes, I'm just surprised. I had no idea you were going through that when I walked into the bookstore. You gave me the most disarming smile. I immediately felt welcomed and not afraid to ask you where the sapphic books were located."

"I don't think you asked. If I remember correctly, I led you in that direction and I don't know why."

"Maybe you have some kind of book gaydar."

Cat chuckled as Elena poured them more wine.

"So, you know I'm going to ask questions," Elena said, setting the bottle back on the table. "If that's okay?"

Cat nodded.

"What would you do?"

Cat furrowed her brow. "Do?"

"What would you do if Hattie walked into the bookstore? If I saw her talking to you, I'd probably—yes, I'd throat punch her."

Cat almost choked on her wine.

"Isn't that right? I've heard Nicolas say that. Throat punch."

Cat took a breath then chuckled. "You'd hit her?"

"Yes! She hurt my friend."

Cat shook her head. She couldn't imagine Elena ever being violent.

"Okay. I wouldn't hit her, but I'd want to."

Cat glanced over at Elena and could see the wheels turning in her head. "What?"

"I think if I walked into the bookstore and saw her talking to you..." Elena narrowed her gaze. "I would walk over and kiss you on the lips."

Cat was about to take another sip and stopped. "Are you trying to make me choke?"

Elena smiled. "I'd kiss you so she'd know she made the biggest mistake of her life. She'd think you've moved on and realize she needs to hit the road," she explained, pointing with her thumb over her shoulder.

Cat giggled. "How much wine did you have before I got here?"

"None. I was waiting for you. I'm not drunk, Cat. I'm looking out for my friend."

Cat smiled at Elena's sincerity. "Thank you."

Elena nodded then leaned towards Cat. "Could you show me a picture so I know what she looks like? I want to be ready."

Cat burst out laughing. "She's not going to come into the bookstore. It's been almost a year and I haven't heard a word from her in months."

"Okay. But just know, I have your back."

"Throat punch," Cat said softly and began to giggle again.

Elena began to chuckle as well. "You do realize I've never hit another person in my life."

"But you'd do it for me?" Cat couldn't resist teasing Elena. "Are you sure you're not coming onto me?"

Elena's eyes widened. "No! I—I..." Elena stammered.

"I'm kidding. How about we get some food and talk about how to fill this bookcase," Cat suggested.

"Do bare shelves make you nervous?" Elena replied.

Cat looked into Elena's eyes. "Not at all. They're full of opportunities."

"I like that." Elena got up. "I'll be right back."

Cat gazed around the room and sighed. She didn't like to talk about Hattie or their time together, but sharing with Elena didn't give her the feeling of sadness that usually accompanied memories of Hattie. And offering to throat punch Hattie didn't hurt either. Cat smiled and an image of Elena walking up and kissing her in the bookstore caught her by surprise.

"Okay, where do you want to order from?" Elena said, walking back into the room with several take-out menus. "We have Mexican, Italian, Chinese, burgers."

"Do you cook?"

"Sometimes, but all I could offer today would be sandwiches. I need to go to the grocery store," Elena replied.

"I love sandwiches," Cat said.

"Really? I do, too."

Cat raised her eyebrows. "I don't mind ordering take-out and I'll pay since you've supplied the wine, but..."

"Come on, let's see what I have to make sandwiches."

They both got up and went to the kitchen. Elena began

to hand Cat the sandwich makings from the refrigerator. Cat set them on the island and turned to Elena. "Bread?"

"Right here," Elena replied, reaching into a cabinet on the other side of the refrigerator.

"Let's create a masterpiece," Cat said.

"You are serious about sandwiches."

"I am. That's another little weirdness about me. You know when you order a burger or a sandwich and they pile it so high you can't get your mouth around it? I hate that," Cat said as she took four pieces of bread out of the package and set two slices on each plate that Elena pushed in front of her.

"How are you supposed to take the perfect bite and taste all the toppings?"

"Exactly," Cat said, pointing a knife at Elena. "You get it."

Elena grinned. "Mustard or mayo?"

Cat tilted her head. "Both."

Elena chuckled. "My kind of gal." She took the lids off the jars and scooted them towards Cat.

Cat began to build her sandwich while Elena worked on hers across the island.

"This is fun," Cat said, looking up at Elena.

"I'm glad you're here. I always see you at the bookstore and this is a nice change."

"I guess you're right. Except, we were at Cory's bar last night."

"Why haven't we gone to dinner or to a movie or something?"

Cat shrugged. "We're having dinner now."

Elena chuckled. "How about we halve our sandwiches and share?"

Cat gazed at the ingredients spread out on the island. "I don't see any onions. I don't care for them."

"Huh, I don't either. What are you making?"

"Turkey, Swiss cheese, lettuce, tomatoes, and avocado," Cat replied.

"I have salami, cheese, pickles, and lettuce," Elena said.

"I'm in, let's halve them."

Elena reached into a drawer and brought out a knife to cut the sandwiches when the doorbell rang. "Here you go. Be right back." She handed Cat the knife and went to the door.

Cat looked up as Elena opened the door. In walked a very good-looking man who stopped as soon as he saw Cat.

"Oh, no. I'm interrupting," he said.

"The first time I have a woman over and you pop in!" Elena exclaimed.

Cat saw the shock on the man's face then heard Elena laughing beside him.

"You should see your face! Gotcha!" Elena said.

"Oh, you! That was not funny," the man said, giving Elena a menacing look.

"Cat, this is Nicolas," Elena said, pulling him over to the island.

"Oh! It's so nice to meet you."

"Uh, it's nice to meet you," Nicolas replied. He tilted his head and narrowed his gaze. "You're the bookstore Sloan sister."

It was Cat's turn to be surprised. "I am."

Nicolas nodded and glanced at Elena with a big smile. "Nice work, Ms. E. She's a looker."

"A looker?" Elena asked, chuckling.

"That's what my dad says when he sees a beautiful woman."

Elena glanced over at Cat and said, "Cat is definitely a

looker, but I was teasing you. I invited her over to see the bookcase."

"Uh, thank you," Cat said.

"I know who you are. Ms. E goes to see you every day," Nicolas said, nodding and grinning.

"So, this is who taught you throat punch?" Cat asked.

"What?" Nicolas said, looking from Cat to Elena.

"Okay, back up. Cat, this is Nicolas Navarro," Elena said.

"Hi Nicolas."

"Nicolas, this is Cat Sloan," Elena said, finishing the introductions.

"Yeah, I already said that." Nicolas reached out his hand and Cat shook it.

"Elena asked me over to show me the beautiful bookcases. Now I know who to call if I need any construction done."

"Thanks," Nicolas said with a proud smile. "Let me see, I have a card in one of these pockets," he added, putting his hands in his back pockets.

"You have a business card?" Elena asked, amused.

"Yeah. You never know when you'll find a new client," Nicolas said. He pulled out a card and handed it to Cat. "At your service."

Cat grinned. "Thank you." She immediately liked this friendly man. "So, Nicolas, Ms. E," Cat said, glancing over at Elena, "tells me you were once her student."

Nicolas looked at Elena and smiled. "That's right. She taught me how to read."

"Oh, that reminds me, I brought you a book," Cat said, walking around the island and grabbing the book off the coffee table.

"*You* brought *me* a book?"

"Yes, Elena didn't come by the bookstore today and..."

Cat looked at Elena then back at Nicolas. "It's a long story. Anyway, this came in today." Cat handed him the book and watched his eyes widen.

"This is one of my favorite authors. Thank you," he said.

"You've got to come by my store sometime. I have a lot more to choose from," Cat said. "And while you're there maybe you can tell me the dirt on Ms. E."

His face brightened. "Oh, I like you. Hell yeah, I'll spill the tea on Ms. E."

"What? There's no dirt on me and I don't drink tea," Elena protested.

Cat and Nicolas laughed. "We'll see about that," Cat said with a grin.

"I came by to make sure the paint dried to a smooth finish. I didn't mean to interrupt your date," Nicolas said.

"It's not a date," Elena and Cat said in unison.

"Okay!" Nicolas held up both his hands. "Let me take a look in here then I'll be out of your hair."

"Would you like to have a sandwich with us?" Elena called to him.

"No," he said, coming back into the kitchen. "I've got a date."

"Ohhh!" Elena exclaimed. "Is this the guy you told me about?"

Nicolas scoffed. "No. He's so last week. I'm meeting someone for drinks. You know, like you did last night."

Cat looked over at Elena and raised her eyebrows. *This is getting interesting*, she thought.

"I had a drink with Cat last night. That wasn't a date either. Yours, however, *is* a date."

"Whatever," he said, once again looking at Elena then at Cat. "It was nice to meet you."

"You, too."

"Thanks for the book. I'll come by and see what else you've got," he said with a grin. He winked at Elena. "Bye, Ms. E."

Elena walked him to the door. When she closed it she turned to Cat. "That's Nicolas."

"He is adorable," Cat said.

"He's a mess," Elena said, walking back over to the island. "Let's eat over here."

They carried their plates and glasses to the table in the dining area. Elena sat at the head of the small table and Cat sat at a right angle to her.

"I can see y'all have fun together," Cat said.

Elena smiled. "We do. He's always talking about the various guys he meets. That's why I teased him about you being here."

"What? You don't have various women over most nights?" Cat said playfully.

Elena scoffed. "About as often as you do."

Cat laughed. "You've got me there." She took a bite of the sandwich Elena had made and nodded. "Mmm, this is good." After she swallowed she glanced at Elena and said, "It won't surprise you, but I haven't been on a date or even thought of another woman in that way since Hattie left."

"Same," Elena said, taking a sip of wine.

"Liar," Cat said, taking another bite.

"I beg your pardon?"

"What about the library girl? You've had a thought or two about her," Cat replied.

"That doesn't count," Elena said, taking a bite of her sandwich.

"Sure it does. You've thought about that kiss."

Elena chewed and stared at Cat. "And you mean to tell

me you haven't looked twice at anyone who's walked into the bookstore? I thought you looked for beauty in everyone."

"I am, but that doesn't mean I want to go out with them," Cat said.

"Hmm, I guess you don't need to when you have one of those little toys from The Bottom Shelf," Elena said, pinning Cat with a look.

Cat put her sandwich down on her plate and leveled her gaze at Elena. "Do you want to talk about vibrators?"

8

"Why not? You know me and my questions." Elena shrugged. She didn't want to make Cat uncomfortable, but couldn't help wanting to know more about her. It seemed that every new thing she learned led to more questions.

"Who else am I going to talk to about them?" she continued. "You're the woman with the sex toys in the back of her store."

"True," Cat said as she slowly spun the stem of her wine glass between her finger and thumb.

"Uh oh, you pulled your teeth across your bottom lip," Elena said.

"I what?" Cat said, looking up at Elena.

"You do that when you're thinking about what you want to say." Elena shrugged. "I've noticed."

Cat tilted her head. "You know if someone else told me that it would unnerve me, but not you. Anyway," Cat said, "I don't want you to get the wrong impression about me and vibrators. Yes, I opened a place for women to purchase vibrators, but I do not think they replace intimacy."

"I didn't think that. I thought it was a way to explore my body, my sexual desires. I do hope to have sex again someday and I want to be able to ask for what feels right to me."

Cat smiled. "Good. I didn't mean to imply a vibrator could replace..."

"Love? Or intimacy, as you said. I want a partner for that. Don't you?"

Cat sighed. "That's a hard question for me." Cat smiled at Elena and continued. "I don't ever want to feel the way I did when Hattie left. Ever again. In order to protect myself from that, it seems the easiest thing to do would be to *not* fall in love. However, I'm not one for casual sex. I've never been able to do the friends with benefits thing. My heart gets involved."

"Hmm, I can understand your heartache. I've certainly been there, although for different reasons. But..."

"There's always a but." Cat smiled.

"I don't want to close off my heart to love and..."

Cat looked up and waited. "And?" she finally said when Elena didn't continue.

"I don't think you should close your heart to love either." Elena quickly added, "Let me explain before you get upset."

Cat smiled. "I won't get upset with you." She reached for her wine. "Maybe."

Elena raised her eyebrows. "You have too much love inside your heart not to give it to someone. It's like you're depriving the world."

"What?" Cat laughed.

"Sure. People who have some kind of talent or gift should share it with others. They shouldn't keep it to themselves. I happen to be able to make kids connect letters to make words and help them read. Can you imagine what would've happened to Nicolas if he hadn't learned to read? He wouldn't be the outgoing, accomplished person that he is."

Cat tilted her head. "You're trying to equate your ability to improve peoples' lives to me falling in love?"

"No." Elena shook her head. "You have so much love in your heart, Cat. I can see it in the way you help others or when you're with your sisters and friends. I can feel it with how you've befriended me. Don't deny someone, and there will be someone someday, that exquisite love that is only you."

Elena could tell Cat was thinking about what she said. "I know it's hard and you don't want to feel that pain again, but someone is going to love you and when you feel that rush of emotion and it overflows inside of you then you'll barely remember who Hattie was."

Elena smiled and waited for Cat to meet her eyes. She could see a hint of the pain or perhaps that was the wall receding where it'd been around her heart.

A slow smile crept onto Cat's face. "I remember how it feels to give love, but will I get love back?"

"You will. I promise."

Cat scoffed. "How can you promise that?"

Elena shrugged. "I don't know. Maybe I'll become a matchmaker and find your forever partner."

"Let's talk about you."

"Nope. We're talking about you," Elena said, pointing at Cat.

"Okay," Cat said, leaning back in her chair. "I'll make a deal with you. If I see someone who interests me I'll let you know."

"Oh? Let me know?"

"Yes. In order to do that I will have to open my closed off, black heart."

Elena laughed. "Cat Sloan, your heart could never be black."

"It feels like it some days."

Elena reached over and squeezed Cat's hand. "Not anymore. What do you say we go in the other room and gaze at the empty shelves? I have brownies for dessert."

"How could I say no to a brownie?" Cat grinned.

They got up and Cat took their plates to the sink while Elena got the brownies.

"Don't you dare try to do the dishes. I'll put those in the dishwasher later," Elena said, giving Cat a menacing look.

"Okay, okay."

Elena led them into the other room and they once again sat on the loveseat.

"So, you like the blue vibrator?" Cat asked.

"I thought I was the one who asked the questions," Elena said.

Cat chuckled as she took a bite of her brownie. "Mmm, this is good."

"Thanks. To answer your question, yes, I do like Aqua," Elena said.

"Aqua?"

"Yep. I named her."

"Her? You know that means something."

Elena giggled. "I do. I've thought about getting her a friend."

"A friend?"

Elena nodded. "Will you take me to The Bottom Shelf tomorrow?"

"Of course. Do you have another in mind?"

"Yes and I want to get lube."

Cat's eyes widened. "Okay."

"Which ones do you have?"

"I'm learning not to be surprised by you." Cat chuckled. "Well, I have the same one you have and it's my favorite."

"What others?"

"That's the only one."

"Really? Hmm, I guess I'll have to try out some of the others and report back to you."

Cat giggled. "Okay, you do that."

Elena smiled at her. "Thanks for talking about this with me." She tilted her head and stared at Cat for a moment.

"What?"

"Thanks for being my friend. You have no idea how much I needed you when I walked into your bookstore."

"It is becoming clear to me that I needed you, too."

"It's your turn to ask me out on our next friend date," Elena said, taking the last bite of her brownie.

"Deal," Cat said, holding out her fist.

Elena bumped her fist to Cat's and grinned.

"I love this room. Thanks for sharing it with me," Cat said.

"You're going to help me fill it."

"If I had a room like this, I'd be sitting in it all the time. It gives me calmness and excitement all rolled into one. That doesn't sound possible, but it does."

"I feel peace in here, but also excitement with how the room will take on a life of its own. So, what you described isn't any less impossible than me thinking a room can live."

"Maybe a room is full of memories that were made in it and that's what brings it to life. I think I hear laughter because you and Nicolas have been in this room together," Cat said.

Elena chuckled. "He really knows how to tell a story."

Cat sighed. "I must be the most boring person alive."

"What? Why would you say that?"

Cat shrugged. "I'm not athletic like Cory and I don't love to socialize like CeCe. I just really like books. And who gets off on a room with empty bookshelves in it? Talk about boring. Even though they are beautiful."

"I do! Why do you think I had them built? I wanted a room I could sit in and simply enjoy being in it," Elena said. "Not many people would understand that, but you do."

Cat smiled. "I do get it."

"You know, I had to attend social events with Dean and occasionally hosted clients and some of his partners in our home, but I never enjoyed it. I had nothing in common with those people. Don't get me wrong, most of them were lovely people, but we didn't share the same interests. As for athletics? That ship sailed long ago," Elena said. "I enjoy walking."

Cat chuckled. "Walking? Care to elaborate?"

"I like walking through an interesting area. It can be in nature or simply along a quaint street."

"You don't mean hiking?" Cat asked.

"No. I mean walking along the lake or perhaps along tree-lined streets of a neighborhood."

"That sounds nice."

Elena smiled at Cat. "That would be boring to most people."

Cat narrowed her gaze. "So you're trying to say you're boring, too?"

Elena laughed. "No, we're not boring. We happen to like a lot of the same things. Don't you agree?"

Cat nodded. "I do. However, you didn't mention vibrators."

"That's between you and me, my friend."

"Of course it is. I'd never tell anyone about Aqua."

Elena giggled. "Are you making fun of me?"

"Would I do that to my friend?" Cat grinned as Elena eyed her for a moment.

"I mentioned to you that my sex life with Dean wasn't the greatest," Elena began.

Cat nodded then put her arm on the back of the couch and turned towards Elena. Her knee rested against the outside of Elena's thigh. The simple touch brought her a feeling she couldn't quite name and that was okay. There were several things about Elena that Cat avoided thinking about because if she did they might overstep the boundary of friendship.

Elena looked over into Cat's eyes. "Please don't think I'm complaining or was unhappy in any way. Dean was wonderful and I loved him very much and I knew without a doubt that he loved me."

Cat gave her an encouraging smile.

"I've never talked about sex with anyone and I don't know why I want to talk about it with you. But..." Elena took a deep breath and rested her fingers on Cat's knee.

"For something that makes you feel so good, it can be hard to talk about," Cat said softly.

"That's just it. I loved the intimacy Dean and I shared when we held each other, but sex rarely made me feel good. There was always this desire of wanting to feel the way people feel in the books we read, but we just couldn't get there."

Cat put her hand over Elena's and asked, "Did you ever have an orgasm?"

Elena looked up. "If I ever had one with Dean, it was a long time ago."

Cat nodded. "I've faked an orgasm or two in my life."

Elena's eyes widened. "Haven't we all?"

Cat chuckled and Elena felt the tension ease in the room.

"But let me tell you something, Cat Sloan. That little vibrator has given me more orgasms in the last few weeks than the rest of my life combined."

Cat could see the twinkle in Elena's eyes. "Good for you."

"I don't feel guilty about it either."

"You shouldn't."

"It seems a little bizarre for a forty-seven-year-old woman who was married for nearly twenty-five years to all of a sudden be this interested in sex."

"But is it just the sex?"

Elena smiled. "No. You told me I might discover things about myself and it was a good thing."

Cat smiled.

"One thing I have discovered is that I will not settle for a ho-hum sex life with my next partner," Elena stated.

"Okay! Now, are we looking for a man or a woman?" Cat asked.

"We're not looking," Elena said. "At least not right now. There is more to me than sex."

9

"Well, duh! Of course there is," Cat said, squeezing Elena's fingers.

"I think what I'm discovering is that all the parts of me need to be nurtured, not just some of them."

"Go on," Cat encouraged her.

"I'm engaging mentally by reading the books I've wanted to read since college," Elena began. She leaned in closer and lowered her voice. "We both know how I'm nurturing myself physically."

Cat grinned. "You mean with walks by the lake or through nice neighborhoods?"

Elena threw her head back and laughed. "Oh my God! Yeah, that's it."

"What about emotionally? You've suffered a great loss, Elena. You can't neglect grief."

"I'm not. I have worked through the steps of grief and saw a professional for a time. It helped immensely." Elena smiled at Cat. "I hope this doesn't put any pressure on you, but emotionally I'm nurtured by our friendship. That also includes Cory and CeCe and the other people I've met at the shopping center."

"And you have Nicolas," Cat added.

"I do," Elena said fondly.

"I'd say you're figuring this out and doing your best."

"Thank you."

"Not to put any pressure on you," Cat said with a lilt to her voice, "but you know our friendship is important to me. I closed myself off to most of my friends, but somehow you walked into my life and showed me I can trust myself again."

"I'd say we're both figuring it out, together."

Cat nodded as thoughts swirled through her head. So much of what Elena said rang true in her life as well.

"I can see the wheels in your brain turning," Elena said.

"I'm not chewing on my bottom lip."

"No, it's the faraway look in your eyes."

"I was thinking about everything you said and what resonates is: don't settle."

"You shouldn't either," Elena said.

"I know. I agree. I hadn't thought about it, but we shouldn't settle for anything other than what nurtures us, to use your words," Cat said.

"Here's to not settling." Elena held out her fist.

Cat made a fist and hit hers against Elena's. "I think this takes us past the 'easy to talk to because we don't know each other as well' theory," Cat said, making air quotes.

"Perhaps we have wandered into the 'you're the only person I can talk about this with' territory."

Cat giggled. "Oh, yeah. There's no one else I'd have these conversations with."

"Not even your sisters?"

"Especially them!" Cat laughed.

"Perhaps we'll talk about your orgasms next time," Elena said.

Cat sat back and smiled as Elena's words hung in the air of this very nice room with beautiful bookcases.

An hour later Cat was back home in her bed, propped up on pillows. She'd planned to read for a while, but if thoughts had been swirling around in her head while she sat in Elena's sapphic study, they were now making her dizzy. Yes, the sapphic study—she giggled because that was the name Elena had come up with for her room with the beautiful bookcases.

Did Cat want to talk about the intimate parts of her sex life? She'd never done that. Did she want to tell Elena that she loved kissing? Or that simply holding hands was one of her favorite things? She wasn't big on public displays of affection, but holding someone's hand while walking along had always given her a thrill.

Cat knew she could trust Elena with these intimate details inside her heart, but she'd just gotten used to the idea of trusting someone again. Who was she kidding? She wouldn't trust just anyone, not yet. It was only Elena.

The talk about vibrators suddenly thrust to the front of her mind. Elena was so honest and the delight on her face as she'd talked about her discoveries was adorable. She talked about her love for Dean, but she must have buried her desires along the way.

Cat wanted Elena to find someone who was willing to explore all these discoveries with her and embrace them and her for the incredible woman she was becoming. *Elena is incredible.*

Cat smiled and reached into the drawer of her bedside

table. Perhaps Elena wasn't the only one who needed to explore and discover.

In the middle of the night, Cat's eyelids slowly fluttered open. She felt something squeeze her forearm and realized it was her own hand. "What the..." she mumbled. Her head rested on her pillow and she looked down where her hand now rested on her stomach. A vague dream was swirling around in her head. She tried to remember what she'd been dreaming about before she'd woken. Fragments began to come back to her.

She was walking and there was someone with her. They had paused to look out over a body of water. Cat recognized the familiar stretch of water as the lake where Lovers Landing, the sapphic Hollywood hideout, was located. She had become friends with the women who owned the resort and had been there several times.

It didn't seem odd to Cat that she'd dreamed of this particular place because she loved it there. She tried to relax and see if more of the dream would come back to her. Cat was walking with another woman beside her and they were... She tried to remember. They were holding hands!

Cat gasped and sat up in bed. "Who was I holding hands with?" she muttered. She eased back down on the bed and closed her eyes. Her idea was to relax and think back on the dream hoping she could see who was with her. She could see them walking along the beach and she could almost smell the water. The contentment of being with this woman was obvious. She could still feel it even now while she was awake. But every time she tried to look at the woman's face, she couldn't see who it was.

Cat sighed and tried to get comfortable again. Maybe if she went right back to sleep the dream would continue. A smile played at the corners of her mouth. "Come on, mystery woman. Reveal yourself." She closed her eyes and the last thought before sleep came again was: *we're holding hands.*

As music began to filter through her bedroom, Cat once again opened her eyes. It was the familiar tune of the song she chose for her alarm. She yawned and stretched her limbs. Suddenly she remembered waking up in the middle of the night to the dream she'd been having. She rolled over and thought back through the parts of the dream she could remember, but the woman's face was still a blur.

"Oh well," she said, getting up. It was time to get ready for work. Maybe parts of the dream would come to her during the day. What she remembered most was the happy feeling she had during the dream. She was with someone who made her feel that way. If nothing else, maybe that meant her heart was shedding the pain and perhaps she could be happy like that again with someone new.

* * *

It had been a busy morning at the bookstore and now that Jessica had come in, Cat was ready for a break.

"Hey, I'll be back in a few," she said to Jessica as she walked through the opening into CeCe's salon. She looked towards the back but didn't see her sister.

"She's in the back room," Ryan said as he blew his client's hair dry.

"Thanks." Cat smiled as she walked by, then she stopped. "Alone?" she asked Ryan.

He grinned and nodded.

Cat walked to the back of the store which was similar to hers. There was a hallway with restrooms and the door at the end of the hall opened into CeCe's back room. She had made it into the cutest little sitting area and break room for her clients and the other stylists.

"Hi, baby sister," CeCe said when Cat walked into the room.

"Really? Baby?"

CeCe chuckled and patted Cat's cheek. "You'll always be my baby sister. I remember when Mom brought you home from the hospital."

"Yeah, yeah, yeah." Cat had heard this story a million times and she was only thirty-seven.

"I can't believe you don't remember meeting me for the first time," CeCe teased.

"Someone is in a chipper mood today. Let me guess, Alexis spent the night?"

CeCe smirked. "We spend every night together. There's no way I'm letting her go."

"CeCe and Alexis, sitting in a tree, k-i-s-s-i-n-g," Cat sing-songed.

"Don't be jealous."

Cat scoffed. "Jealous! Okay, maybe I am a little. Not of Alexis, but the kissing part."

"She is a good kisser," CeCe said dreamily.

"Would you say that you and Alexis started out as friends with benefits?" Cat asked.

CeCe furrowed her brow and stared at her sister. "No. We were friends, began flirting, and then we kissed. From there it was on!"

Cat chuckled. "That's so romantic."

"It was. I'm leaving out all the good parts because I know your heart is a little tender," CeCe said, then she gasped. "Wait a minute, has your heart returned from the dark depths?"

Cat groaned. "Please don't make me regret talking to you about this."

CeCe put her hands on Cat's upper arms and smiled. "Okay, dear sister. Sorry about that. What do you want to know?"

"I remember you talking about friends with benefits with one of your clients," Cat began.

"It was her, not me."

"I know, but how do you think it works?"

"Well, she and this guy were really good friends and—"

"What I don't get is aren't there feelings involved?" Cat asked, interrupting CeCe.

"Well, yeah, because they're friends to begin with, but with them, neither one was looking for a forever type thing. It was more like helping each other because, you know, you have needs. And where is all this coming from?"

Cat shrugged.

"Is there someone you want to explore this with?"

Cat shook her head. "No, I'm not ready for anything like that. Love is the furthest thing from my mind." Cat knew CeCe and Alexis were falling in love so she quickly added, "But I want that for you." She smiled. "Alexis is one lucky woman."

CeCe returned her smile. "I'm pretty damn lucky myself, but we're not there yet."

Cat raised her eyebrows.

CeCe sighed. "There's more to it than love. I'm not sure I fit in her world."

Cat scoffed. "Please. You don't believe that anymore. Let Alexis show you exactly where you belong. I think we both know where that is."

CeCe smiled again and sighed. "Wait a minute! Why are

we talking about me and Alexis? We were talking about you."

Cat chuckled. "It's hard not to talk about you and Alexis. I'd better get back to the bookstore."

"I'm not sure what just happened, but did I answer your question?"

"Yes you did." Cat gave CeCe a quick hug. "Love ya, sis." She walked out before CeCe could ask her any more questions. Just as she suspected, friends with benefits wasn't for her. She wasn't even sure why she'd thought about it in the first place. She'd never been attracted to any of her friends in that way. Talking to Elena last night and then the dream had her feeling off balance today.

She waved at Ryan as she walked out of the salon and back into her little haven. Books were her friends and made her feel safe. "Ahh," she sighed, gazing happily around her bookstore.

10

"Hey there," Elena said, walking up to Cat at the register.

"Hi. Hey, have you ever been attracted to any of your friends?"

"What?"

"Oh, sorry. I was just wondering."

Elena walked around the register and looped her arm through Cat's. She led them over to the reading nook and turned to her. "What's going on?"

"Nothing. I was talking to CeCe about friends with benefits and that's something I've never quite understood. I mean, I get it, but... I guess all our talk about sex and vibrators last night got me thinking."

Elena was trying to connect the dots from last night to what Cat was saying now and must have had a confused look on her face.

Cat reached out and put her hand on Elena's arm. "I didn't tell CeCe anything about our conversation."

"Are you..."

Cat furrowed her brow then realization dawned on her

face. "Oh, God! No, Elena. I didn't mean you and me."

"Whew, okay," Elena said. "I thought I'd missed something."

Cat chuckled. "It's been a strange day. I had this dream and our talk..."

"Dream?"

"It's nothing. Really." Cat sighed. "It seems you have made this nice wall, that I had so expertly built around my heart, begin to come down. All kinds of thoughts about all kinds of things have swirled through my head and you, my friend, are getting the random blips. Don't ask me where the friends with benefits came from because I don't even know." Cat paused and stared at Elena. "But it makes me wonder, have you ever been attracted to any of your friends?"

"No, I haven't. I guess I can see where you might think that since I repressed all those feelings from college, but there's no one. Friends are friends. Dean was my lover."

Cat nodded. "I didn't mean to make you uncomfortable."

"You didn't. But have *you* been attracted to any of your friends?"

"Never." Cat shrugged and held her hands up. "See what I mean? I don't get it."

"Hmm, I've never thought about it, but I guess I can see how it could happen. You see it in the movies all the time."

"Well, if it's in the movies, it must be true."

Elena laughed. "Absolutely."

Cat leaned in and said, "I think Aqua might be my kind of friend with benefits."

Elena giggled. "You're being weird today, but okay. Yeah, I did refer to her as my little friend."

Cat shrugged. "Exactly."

"Do you have time to sit for a minute?" Elena asked.

Cat looked around the bookstore and saw Jessica

helping a customer, but there was no one else in the store. "Sure. If someone comes in I'll need to help them."

"Of course, just like every other day when I come in." Elena smiled. "Do you want to tell me about this dream?"

Cat sat in what had become her chair when Elena visited the bookstore. "It's nothing, really. I was walking..." Cat gasped. "It's because of what you said last night!"

"What did I say?" Elena thought about their conversation, but they'd talked about a lot of things.

"You mentioned walking along the lake. That's what happened in my dream," Cat explained.

Elena listened and hoped Cat would continue. She wondered if it had upset her and that's why she was a little off today.

"I was walking along the lake near Lovers Landing," Cat began. "Do you know it?"

Elena nodded. "Yes, that's where Krista Kyle has her resort. I've never been out there. Have you?"

"Yeah, several times. Krista is a friend. Anyway, I was walking along the lake at Lovers Landing and I was holding someone's hand."

Elena's brows rose up her forehead. "Someone?"

"Yes, a woman, but when I tried to see who it was her face was a blur," Cat said.

"But you know it was a woman."

Cat nodded.

"Did this dream upset you?"

"No. I remember feeling...contentment. I was happy and belonged with her."

Elena smiled. "That's a good thing, isn't it?"

"I think so. I tried to see who the woman was and even went back to sleep in hopes the dream would continue."

"No luck?"

Cat shook her head. "The more I think about it, I probably dreamed about the lake because you mentioned it. But I also think it means it's time for me to lose the anger and hurt Hattie caused me. I mean, come on! I'm not the only one whose girlfriend broke up with her."

"No, but still, you have to work through that pain in your own way. Everyone is different."

"How long has it been since you lost Dean? I don't think you've ever told me."

Elena smiled. "It's been almost a year."

Cat nodded. "Hmm."

"That's about when Hattie left, isn't it?"

"Yeah. I was just thinking we were both hurt around the same time."

"I'm sorry we share that pain, but at least we're not going through it alone."

Cat smiled compassionately at Elena. "That's probably why we became such fast friends. Our heads might not have seen it, but our hearts did."

"You know, at this point, I don't care so much how it happened. I'm just glad it did."

"Me too." Cat grinned. "Do you have plans tomorrow night?"

Elena leveled her gaze at Cat. "Really? Do I ever have plans?"

Cat chuckled. "I have some things for your sapphic study."

Elena giggled. She couldn't believe she'd come up with that name, but Cat latched onto it and that's how the bookcase room would be known going forward.

"I'll bring dinner," Cat added.

"I have wine. You know I'm a regular customer of Cory's, too."

Cat laughed. "You may become a Sloan sister."

"CeCe is doing my hair this afternoon, too."

"It looks beautiful," Cat stated.

Elena grinned and felt her heart jump. For Cat to notice and give her a compliment made Elena feel beautiful. She hadn't felt like that in a long time.

"It does," Cat said. "What are you having done?"

Elena gave Cat a radiant smile. "You'll just have to wait and see."

Cat laughed. "Can't wait."

The bell above the door echoed around the bookstore. "It's time to make someone's book dreams come true," Cat said.

Elena watched her walk away and couldn't keep from smiling. She'd been afraid things might be awkward after their conversation last night, but if anything, she felt closer to Cat. This friendship was becoming more and more important in Elena's life.

I don't know what I'd do without her, Elena thought.

* * *

Cat and Elena settled into a nice routine. Elena still came into the bookstore every day and Cat went to Elena's several nights each week. It was Cat's turn to bring dinner tonight and she knew Elena would be excited with her choice. She'd also brought something for Elena to put in the bookcase and this time it wasn't a book. Cat was a little hesitant about this addition and butterflies swirled in her stomach as she pulled into Elena's driveway.

She took a deep breath and looked into her rearview mirror. "What is wrong with you?" she said to her reflection. "It's just Elena."

Cat smiled and thought there was so much to Elena that *just* couldn't be further from the truth. She was Cat's best friend and there was no one she'd rather spend time with. If either of them ever met someone else—Cat couldn't imagine and she didn't want to.

"Hey," Elena called from her front porch. "Are you coming in?"

Cat smiled, gathered her things, and got out of her car.

"What were you doing?"

"Nothing. What were *you* doing?" Cat replied. "Staring out the front window?"

Elena chuckled. "No, I was in the kitchen and saw you drive up. Is that what I think it is?"

"Tacos from the food truck down the street from the bookstore," Cat said, holding up the bag.

"Get in here!" Elena exclaimed, holding the front door open for Cat. "You know how much I love their tacos."

Cat laughed. "I do!"

They went inside and Cat set the food sack on the island along with her purse and a bag from the bookstore.

"Did you bring something for the bookcase?" Elena said, leveling her gaze on Cat.

"I did, but it's not a book."

"Oh?" Elena's eyebrows rose up her forehead.

"I think you have enough books to read until the end of the year," Cat teased.

Elena scoffed. "Not if you help me."

Cat looked up at her and tilted her head. "You want me to read them?"

Elena nodded. "Yeah, to me."

"What?"

"I was thinking..."

"Yes," Cat said, drawing the word out.

"Do you remember the other day when you read part of that book to me?"

Cat nodded. Sometimes after dinner they would sit in the sapphic study and simply read. Cat had come to enjoy these evenings doing something they both loved together. She knew she could just as easily go home and read, but there was something nice about sitting with her friend in that beautiful room.

"I thought maybe we could read to each other. You know, just like you did the other night. You wanted me to hear how the author described that lake and it was beautiful." Elena gasped. "Maybe you should produce audiobooks."

"No! I have enough to keep me busy with the bookstore."

"Your voice is very pleasing and I enjoyed it." Elena shrugged. "Is that weird?"

"No, it's not weird. You read to me that night, too."

"Are we weird?" Elena asked, leaning in, her voice low and quiet.

Cat grinned. "No, we're not weird and if we are, who gives a fuck. It's you and me."

Elena laughed. "And that's why you are my friend. Who else can you be weird with and it be okay?"

Cat joined her laughter. "But it's not weird."

"Okay," Elena said. "Now, what did you bring for the bookcase?"

Cat shyly looked into Elena's eyes. "If reading to each other isn't weird then this might be." Cat reached into the bag and brought out a framed picture.

"Oh, Cat!" Elena exclaimed. "I love it!"

Cat released the breath she was holding. Jessica had taken a picture of them last week when Elena was in the bookstore. They were standing in the reading nook and Elena had put her arm around Cat's shoulder when Jessica told them to smile. Cat printed the picture and put it in a frame thinking it could take up some of the empty space in the bookcase.

Elena gazed at the picture and then looked down at Cat. "Am I that much taller than you?"

Cat leaned over and gazed at the picture. She was a few inches shorter than Elena, but what she remembered about that day was the feel of Elena's hand on her shoulder. It felt nice to be touched by someone she cared about and knew cared about her. "Yeah, you are."

Elena looked down at her and smiled. "I remember that day. I just came from CeCe's salon."

"Yeah, you had her highlight your hair. It looks beautiful," Cat said, gently touching the ends that didn't quite reach Elena's shoulders.

Elena smiled at Cat, looked back at the picture, and continued. "I was happy she took the picture and wondered why we hadn't done that before. Nicolas took selfies of us nearly every day while he worked on the room. We should do that!"

"What? Take a picture in the sapphic study?"

"Yes, come on." Elena grabbed Cat's hand and pulled her into the room.

"What about the tacos?"

"It'll only take a minute." Elena had her phone in her hand before Cat knew what was happening. "Let's stand in front of the shelf that has books on it." She chuckled.

Cat smiled as Elena held her arm out and put her hand on Cat's shoulder. "Smile!"

"I am smiling," Cat said, trying not to move her lips.

Elena took several photos then turned to Cat. "Let's put our picture right here."

Cat watched Elena place the framed picture on an

empty shelf across from the love seat. "I'll see it every time I walk into the room."

"It looks perfect there," Cat said, but her eyes were on Elena and the delight that covered her face.

"One more, with our picture in the background," Elena said, turning to Cat with a big smile.

Cat turned around and waited for Elena to step beside her. "Uh, you can't see the picture."

"But we look good." Elena grinned. "Smile for me, Cat."

Cat giggled and smiled again as Elena took several more pictures.

"Thank you," Elena said, beaming another smile at Cat. "Let's have those tacos."

Cat followed Elena back into the kitchen and couldn't believe how excited Elena was over the picture. She didn't tell Elena that she had one framed for herself and it was on a table in her living room with her other favorite pictures of her family.

11

"I'm going to The Bottom Shelf to replenish the stock," Cat told Jessica.

"That place has been very popular lately," Jessica commented.

"I know," Cat said. "Is there something going on we don't know about?"

"I think today is national hot dog day," Jessica replied. "I don't remember there being a national sex toy day, but we could start one."

Cat chuckled. "Why not? They have a day for everything else. Holler if you need me." She walked to the back of the bookstore and shook her head thinking about all the designations someone had come up with to celebrate each day.

She straightened up the displays where people had touched the merchandise. Then she made sure there was plenty in stock in the cabinets underneath the displays. Her phone dinged with a text and she reached into her pocket. She saw a notification of a text from Elena. She opened it and smiled.

Elena was supposed to share the pictures from the sapphic study with her, but forgot to send them last night.

Cat studied the pictures for a moment and the ease and contentment she usually felt when she was with Elena settled over her.

She read the caption under the pictures. *Whatcha doing?*

Cat took a couple of pictures of the vibrators and other toys on display. Then she typed: *Guess?*

She immediately saw the ellipses as Elena typed her reply. *I'll be right there!*

Cat chuckled but warmth began to spread through her at the thought of Elena and her little vibrator friend, Aqua.

"Oh, no, no, no," Cat said out loud. She shook her head then stopped and looked at the mirror behind the display shelves. Her cheeks were red and her clear blue eyes stared back at her. She and Elena had become closer and closer with each passing day. Cat had never had a thought like that about any of her other friends and wondered why she was having this thought about Elena now.

She had to get out of there. Maybe it was the sex toys coupled with the pictures Elena had sent. They both looked so happy as they stared into the camera. There was Elena's hand resting on Cat's shoulder again. Cat closed her eyes, remembering the moment, and she could feel Elena's fingers pressing into her shoulder just as they had last night.

"Stop it!" she mumbled. She closed the cabinets below the display and hurried out of the room. Instead of going to the front of the store she went into the break room and got a bottle of water out of the refrigerator.

She sat down on the couch and took a big drink from the water bottle.

"There you are," Cory said, walking into the room.

"Hey," Cat said, appreciating the distraction.

"Is everything okay?" Cory asked, her brows knit in concern.

"Sure. Why wouldn't it be?" Cat replied, taking another big drink of water.

Cory sat down next to her and shrugged. "Jessica said you were in the toy room."

"I was, but came in here when I finished up. Why?"

"Your cheeks are red and you look a little frazzled." Cory eyed her with a discerning look.

"I'm fine."

"If you say so," Cory acquiesced.

"I do."

"I haven't seen much of you the past few weeks," Cory commented.

"That's because you've been at volleyball practice or out selling booze."

Cory chuckled. "True. What have you been up to?"

"Mmm, I've been selling books," Cat said.

"Duh, I know that. What about Elena?"

"What *about* Elena?" Cat furrowed her brow.

"Come to think about it, I've seen Elena more than I've seen you lately."

Cat shrugged. "We've come to your bar a couple of times, but you haven't been there."

"I like her," Cory stated.

Cat couldn't keep from smiling. "I like her, too."

"Where is she? Doesn't she come in every day?"

Cat nodded. "She'll be here." She smiled and realized Elena coming into the bookstore every day was something she could count on. The thought made her heart skip a beat.

The door into the room opened and Elena came striding

in. "Hey there. I found you," she said with a big grin aimed at Cat.

Cat was enjoying the purposeful steps that landed Elena in front of her. She imagined this was her commanding walk when entering a classroom. With Cat they were usually strolling among the shelves or to whatever their destination might be. "Here I am. Did you lose me?"

Elena chuckled. "Hi Cory."

"I was wondering where you were. I need your help," Cory said. "Both of you," she added, looking at Cat.

"What's up?"

"Tonight my team plays Vi's and it would really be nice if you two could come cheer me and CeCe to victory," Cory said.

"CeCe's playing too?" Cat asked.

"Yeah, we're short a couple of players," Cory replied.

Cat looked up at Elena and raised her brows. "Do you feel like a little volleyball tonight?"

"Sure I do. I'm the Sloan sisters' biggest fan," Elena said.

Cat and Cory laughed. "With as much time as you spend here you may become an honorary sister," Cory said.

Cat smiled. *I don't want her as my sister.* Cat sat up straight and couldn't believe that thought slammed to the front of her head.

Elena furrowed her brow. "Are you okay?"

"Yep," Cat said, slapping her legs and getting up. "I'd better get back out there. Jessica is going to wonder what happened to me." Cat hurried to the door and took a deep breath.

Elena and Cory followed Cat out of the back room. "Thanks. I'll see you tonight," Cory said, exiting through the entrance to CeCe's salon.

Cat wasn't sure what just happened, but after a couple of

deep breaths she felt like herself again. She chuckled as Cory left the bookstore. "This should be interesting. I've never known Cory to have an enemy. She's mentioned that Vi thinks of her that way."

"How long do you think it will take for Cory to wear her down?" Elena asked. "Want to bet?"

Cat laughed. "You've come to know my sister pretty well. I think she's already done it."

"You do?"

"Yep. Cory's been practicing at the gym and I'm sure she's found ways to run into Vi."

Elena giggled. "This should be fun. Another Sloan sister falling in love."

Cat turned to Elena and tilted her head. "You make it sound like a spectator sport."

"We're watching CeCe fall in love right before our eyes. Don't you think so?"

Cat nodded. "I guess."

"Cory may be right behind her."

Cat shrugged. "Maybe so. But don't get any ideas about me."

Elena put her arm around Cat's shoulder. "I have all kinds of ideas about you, my friend. We'll be looking for prospects at the volleyball game."

"If you're looking for me then I'm looking for you," Cat said, gazing up at Elena with a smirk.

Elena narrowed her gaze. "Okay, I'll pick you up."

* * *

Elena and Cat walked into the gym at the Your Way fitness center.

"There's my mom," Cat said, waving at her. "I figured she'd be here."

They walked onto the bleachers and Cat sat next to her mother. "Mom, you remember Elena," Cat said.

"Of course I do. We've had several nice conversations at the bookstore. How are you, hon?" Christine Sloan asked.

"Hi Christine. I'm ready to cheer on the Sloan sisters," Elena said enthusiastically. She knew where Cat got her blue eyes as Christine's sparkled at her. "I'm a big fan."

Christine chuckled. "I'll say you are. They're lucky you're such a good customer. You mentioned you were a teacher. Do you not do that any longer?"

"No," Elena said. "I'm a widow, like you."

Christine gave her a compassionate look. "I wondered."

"After my husband died I couldn't find the motivation to do what I once did. Does that make sense?"

"It does to me." Christine nodded. "I suppose you have the time to find what's next and create a different kind of life."

"Mom!" Cat exclaimed.

"It's okay," Elena said, patting Cat's knee. "I am fortunate Dean and I made some good investments. The house we lived in was way too big for me, so I downsized and the market was in my favor. So yes, I don't necessarily have to work and that's where Cat's beautiful bookstore has saved me."

"Most people think Cory is the sweetest sister," Christine said, putting her arm around Cat. "But Catarina is my baby with the biggest heart." She smiled affectionately at Cat.

"Don't I know it," Elena said, smiling at Cat. "Shhh," she added, putting her finger to her lips. "She doesn't like people to know."

Christine chuckled. "You know my Cat."

"I do," Elena said, winking at Cat.

"Stop, you two are going to embarrass me."

Elena leaned over and softly said, "Your cheeks are the most adorable shade of pink."

Cat groaned. "I saw Alexis over there, I think I'll go say hi."

"Oh, no you don't," Christine said, pulling Cat back down. "They're getting ready to start."

Cat sat back down and smirked at Elena which elicited a soft chuckle.

"According to Cory, this team is good," Christine said.

"Cory always wins, Mom," Cat said.

"I don't know. She seemed concerned."

"We'll do all we can from up here," Elena said in an encouraging voice and clapped her hands.

The first game started and both teams were evenly matched.

"Wow, your sisters are good," Elena commented.

"Yeah, like I said, they got the athletic ability," Cat said.

"That's not everything," Christine commented.

"Who is the dark-headed woman that glanced our way a few times?" Elena asked.

"The one Cory keeps looking at?" Cat chuckled. "That's Vi. She also sells liquor and thinks she's Cory's nemesis."

"Hmm, I don't think so," Elena said.

Cat laughed. "Exactly. They're perfect for each other but haven't realized it yet."

"Sounds like someone else I know," Christine mumbled.

Elena furrowed her brow and snuck a glance at Cat who shook her head. *She must be talking about CeCe and Alexis*, Elena thought.

The first game ended with a loss for Cory and CeCe, but they came right back in the second game to even the match.

"Who do you think will win?" Elena asked as the teams started the third and deciding game.

"Cory will win," Cat said. "She may not win this volleyball game, but believe me, she'll win."

Christine chuckled. "She's right."

"Is this the Sloan sisters cheering squad," Alexis said, plopping down next to Elena. "Do you think they can pull it out?"

"We'll see," Christine replied.

"We have a mutual friend," Alexis said to Elena.

"Oh?"

"Yes, Victoria Stratton. I ran into her the other day and was telling her about Cat's bookstore and I don't remember how your name came up, but it did."

Elena smiled. "I haven't seen her in ages. I think it's because she spends all her free time with Shelby."

Alexis chuckled. "I think she wants to spend *all* her time with Shelby. That's why they started a business together."

"They do great work," Elena said. "I've sent some of my former students her way and she's found them houses."

"That's how CeCe got her house. I love her place," Alexis said.

"Please tell her hello if you see her again."

"Maybe you'll run into her at the bookstore. When I explained Cat had any sapphic book you could want, she said she plans to check it out."

"Thanks, Alexis," Cat said.

"I love your bookstore. Hey, we should all meet at Cory's bar some evening."

"Let's do that," Elena agreed.

"Uh, oh," Cat said. "This doesn't look good."

Vi jumped up and spiked a ball over Cory and just past CeCe's outstretched arms.

"Oh, no. They lost," Alexis said, getting up and going down the bleachers to console CeCe.

Christine smiled. "Now we get to meet Vi. This is the good part."

12

"Mom, be nice," Cat said.

"I'm always nice. You know how much I love meeting your friends."

Cat held out her hand for her mother as they traipsed down the bleachers and joined CeCe and Alexis.

They turned to watch Cory as she walked over with Vi.

"Mom, I'd like you to meet Vi Valdez. Violet, this is my mom, Christine Sloan."

Christine smiled warmly at Vi. "It's nice to meet you."

"It's nice to meet you, too."

"You're a good player. It was entertaining watching you and Cory try to outdo each other." Christine leaned in a little closer. "Cory still thinks she's an athlete, but..."

"Mom!" Cory exclaimed.

Vi chuckled. "It's okay, Cory. I'm the same way."

"Y'all should've been on the same team!"

"No way, Mom," CeCe spoke up. "Then no one could beat them."

"It's okay, you'd be on our team!" Cory said to CeCe.

They all laughed.

"I know you just played against her, but this is my sister CeCe and her girlfriend Alexis," Cory said.

"Hi, Vi. It's nice to finally meet you," CeCe said, raising her eyebrows.

Before Vi could respond, Cory said, "And this is my sister Cat, she owns the bookstore."

"Oh right," Vi said. "I've been meaning to stop in."

"This is Elena Burkett," Cory said. "I'd say you're Cat's friend, but you're our friend too."

"I spend a lot of time in the bookstore," Elena said with a glance over at Cat.

"It's nice to meet all of you," Vi said.

"I've got to go, girls. It was a good game. Vi, it was nice to meet you. I hope to see you again," Christine said. "Oh, and girls, I'll see you Sunday."

"Yes ma'am," Cory, CeCe, and Cat responded in unison.

Elena glanced over at Cat and she rolled her eyes.

"We try to have Sunday lunch with Mom every week and we've missed the past few," Cory explained.

"That's nice," Vi said.

Cory looked at her and smiled. "You'll have to come with me some Sunday."

"See y'all later," CeCe said, grabbing Alexis's hand and walking away.

"CeCe's good. Why doesn't she play with y'all all the time?" Vi asked.

Cory smirked. "Because she'd rather play with Alexis."

Cat laughed. "Can you blame her?"

"Oh my, your heart *is* still beating," Cory said to Cat.

"Sister," Cat said, which sounded like a warning.

Cory held up both hands and nodded. "Thanks for coming, Elena. It was nice to have you here cheering for us."

"It was fun," Elena said. "It was nice to meet you, Vi."

"You, too."

Cat and Elena turned to walk out and Elena bumped her shoulder against Cat's. "There was so much going on in that little meet and greet."

Cat giggled. "I know. Cory is taking Vi back to the bar at The Liquor Box. I think this enemy situation will soon be resolved."

Elena chuckled. "Was there really an enemy thing going on in the first place?"

"Maybe in Vi's mind, but not in Cory's."

"Hey!" Elena exclaimed as they reached the door to leave the fitness center. "We were supposed to be looking for someone for you."

"And you," Cat said, opening the door.

Elena walked through the open door. "I'm not ready for that. I'm happy with my books and Aqua."

"I'm not ready either."

"What about your dream?"

"It was only because you were talking about the lake. I haven't had it again."

"It could happen," Elena softly said. "You can feel that with someone."

"You can, too."

Elena put her arm through Cat's as they walked to her car. "I've got you. That's all I need for now."

Cat smiled over at her and nodded. Elena drove them back to Cat's house and pulled into the driveway.

Cat turned to look at Elena. "Would you like to come in for a while? I'm always at your place, but you've only been to mine once."

"Sure." Elena smiled and turned off the car.

"I don't have a fancy sapphic study to hang out in, but I

do have wine," Cat said as they walked through the front door.

Elena chuckled. "If you had a fancy sapphic study you wouldn't want to hang out in mine."

Cat raised her eyebrows. "I don't come over just for the books." She went into the kitchen and took a bottle of wine out of the refrigerator.

"Glasses?" Elena asked.

Cat pointed to a cabinet and Elena retrieved two wine glasses.

"Let's go in here," Cat said, leading them into the living room.

They sat down on the couch and Elena held out the glasses. Cat filled them both then set the bottle on the coffee table.

Elena held out one of the glasses to Cat and as she reached for it, Elena let go too quickly and wine sloshed onto Cat's shirt before she grasped the glass.

"Oh, no. I'm sorry," Elena exclaimed, setting her glass on the table.

Cat pulled the wet shirt away from her body.

Elena began to unbutton Cat's shirt. "Let's get that off and run cold water on it so it won't stain."

They both went into the kitchen and Cat took the shirt off as Elena turned the water on.

"I can get it," Cat said as Elena took the shirt from her.

"I did it and I'll fix it," Elena said, holding it under the water. "I hope."

"It'll be fine, Elena. It's white wine."

Elena glanced at her and smirked then turned back to her task.

A moment later Elena glanced back at Cat and looked down at her chest.

Cat raised her eyebrows. "Do you see something you like?"

Elena looked up into her eyes. "Yes, that bra."

Cat giggled. "You wouldn't expect me to wear something like this?"

"No, uh, It's not that," Elena stuttered.

"What then?" Cat asked suggestively. She could see Elena's cheeks start to pinken and thought this might be fun.

"That's a beautiful bra," Elena stated, turning the water off.

"Thank you. I have the undies to match."

A smile slowly crossed Cat's face as Elena's cheeks flamed even brighter.

"Can you imagine a mild-mannered tax accountant wearing sexy lingerie under her nice dresses and suits?"

Cat watched Elena wring the excess water out of her shirt then she turned to Cat. "Is there something you want to tell me?"

Cat ran her teeth over her bottom lip. "Well, since you've got my shirt off." Cat took the wet shirt from Elena. "Let's put this in here."

They went back to Cat's bedroom and she hung the wet shirt over her shower door. When she walked back into the bedroom, Elena was sitting on the end of the bed. Cat pulled open a drawer, took out a T-shirt and put it on, then sat down next to her.

"After Hattie left, I was so down that I decided to try and do something to feel better about myself," Cat began.

Elena patiently listened.

"I came across this pretty lingerie set while I was mindlessly scrolling on the internet. After a few clicks, I ordered the set."

Elena grinned. "Good for you."

"I couldn't believe how it made me feel," Cat said. "So I bought more."

Elena shook her head and smiled. "If those other accountants or your clients knew what you were wearing while you crunched their numbers!"

They both started to giggle.

"I don't have to dress up for the bookstore," Cat said. "I wear these cute dresses and pants, but underneath..." Cat shrugged.

"Oh my God! If your customers knew what you were wearing when you sell them a sapphic romance."

"Or erotica," Cat added.

Elena's eyes widened.

"Do you want to see?"

Cat thought Elena's eyes were going to pop out of her head. "The other ones, Elena. Not the rest of what I'm wearing."

"I didn't think you meant that," Elena stammered.

Cat chuckled. "Come here." She walked over to a chest of drawers and opened the middle drawer. "I have a variety of colors. Some lacey, some not."

Elena gasped and reached out to touch one of the silky bras. "They're beautiful."

"You can touch it," Cat said.

Elena looked up at her and grinned. "Wow, that's nice," she said as she ran her fingers over the fabric of a deep red bra.

Suddenly an image of Elena running her fingers over the bra while Cat was wearing it flashed through her mind. She shook her head, casting the image away. *What the fuck!*

"It's become a guilty pleasure of mine," Cat said, taking a settling breath.

"You shouldn't feel guilty about something that makes you feel beautiful, but..." Elena said, looking into Cat's eyes. "You're beautiful without them."

Cat smiled and closed the drawer. "Thank you. Let's try that glass of wine again."

They walked back into the living room and Cat took her glass off the table. "I'll be right back." She walked into the kitchen and wiped the outside of the glass dry.

"You know, now I'm going to be wondering what you're wearing underneath your clothes every time I come into the bookstore," Elena said.

Cat sat down on the couch. "If you're a good girl, maybe I'll give you a peek." She took a sip of her wine and couldn't hold in the laughter.

Elena chuckled. "You are something else, Cat Sloan."

Cat shrugged. "It's the quiet ones you have to look out for."

"Were you ever going to tell me?"

"I almost did the other night when you were reading that passage describing the woman's undergarments. I guess you have your sapphic study and I have my sexy lingerie."

"Good for both of us," Elena said, clinking her glass to Cat's. "Is that how The Bottom Shelf came about?"

"My vibrator serves a purpose just as Aqua does for you. I really wanted a place where they didn't seem quite so taboo. I mean, there's going to be a little hint of naughtiness attached to The Bottom Shelf and there's nothing wrong with that."

"I think it's good to feel naughty as well as beautiful. Cheers to you for providing this public service."

Cat nearly spit out the wine she was drinking then snorted. "Public service! Oh, I love that."

They sipped their wine and Cat gazed at Elena. "Hey,

why don't you come to my mom's with me on Sunday? She's a great cook."

"Isn't it a family thing?"

"Alexis will be there with CeCe and you heard my mom say she loves meeting our friends."

"Okay, I'd love to."

"I'll let you know what time and I'll pick you up."

After Elena left, Cat rinsed out their glasses and put them in the dishwasher. She went back to her bathroom and felt the still damp shirt then took it to the laundry room. There wouldn't be a stain and Cat laid it on top of the washer to continue to dry. Elena hadn't hesitated to unbutton her shirt and Cat hadn't felt awkward standing next to her in just her bra.

It was kind of a thrill if she was being honest with herself. She'd purchased the lingerie for herself and never showed it to anyone else. The expression on Elena's face was curious but there was also something else.

"Elena is your friend," Cat said, walking back into her bedroom.

But why did the idea of Elena touching her in the bra waft through her head?

"Too many sapphic romances," she muttered.

She got ready for bed and wondered what kind of dream she'd have tonight. It didn't matter because they'd both said they weren't ready for anything like romance. They had each other; that was enough for now.

13

"I went by to say hi to Cory, but she wasn't there," Elena said, joining Cat at the register of the bookstore.

"She has a big plan today," Cat said.

"Oh?"

"She has come up with something for Vi to sell liquor in another area. That way they won't be competing for the same accounts."

"And they can be friends," Elena said, nodding.

Cat chuckled. "They are already friends, but this way they can be more."

"Hmm, is love in the air?"

Cat raised her brows and grinned.

Elena looked around and could see no one was near them. She leaned in closer. "What color are you wearing today?"

Cat giggled. "You have asked me that every day since I told you about my...drawer."

It was Elena's turn to giggle. "Drawer?"

"Well, yeah."

Elena's giggle turned into laughter. "I've been in your drawers."

"Oh my God! Have you turned into a teenage boy?"

Elena shook her head and controlled her laughter. "Nicolas has been by for a visit. He can be so funny and sophomoric at times."

Cat chuckled. "That's why we love him."

"We do." Elena eyed Cat and wasn't letting her off the hook. "So, what color?"

Cat smirked. "Let's go to our favorite little hideout."

"The reading nook isn't exactly a hideout," Elena said, following Cat through the bookstore. "The Bottom Shelf is more of a hideout."

"Someone is in there," Cat said, standing behind a set of bookshelves. She took a quick look around and saw Jessica with a customer. There wasn't anyone else in the store. "Psst," she whispered quietly.

Elena walked over and Cat unbuttoned the top two buttons on her shirt. She held it open discreetly so Elena could get a peek.

"Ohhh," Elena softly said. "It's the red one! I love that one." Elena suddenly imagined them in the toy room surrounded by all those vibrators as she looked down Cat's shirt. Warmth spread through her body and when she looked up into Cat's eyes she saw amusement.

"I swear you love my bras as much as or more than I do."

Elena's throat was dry and she was afraid to speak. She swallowed and murmured, "They're beautiful."

Cat smiled and Elena knew she had no idea she wasn't talking about the bra. She would never do anything to risk their friendship, but her feelings for Cat were beginning to shift and she didn't know what to do with them.

"Hey, is everything okay?" Cat asked with concern in her

eyes.

"Yep." Elena smiled. "Let's sit."

They sat in their customary places and Elena took a deep calming breath.

"What should we have for dinner tonight? It's my turn to bring the food," Cat said.

Elena breathed a sigh of relief that Cat started in on their normal conversation as if nothing was amiss.

"Where did the pizza come from that we had at your mom's last Sunday?"

"You liked it." Cat grinned. "It came from an Italian place not far from here. I can pick one up when I come to your house. Any requests?"

Elena chuckled. "You know what I like." It wasn't lost on Elena that they had settled into a comfortable friendship that was similar in some ways to her marriage. Another deep breath should calm all these crazy thoughts running through her head. *What is wrong with me today?*

"I do, but maybe I'll surprise you."

You seem to be surprising me with everything you say today! Elena glanced over to the opening between Cat and CeCe's stores, hoping for a distraction. With a stroke of luck , CeCe came strolling into the bookstore.

"Hi sis," Cat said, waving at her from her chair in the reading nook.

"Hi," CeCe said with an excited smile. "I need your help."

Cat got up and said, "Sit."

"You don't have to get up," CeCe replied.

"It's fine. I'll sit right here," Cat said, plopping down on the ottoman in front of Elena's chair. "What's up?"

CeCe gazed around the store then leaned in and said, "I'm going to propose to Alexis."

Cat covered her gaping mouth with her hands and Elena gasped.

"That's wonderful," Cat said. "No more doubts."

CeCe grinned. "I haven't had any for a while."

"Doubts?" Elena asked.

"Yeah, I wanted to fall in love with Alexis, but I held back because I couldn't see myself in her world."

"We tried to tell her she was wrong," Cat said, glancing over at Elena.

"What did Alexis do to change your mind?"

A dreamy smile grew on CeCe's face. "She knew about my doubts and simply said, 'I can tell you over and over that we are a perfect fit, but to make you believe me, I know I have to show you.' So that's what she did."

"How?" Elena asked.

"She simply loved me every day and showed me over and over."

"It helped when she sold her house and moved in with you. That's a show of commitment," Cat said.

"The doubts were long gone by then. Instead of belonging in her world or my world, we created our own world and it's amazing."

Cat and Elena both beamed smiles at her.

"I've been trying to figure out how to propose and then it finally occurred to me that I don't need some kind of big production."

"What! You're the lavish Sloan sister," Cat stated.

CeCe chuckled. "I know, but this needs to be about us and just us."

"How are you going to do it?" Elena asked.

"First, I'm going to take her next door to the diner for an ice cream cone," CeCe said. "The first time she had a bad day and chose to come by here instead of going home, I took her over there for ice cream. It surprised her because I'm pretty sure she was expecting wine."

Cat laughed. "You can't beat one of their soft serve cones."

"Right?" CeCe chuckled. "I think that's when we started to fall in love."

"What's next?"

"I'm going to have Cory order her favorite bottle of wine and we'll come by here to pick it up on our way to the back room of the salon."

Cat raised her eyebrows.

"That's where it all started and that's where I'm going to tell her how much I love her and want to spend all my days with her."

"Aww, CeCe. That sounds perfect," Elena said.

"What do you need from us?" Cat asked.

"After she says yes, I hope." CeCe crossed her fingers on both hands.

"You know she will," Cat said.

"I want you and Cory to come in with a bunch of champagne and we're going to have a big ass party!"

"That's the sister I know." Cat grinned.

"I want all our friends to come in right behind you and celebrate with us. Elena, I hope you'll come. You're our friend, too."

Elena clutched her hand to her chest. "I would be honored."

"You know, so many good things have happened to me since we decided to open this shopping center." CeCe gave Cat a pointed look. "Good things are here for you, too, little sister. Open that big heart of yours just a smidge." CeCe held her finger and thumb apart, almost touching.

Cat smiled at her sister. "I'm trying."

"Hey, you don't know where Cory is, do you? I went there to get her so I could explain this to all of you at once, but she must be on a delivery."

"Nope. This is the day she reveals her big plan to Vi."

"Oh, that's right." CeCe smiled. "I hope they can work through their business stuff. Vi seems right for Cory, don't you think?"

"She's been in here a couple of times to buy books and they do have a lot in common. Vi could be the one to tame our big sister," Cat said.

CeCe slapped her knees and stood up. "Okay, I have a client in a few minutes."

"Wait," Cat said. "You haven't told us when you're doing this."

CeCe's face brightened with excitement. "Saturday."

"I'm so happy for you," Cat said, hugging her sister.

"We'll be ready," Elena assured her.

CeCe grinned as she turned to leave.

"Isn't this exciting," Cat said. "You could feel the love radiating off them through all the flirting and now CeCe is getting married."

Cat slung her arm over Elena's shoulder as they watched CeCe walk away. "That could be you again."

"Or you," Elena said.

"Mmm, I don't think so," Cat said quietly.

* * *

Saturday was here before they knew it. Cat and Cory had helped CeCe contact all their friends, the champagne was chilling, and excitement was in the air.

Cat was so happy for CeCe and felt like she'd had a front row seat watching her and Alexis fall in love. Cory had told her that Vi was receptive to her business proposal and Cat thought she may be watching Cory and Vi follow the same path. She sighed and a stab of sadness went straight to her heart.

"Is everything ready for the big ass party?" Elena asked, walking up beside her. "Hey, what's wrong?"

"Hi," Cat said, giving Elena a smile that didn't quite reach her eyes. "I was just thinking about how happy I am for CeCe and I think Cory may be next."

"Oh?"

Cat nodded. "Vi was interested in her business proposal, so you never know."

"Then why do you look so sad?"

Elena's kindness made tears sting the back of Cat's eyes. She wasn't an outwardly jovial person like her sisters, but she certainly wasn't sullen either. Elena always seemed to know when she was having a down day.

Cat sighed again. "I always thought I would be the first one of us to get married. Hattie and I were together for a long time and Cory and CeCe haven't had serious relationships in several years."

Cat felt a gentle hand rest on her shoulder. "Here's the bright side," Elena said. "Hattie is obviously an idiot and you, my friend, deserve the best."

Cat leaned into Elena's side and rested her head on Elena's shoulder. "Thank you."

"Anytime."

"You always find a way to make it all better."

"That's what friends are for," Elena said.

Elena squeezed Cat's shoulder then dropped her hand. Cat immediately missed the affectionate touch.

"So, is everything ready for the party?"

"Don't you mean the *big ass* party?" Cat chuckled. "CeCe

will settle for nothing less, but yes, everything is ready. She texted and said they aren't doing the ice cream, but are on their way to the salon."

"Hey, is that Vi I see over at Cory's?" Elena asked, looking through the opening to the other stores.

"Yeah, it is. Maybe things are working out for her, too."

Elena gasped. "Here they come."

CeCe and Alexis walked through the front door of the salon and headed for Cory's store.

"It's happening. Cory has the wine at the register for them."

They both looked on and neither said anything as they watched CeCe take a sack from Cory.

"Uh oh, they're coming this way," Elena said. "Was that part of the plan?"

"I'm not sure," Cat mumbled as CeCe and Alexis walked into the book store. She turned around and noticed Elena had retreated to the reading nook.

"Hi, you two," Cat said happily. "Alexis, there are new toys," she added, pointing with her thumb to the back of the store.

"I heard." Alexis grinned.

"Maybe we should get something to go along with your cute little turquoise friend," CeCe suggested in a sexy voice.

Alexis chuckled. "It never hurts to look."

"That's my girl," CeCe said.

Cat waited until they'd started towards the back of the store and went to join Elena.

"Why did you leave? One minute you were there then poof, you were gone," Cat said.

"I didn't know what to do. I was afraid I'd give it away," Elena replied.

Cat raised her brows and gave Elena an amused look.

14

Cat chuckled. "You're excited about this, aren't you?"

"I am," Elena said. "You can see the happiness on CeCe's face along with some nerves. They're a beautiful couple."

"Yeah, they are."

CeCe and Alexis weren't in The Bottom Shelf long and CeCe waved to Cat as they left the bookstore and went back into the salon.

"I think they picked up a toy," Elena said.

Cat chuckled. "I don't think they'll be needing it tonight."

Elena laughed.

They both crept to the opening between the stores and stole a look to the back of the salon. CeCe and Alexis were nowhere to be seen.

"They must be in the back room," Cat said. "I'm going to check with Cory." She turned to Elena. "I'm glad you're here. We may need your help carrying in the champagne."

"I'm happy to do whatever you need."

Cat smiled at Elena and thought about just how accurate her statement was. She was always ready to give Cat a hand or just be there for her.

Their friends were quietly gathering in the front part of the salon when Cat walked through to The Liquor Box. She saw Cory and Vi smiling at each other. This felt like an intimate moment and she hated to intrude. Finally she cleared her throat. "Hi y'all."

"Hi, Cat," Vi said, tearing her eyes away from Cory's. "I better get out of here. I heard about the big proposal and y'all have jobs to do."

"Wait, I'll walk you out," Cory said.

Cat smiled as they left the store.

"They looked very friendly," Elena commented from behind Cat.

"I noticed that, too." Cat grinned. "I guess we'll get the champagne from the back."

"Lead the way."

Cat chuckled. "Is love in the air or what? Cory has the champagne loaded into coolers so we can roll them into the back room."

"I've got the glasses," Elena said, taking two sacks off the bar.

Cat rolled one of the coolers into the salon with Elena walking beside her. "CeCe's co-workers have the food ready."

Everyone waited quietly and Cat could only imagine how surprised Alexis would be, but also happy.

Cory rolled the other cooler beside Cat's and grinned.

"I take it Vi is happy with your business idea." Cat smiled at her sister.

"She asked me out," Cory said excitedly.

"That's great," Elena said.

"I know, she wanted to celebrate our agreement tonight," Cory said.

"Oh, bummer," Cat commented.

"No, it's okay. She's going with me to make a delivery at Lovers Landing tomorrow."

"I don't guess you'll be swimming and hanging out at the beach?" Cat asked.

"That's the plan," Cory said with a sparkle in her eyes.

"Be careful, big sister. You know what they say about Lovers Landing."

Cory grinned and raised her brows.

"What happens? What don't I know?" Elena said.

"There's magic at Lovers Landing," Cat said. "It's where women fall in love."

"I'm going to see if I can hear them." Cory walked to the door and put her ear against it.

"You're right," Elena said quietly next to Cat. "Love is in the air."

"Told you." Cat gave Elena a grateful smile. "I was in such a bad mood when you came in earlier and now all I feel is happiness."

Cory knocked on the door and they could hear CeCe yell, "Come on in! She said yes!"

They wheeled the coolers through the door and the party began.

Cat and Cory began filling glasses with champagne as their friends streamed in and surrounded the happy couple. Alexis showed off her ring and Cat could feel the joy from across the room.

"Do you need any help?" Elena asked, sidling up next to Cat.

"No, I think everyone has a drink in this first wave of

people," Cat said. "Do you see those women talking to CeCe and Alexis?"

Elena nodded. "Oh! That's Krista Kyle."

Cat smiled. "It is. She's with her wife and friends. That's the Lovers Landing crew. Give me a minute and I'll introduce you to them."

"It's okay. I know you're busy," Elena said shyly.

"It'll slow down and I'll introduce you. I want them to meet you, Elena," Cat said with a smile.

"There's Victoria Stratton and Shelby. Dean did some work with them. I should say hello."

"Oh, that's right. Alexis mentioned that you two knew each other. Enjoy the party. I'll come find you," Cat said.

Sometime later, Cory left a few bottles of opened champagne on the table so she and Cat could join the party.

"Uh oh," Cat said, coming around from behind the table. "Mom has them cornered. We should save our sister."

"Let's go," Cory said.

CeCe sighed as she watched Cory and Cat walking toward her.

"Mom must have mentioned the big wedding," Cory whispered.

"Several years ago Mom entered us in this contest," CeCe began when her sisters arrived at her side.

"And we won!" Christine exclaimed.

"Won?" Alexis looked at CeCe.

CeCe nodded. "We won an exclusive wedding."

Alexis's eyes widened. "Wow!"

"But it's for all three of us," Cory added.

"All three?" Alexis asked.

Cat nodded. "All three of us have to get married in one big wedding," Cat said with zero enthusiasm.

"Three sisters and their loves," Christine said, clapping her hands.

"CeCe is the first to get engaged." Cory grinned. "I'm so happy for you both. You are perfect together!"

"Thanks, Cory," Alexis said. "So we're all getting married together?" she asked, sounding confused.

"We can talk about it later, babe," CeCe said.

"You'd better get busy finding Cory and Cat their soulmates. Oh wait, you say the love of your life now, right?" Christine said dramatically, holding her hand to her chest.

"I'm sorry, CeCe," Cat said. "There's no way I'm getting married, so I guess none of us will get the fancy wedding."

"Hold on, Cat," Alexis said. She looked at CeCe and smiled. "I never thought I'd fall in love again. And there was no way I was ever getting married."

"That's right. Lex told me that from the beginning, but our hearts had a better idea."

"And here we are. I never imagined I'd ever be this happy," Alexis said, putting her arm around CeCe.

"Keep your heart open, Cat." CeCe smiled at Alexis. "You never know what can happen."

Cat wanted to believe she could find the kind of love CeCe and Alexis shared. At one time, she thought she'd had it. How could she trust her heart to know? Because it didn't with Hattie. But right now, watching her sister, she wanted that. She wanted to love and be loved like that.

Tears stung Cat's eyes. To keep from crying, she quickly turned around and her eyes locked on Elena's. *Could I love again? Could it be...*

Cat shook those thoughts out of her head and took a couple of steps towards Elena.

"You never mentioned this big wedding," Elena said, raising her eyebrows.

"That's because it's my mom's dream, not mine," Cat said.

Elena gave Cat a sad smile and she couldn't help but wonder what that was about. She reached out and put her hand on Elena's arm. "Is this making you miss Dean or think about your wedding?"

Elena shook her head. "No. I just want that for you someday, Cat."

Cat followed Elena's gaze and saw CeCe and Alexis sweetly sharing a kiss as Alexis showed her ring to another friend.

* * *

"Thanks, Elena. That would require trusting someone with my heart. You know how I feel about that."

"But you're working on it," Elena encouraged her.

Cat scoffed. "Outside of my family, you're the only person I trust. I know you wouldn't hurt me."

Elena smiled at Cat but her heart was breaking in her chest. She wanted to kick Hattie Tucker's ass into next week for hurting Cat and taking her self-confidence with her when she left.

"Did you have a nice chat with Victoria and Shelby?" Cat asked.

Thoughts ran through Elena's head on how she could help Cat restore her trust in herself. Cat was an amazing woman and should have an equally amazing partner to live this life with.

"Elena?" Cat said, putting her hand on her shoulder.

"I'm sorry," Elena said, meeting Cat's stare. "It was great to talk with them. I met the other partners in their business."

"They are a great group."

Elena nodded.

"Are you okay?"

"Yeah," Elena said, trying to smile. "I'm going to take off. This was a great party. Well done, Sloan sister."

Cat smiled. "You know it wasn't just me. Let me walk you out."

"No, that's okay. You stay and enjoy the party. I'll see you tomorrow."

Elena headed for the door and could feel Cat's stare on her back. She couldn't stand there another minute with all those jumbled feelings racing inside her. She wanted to go home, sit in her sapphic study, and get lost in a book. That way she could wrestle with someone else's problems instead of facing her growing feelings for Cat.

Elena pulled into her driveway and noticed a pickup pull in behind her. She looked into the rearview mirror and watched as someone got out of the car.

"It's me!" Nicolas said loudly, holding up both hands. "I don't want to scare you."

Elena smiled and got out of her car. "Hi," she said, walking towards him.

Nicolas peered into Elena's car. "Where's Cat? I thought she might be with you."

"Not tonight. She's at an engagement party for her sister."

"Aww, CeCe proposed," Nicolas said, nodding. "I could tell she was thinking about it when she did my last haircut. Good for her."

"What are you doing here? I thought you'd be out on a Saturday night," Elena said.

"I wanted to come by and check on my two best girls." Nicolas grinned. "Why aren't you at the party?"

"I was."

"But..."

Elena shrugged. "Come on in. I'll tell you all about the party."

Nicolas followed her inside and as she put her purse down he said, "Let's sit in this beautiful room the three of us created."

They walked into the sapphic study. "The three of us?"

"Yeah, you, me, and Cat."

Elena sat down on the love seat and chuckled. "I guess that's true."

"I built these exquisite bookcases and you and Cat are filling them," he said, sitting in one of the chairs across from her. "I never thought I'd love sitting around a bunch of books, but this room is beautiful."

"Yeah, it is," Elena said, gazing around the room. She was glad Nicolas was here, but it seemed empty without Cat.

"Are you okay?"

"Yes," Elena said, trying to perk up. She told Nicolas about CeCe's proposal and then the party.

"What fun! Alexis must have been surprised." Nicolas chuckled.

"They are so happy," Elena said wistfully.

"Why do you seem sad then?"

Elena looked into his eyes and sighed.

"Come on, Ms. E," Nicolas said with a kind smile. "Talk to me. I was once your student, but I've been your friend for a long time."

Elena smiled. "You are my friend."

"What happened?"

"I don't know," Elena began. "CeCe and Alexis are so happy and so in love..."

"Yeah?"

"I want that for Cat."

"What about you?"

"What about me?" Elena furrowed her brow.

"You both should be happy and so in love, as you put it." Nicolas gave her a knowing smile. "Are you going to make me say it or are you going to admit it?"

"Admit what?"

There was that kind smile again. Elena imagined Nicolas's smile charmed many men. She could see he was waiting on her. "Have you ever had a friend who you developed feelings for?" she asked.

"I think you mean more than just friendly feelings," Nicolas said.

Elena nodded. "Something has changed inside me. These images flash through my head."

"Like what?"

"I overheard Cat's mother explaining to Alexis that she won an exclusive wedding for the girls. But they all have to get married at the same time."

"Oh damn," Nicolas exclaimed, placing his hand over his chest. "That would be some wedding!"

"Wouldn't it?" Elena replied. "I overheard Cat tell CeCe she was sorry because it would never happen. She's never getting married."

Nicolas nodded. "Her ex really did a number on her."

"Exactly! If Hattie Tucker had been standing in front of me I would've throat punched her."

Nicolas's eyes widened. "You go, Ms. E!"

Elena groaned. "You know I'm not like that! I mean, where did that come from?"

15

Nicolas stood up and walked over to sit on the loveseat next to Elena. He smiled and took her hand. "You care about Cat."

"Yes, I know that. I'm so mad because Hattie took a piece of Cat's confidence with her and I want her to find it again. She has the biggest heart and so much love to give, but she's afraid to trust herself."

"What happened when Cat said that she's never getting married?"

Elena shook her head. "Alexis told her to open her heart. She said she didn't think she'd ever love anyone again or get married, and look at her now."

Nicolas smiled. "They're a great couple."

"CeCe once told me that when she and Alexis started dating, she didn't think she would fit into Alexis's world."

Nicolas nodded. "She mentioned that to me."

"She said Alexis didn't try to tell her that she fit, she simply kept loving her every day and showed her."

Nicolas stared at Elena. "That's your answer."

Elena's brows came together in confusion. "The answer?"

"Let's be truthful, shall we? You have feelings for Cat Sloan. You're falling in love with her."

Elena scoffed.

"Hear me out," Nicolas said, grabbing both her hands. "You want to beat up her ex, you want her to find love and be happy. Those are things you'd want for someone you love."

"Of course I love Cat. How could I not? We spend a lot of time together."

"Un uh." Nicolas shook his head. "There's a difference between love and *in love*."

Elena sighed and slumped against the couch. "I don't know how it happened. One day she's my best friend and the next I'm imagining her in one of her sexy bras."

"Umm..."

"That's too much information."

They sat quietly for a few moments before Nicolas smiled and said, "You don't know what happened? Let me give you the play by play. You go see her every day. She spends most evenings with you in this beautiful room. I know you don't just sit in here and read. You share yourselves with each other through your conversations, your time, and your touches. And now your hearts are beginning to talk."

Elena shook her head. "She doesn't feel the same way."

"How do you know that?"

"Because she said it tonight when she said she'd never get married."

"That doesn't mean she isn't falling in love with you."

Elena gave him a confused look.

"You would not be admitting to these feelings if I hadn't

pushed you. No one is pushing Cat. Don't you think she could be just as confused as you are?"

She tilted her head. "I never thought about that."

"Imagine how confused she must feel since she's afraid to trust herself."

"Oh," Elena mumbled. "What do I do?"

Nicolas smiled. "Maybe Alexis gave you an idea."

"Just be there for her every day and love her until she trusts herself?"

"Maybe show her she can trust herself and you."

"She already trusts me," Elena said, looking out the windows. "Wait!" She turned back to Nicolas. "If I screw this up, I'll lose her. I can't lose her, Nicolas," she said frantically.

Nicolas patted her hand. "You're not going to lose her. Take a breath."

"Fuck, I don't know what I'm doing," Elena groaned.

"Didn't you just tell me that Cat trusts you?"

Elena nodded.

"Then trust yourself. You want Cat to be loved and happy. Who better to give that to her than you?"

Elena stared at him.

He softened his gaze. "She'll feel it and things will change. Love does that."

"How do you know? You're only twenty-five years old!"

Nicolas smiled. "I know love when I see it and that's what's happening with you and Cat. Trust yourself, Ms. E."

Elena sighed. *Trust yourself.*

* * *

Cat was at the front of the store dusting shelves. She was thinking back on CeCe's engagement party when they were talking about the wedding. Alexis had told her to open her heart and when she turned around there was Elena staring at her. Such a strong feeling of affection—she wouldn't dare call it love—had come over her. The thought of falling in love and trusting someone with her heart wasn't as frightening when she was looking into Elena's soft brown eyes.

"Cat," Cory called to her. "Sisters meeting, now."

She looked up to see Cory and CeCe coming into the bookstore from the salon.

"Uh, I'm the only one here. Jessica won't be in until later."

Cory sighed loudly. "Okay, we can talk here."

"Come over to the reading nook," Cat said. "What's wrong?"

CeCe and Cat both looked at Cory with concern as they each sat in one of the comfy chairs. Cory paced in front of them then stopped. A big smile blossomed on her face.

"Uh oh," CeCe said. "You went out with Vi yesterday, didn't you?"

Cory nodded. "We had the best day!" she exclaimed.

"So you're not battling Vi any longer?" Cat asked with a grin.

Cory looked at her sisters then proclaimed, "I am so in love with Violet Valdez!"

"Wow! That's wonderful and fast! I had to figure out I was good enough for Alexis, but not my big sister. She's a true lesbian!" CeCe said, jumping up to hug her.

"Ha ha," Cory deadpanned.

"Aw, I'm happy for you," Cat said, taking her turn to hug Cory.

"Talk about a turnaround," CeCe said, sitting back down.

"Not really," Cory said, sitting on the ottoman across

from them. "While I've been trying to get Vi to see me as her friend, she was trying to keep me as her enemy, but it didn't work. We've had a connection since the first time she walked into The Liquor Box. But the first time she kissed me, I knew. She's the woman my heart has been waiting for."

"I'm assuming she feels the same way?" Cat asked.

Cory giggled. "She said she didn't have to hold her feelings back any longer."

"Oh my God, CeCe, did you hear her? She giggled," Cat said, laughing. "Cory Sloan doesn't giggle."

"Did all this happen at Lovers Landing?" CeCe asked. "That was a magical place for Alexis and me, but we had to wait and be sure it was our hearts and not something else." CeCe wiggled her eyebrows.

Cory smirked. "Krista and Melanie made us a picnic and let us use the private beach."

"I know exactly where you're talking about. That's where Alexis and I spent our first night together."

"I tried to slow down and not get ahead of myself, but all the emotions came out. I thought I may have messed up, but on the way back to Vi's place she said she knew what she wanted and our time is now," Cory said. "Oh, and she added that our time is perfect."

"Fuck, Cory. How romantic!" CeCe said.

"I knew she had a romantic streak. She buys sapphic romances from me," Cat said with a proud smile.

Cory chuckled. "She mentioned she was one of your best customers. You'll never guess what else we did on the beach."

"Uh, we don't need *those* details," Cat said.

"I'm not talking about *that!*" Cory exclaimed. "We danced on the beach. Vi knows how to salsa."

CeCe gasped. "No way! That is so romantic. You have someone to dance with now."

"I know!" Cory grinned.

"The romantic Sloan sister has been romanced." CeCe laughed. "I'm swooning for you, sister!"

"Don't say anything when you see her. We haven't actually said the words yet, but I'm in fucking love!" Cory looked to the ceiling and spread her arms out wide.

"When will we see her?" Cat asked.

"I don't know. She's coming by to see me after work."

"We'll be on our best behavior," CeCe said, giving Cory a grin. "However, I do remember you telling Alexis I had a crush on her right back there." CeCe pointed to the sex toy shop in the back of the bookstore.

Before Cory could respond, the bell over the front door of the bookstore rang, indicating a customer was walking inside. All three of them turned their heads to the front of the store.

"Hey," Elena said. "Am I interrupting a family meeting?"

"Not at all," Cory said. "Come on in. It's nice to see you."

CeCe stood up. "I think I have your favorite chair."

Elena chuckled. "Do I come in here so often that you know where I sit?"

"Being Cat's favorite customer has perks," Cory said. "We'll get out of your way."

"See y'all later," Cat said. "I'm really happy for you, Cory."

As they left the bookstore Elena joined Cat in the reading nook. "Are you sure I didn't interrupt something?

Cat chuckled. "Cory just proclaimed her love for Vi."

"What!"

"Yep, they went on a date yesterday. Vi went with Cory to make a delivery at Lovers Landing. Krista and Melanie made them a picnic and they spent the afternoon at the private beach."

"Wow, that must have been some date."

Cat nodded. "Oh and they did the salsa on the beach."

"Come again?"

"Cory knows how to dance and found out that Vi does, too. They were doing the salsa on the beach. Cory's found her dance partner and more."

"What do you think about that?"

Cat tilted her head. "I'm happy for them. The more I get to know Vi, she's perfect for Cory."

"Just like Alexis is perfect for CeCe?"

"Yes," Cat replied hesitantly. "Why does it sound like you're asking something else?"

Elena shrugged. "I overheard you telling CeCe there was no way you were getting married. I wondered if you're feeling pressure now that Cory is head-over-heels in love, too."

"Oh," Cat said, then sighed. "Honestly, I don't know what to think anymore. I have so many thoughts swirling around my head that I feel confused most of the time."

Elena furrowed her brow. "About what?"

Before Cat could answer, the bell over the door rang. "I'm the only one here." Cat started to walk towards the customer, but turned to Elena. "I have a new book for you, so don't run off."

Cat helped the customer find the books they requested then left them to peruse another section of the bookstore. She took a book from under the counter at the register and brought it over to Elena.

Before she handed it to her, she looked at Elena and smiled. "Hey, why did you leave the party so early Saturday night? I didn't get to introduce you to my Lovers Landing friends."

"It wasn't that early." Elena shrugged. "I talked to the people I knew and you were busy."

Cat tilted her head. "I wasn't busy. I'll never be too busy for you."

Elena smiled. "What did I miss?"

Cat stood on her tiptoes and looked over the top shelf of the bookcase nearest her to make sure the customer was okay. Then she sat on the ottoman in front of Elena. "You missed me thanking you."

Elena's brows knit in confusion. "Thanking me?"

Cat nodded. "When I made that statement about never getting married and Alexis told me to open my heart... Well, it made me tear up."

Elena reached for Cat's hand and squeezed it.

"When I turned around and saw you, I realized that I wasn't scared of the idea of love anymore."

Elena's eyes narrowed and Cat could still see confusion.

"You have helped me to trust myself again. Before, if anyone mentioned my heart or love or—God forbid—marriage, my heart would race and it scared me. But not anymore."

"That's a good thing."

"It is and I have you to thank," Cat said with a smile.

"Me?"

Cat nodded. "Yes, you're the one who encouraged me to trust my heart. It's beginning to heal. I trust you and look what I have. A best friend."

"You're my best friend, too," Elena said. "Don't ever be confused about that."

If only Cat could tell Elena what had really gone through her mind the night of the party. Elena made her believe she could love again because it was her. Once again thoughts swirled through her head, but she shut them down and gave Elena a sweet smile. "Next time, you're coming to the party with me so you can't slip out early."

"Next time?"

"I predict it won't be long until Cory and Vi will be engaged."

"Love is still in the air," Elena said.

"Hey, let's do something different tonight," Cat said.

16

"Different?"

"Yeah, instead of me bringing dinner to your house, let's go out."

This was new. Cat loved sitting in the sapphic study just as much as Elena did. But the idea of going out with Cat sent a thrill through Elena's body. "Where?"

"We have a bar that we love and it also serves decent food," Cat said.

"We?"

"The Sloan Sisters," Cat said, tilting her head. "Who did you think I meant?" Cat gasped. "Oh, wait. No! I was not thinking of Hattie."

"I didn't think you were," Elena said, holding her hands up. "I didn't know who you meant."

Cat's stiff frame visibly softened. "Sorry. You know what, we're going to Betty's tonight and we're going to have a good time. Hattie never really liked it there. That should've been my first clue we weren't going to last."

"I've seen Betty's, but I've never been," Elena said.

"Perfect. We're going. Let me check this customer out and we'll make plans."

Elena noticed a lightness to Cat's step and couldn't keep from smiling. They were going out to a bar together. It wasn't really a date, but the other people who saw them together didn't know that. Elena sighed and leaned back in her chair. She knew she shouldn't be pretending this way, but maybe someday she and Cat would be in a place where she could ask Cat on a date. Until then, maybe it would be okay to pretend.

Later that evening Cat came to pick Elena up and she was actually a little nervous. When she answered the door all her nervousness instantly calmed. The smile Cat gave her was equal parts excitement and warmth, sprinkled with just a hint of adventure.

"Look at you," Cat said, grabbing her hand.

Elena felt Cat's eyes look her up and down. It had been a long time since she'd chosen her outfit with someone else in mind. She and Cat usually sat around in jeans and casual tops when spending time together. Tonight Elena had chosen a dark blue pair of jeans with a sleeveless top. Over that she wore an oversized button down shirt. She'd rolled the sleeves up to just below her elbows and one side of the shirt hung just off her shoulder.

"You are beautiful, Elena," Cat said with a smile.

"Thank you," she replied and could feel her cheeks warm.

Cat had chosen to wear a T-shirt dress with a denim jacket over it. Her dark, curly hair was down and flowed just below her shoulders. Elena felt little flutters in her stomach and couldn't stop staring at her. "But you're the beautiful one," Elena finally said.

"We both look fabulous," Cat said, exaggerating the last word. "Isn't that what Nicolas would say?"

Elena chuckled. "Yep, and he'd be correct."

"Let's go. I'm excited to show you Betty's. I don't know why I didn't think of this before," Cat said as they walked to the car.

"Because we had that new room to decorate," Elena replied.

"I love your sapphic study and plan to be sitting on our favorite loveseat a little later." Cat grinned as she glanced at Elena.

Once in the car, Cat reached to turn the volume up on the radio. "I love this song." Harry Styles' "Satellite" began to echo around the car.

"I like it, too," Elena commented.

"You listen to Harry Styles?"

"Yes, I listen to all kinds of music." Elena gazed out the window and began to lose herself in the words. It felt like Harry was singing about Elena. She looked over at Cat when Harry sang: "Spinning out, waiting for ya to pull me in. I can see you're lonely down there. Don't you know that I am right here?"

Elena did feel like a satellite going 'round and 'round, waiting for Cat to pull her in.

Cat looked over at her and smiled. "Caught ya, didn't I?"

Elena's eyes widened. Did Cat know Elena was falling in love with her?

"I can see you have a crush on Harry Styles. It's okay," Cat said.

Elena laughed. "I don't have a crush on Harry Styles." *I have a crush on you.*

"Okay, whatever you say," Cat said, keeping her eyes on the road.

"I like his last album. That doesn't mean I have a crush on him."

"I love that album, too." Cat quickly glanced over at Elena. "Maybe one evening we should play songs for each other."

A big smile grew on her face. "I'd like that."

Cat pulled the car into a parking space and they went inside.

"Cory used to work here and is still good friends with the owner," Cat explained to Elena. Just then a man called her name and waved.

Cat took Elena's hand and pulled her towards where the man stood behind the bar.

"This is Chris," Cat said, smiling at the man. "Chris, this is my friend, Elena."

"Hi," Elena said. "It's nice to meet you."

"Hi, Elena," Chris said with a friendly smile. "Any friend of Cat's is a friend of mine. Welcome to Betty's."

Elena immediately liked him. "Thank you. This is my first time here."

Chris gave Cat an incredulous look. "Have you been keeping this beautiful woman all to yourself?"

Cat grinned at Elena. "Yeah, I guess I have."

"Shame on you. Ladies, right this way," Chris said, leading them to a table. "Okay, Elena. Now that you're here, you don't have to be with this one to get the best table at Betty's. Just ask for me at the door," he said with a wink. "Your server will be right with you."

Cat chuckled and gave Elena another grin. "I think he thinks we're together," Cat said over the noise.

"We are," Elena said as she leaned in. She couldn't resist teasing Cat just a little or indulging the idea of them together.

"Right," Cat nodded. "Like someone like you would go on a date with someone like me."

"What does that mean?" Elena was surprised by Cat's words. They had always seemed like equals since the day she walked into the bookstore.

Cat shrugged. "It's hard to explain."

"Try," Elena said, leaning closer.

Cat sighed. "You're a smart, accomplished, confident woman."

"As are you," Elena said.

"No, I'm not."

"Yes, you are. What about a tax accountant-cum-bookstore owner doesn't scream smart and accomplished? Only a confident woman would leave one career for her dream career. So you see, Catarina Sloan, you're talking about yourself."

Cat's smile grew and Elena was tempted to lean over the table and kiss her.

At that moment their server walked up and they gave her their order.

The conversation went from music to movies and TV shows. Sometimes when they spent an evening at Cat's they would watch TV together and Elena had thought about putting a TV in the sapphic study. Cat was passionately opposed to this idea and assured Elena they had plenty to entertain themselves with without a TV. Cat was right.

Once they were back at Elena's and in their spots on the loveseat, Cat said, "What did you think?"

"I loved Betty's and think we should do that more often."

"I do, too. I had a great time tonight."

Elena gazed at Cat and couldn't keep from going back to their earlier conversation. "Do you really think you're not a confident woman?"

Cat sighed. "I did, but I don't anymore. After the way you explained it to me tonight... Hell yeah, I am confident in my business abilities."

"You can be confident in your heart too," Elena said. "I've watched you become lighter and brighter every day."

Cat smiled. "You have helped me find my confidence again, El. I guess seeing myself through your eyes and knowing you believe in me makes me believe in myself."

Elena smiled and felt her heart soar with happiness. Now, if she could just convince Cat to see her as more than a friend.

"Isn't there something you want to ask me?" Cat said.

Elena furrowed her brow and pressed her lips into a line. "Ask you?"

Cat grinned. "You haven't asked me what color I'm wearing."

"Oh!" Realization spread through Elena. Their little game of what color lingerie Cat was wearing was fun, but now that Elena had embraced her feelings for Cat she was afraid it would be harder and harder to keep those feelings under control if they continued the game.

"Do you want to guess?"

Elena studied Cat for a moment and chased away the desire to lean over and kiss her. Maybe someday. "I think today you're wearing that deep blue bra for the Monday blues."

"Nope." Cat shook her head. "Mondays aren't all bad. I got to see you and I didn't yesterday."

Elena chuckled to herself. *Maybe one day after spending the weekend with me, she might change her mind about Mondays.*

"What are you thinking? I can see an evil little twinkle in your eye," Cat said.

"Evil? Me?" Elena said innocently. "Are you going to show me?"

Cat leaned in closer and pulled the v-neck of her dress away from her chest. "I wore the red one today because it's your favorite."

Elena glanced down at the silky red fabric covering Cat's breasts and had to sit on her hands to keep from touching her. She looked back up into Cat's eyes and smiled. "You're beautiful," she whispered.

* * *

On her way home, Cat thought back over the evening. Elena seemed to have a good time at Betty's and Cat did too. But right before she'd left to come home, they were playing the lingerie game and the way Elena had whispered to Cat sent shivers through her.

Elena was a beautiful woman and Cat never hesitated to tell her. In turn Elena had told her more than once that she was beautiful as well. But there was something different in her voice tonight. Cat couldn't be sure because as much as she wanted to trust her heart she still had doubts. She knew Elena wanted to explore her feelings for women. They spent a lot of time together, so it wouldn't be a surprise they'd developed feelings for each other.

But were these feelings progressing past that of a friend? That's where Cat's doubts came in. Maybe she simply needed to ask Elena. That could be risky and could make things awkward between them.

She sighed and let the thoughts swirl through her head as she pulled into her driveway.

A flash of light in her rearview mirror caught her attention when someone pulled in behind her. She got out of her car and recognized Alexis behind the wheel.

"Hey." Alexis waved from her rolled down window.

Cat walked up to the car and could see she was alone. "Did CeCe send you to the store for ice cream?"

Alexis chuckled. "No, I had to check on a patient. I saw you pulling in and thought I'd see what you're doing out so late. Were you at Elena's?"

"You know me too well." Cat grinned. "Actually, we went to Betty's."

"Oh gosh, I remember Cory's birthday party there." A sweet smile grew on Alexis's face.

"I remember it, too. You and CeCe couldn't keep your eyes off each other."

Alexis wiggled her eyebrows. "Can you blame me?"

"Not one bit."

"So, was this a date? Have you opened your heart?"

17

Cat scoffed. "No, it wasn't a date."

"You're dressed like it's a date," Alexis said.

Cat looked down at her outfit and back at Alexis. "I wanted to look nice."

Alexis raised her eyebrows but didn't say anything.

"You and CeCe were friends first, right?"

"Mmm, kind of," Alexis said. "We didn't hang out like you and Elena do, but I considered her a friend."

Cat nodded.

"Do you think you and Elena are moving past friends?"

Cat shrugged.

"Maybe you should see if there's more than friendship between you and Elena."

"I don't think I can do that. I can't risk it."

"You know, CeCe had boundaries. She doesn't date her clients and when she told me I needed to get a new stylist, I had to do something. Look how that turned out," Alexis said.

"Yeah, but what a risk."

"The risk was worth it."

"But what if you had lost her?" Cat said, stepping closer to Alexis's open window.

"But I didn't because I made sure she knew who I was and that we wanted the same things."

Cat ran her teeth over her bottom lip, letting Alexis's words swirl around her head with the other thoughts.

"You could just wait and see how it goes. Maybe Elena is having the same feelings."

"Yeah, but..."

"What?"

"I guess CeCe told you about Cory. She's madly in love with Vi and they'll be engaged before we know it."

Alexis scoffed. "You don't know that."

Cat looked down at her feet and Alexis reached for her hand.

"Cat, I'm going to marry CeCe when it's our time. Same goes for Cory and Vi. Don't let that big wedding thing have any influence on you. This is your life, your love, the way you want it. Everything will be fine with your sisters. I promise."

Cat smiled and looked into Alexis's eyes. She could see her smile illuminated from the lights inside the car.

"You're my family now. I want you to find the happiness I have with CeCe, whether that's with Elena or someone else." Alexis shrugged. "Your happiness is what matters. You don't have to get married to be happy. I know that much about you."

"You do?"

Alexis nodded. "You may be the youngest sister, but that doesn't mean you have to do anything like your older sisters."

"Thanks, Alexis. I'm glad you stopped by," Cat said, returning her smile.

"I'm just around the corner. We need to see more of each other."

"I'd like that."

"How about the next time you and Elena are going to Betty's, invite us. We'd love it."

Cat smiled. "Okay, I will."

"Don't worry about these feelings you have for Elena. Love always finds a way and it will for you, too."

Cat nodded. "You'd better get home. I'm sure CeCe is waiting for you."

"See you tomorrow. I want to buy a book from my sister-to-be." Alexis grinned.

Cat took a step back and watched Alexis drive away.

Maybe she was right. Stop worrying about everything and just let it happen.

* * *

Elena walked into the bookstore and immediately her eyes scanned the area for Cat. She saw her walking towards the front of the store from the back. When Cat saw her a smile widened on her face and she gave Elena a wave.

Elena waved back and walked to meet her. In her mind the smile on Cat's face was just for her. After a few weeks, their routine was still the same in that Elena came to the bookstore every day, they sat in their chairs and talked about books, and Cat caught her up on the latest love blooming at The Liquor Box. Once a week, instead of hanging out in the sapphic study or at Cat's, they went to Betty's. Sometimes CeCe and Alexis met them there and last night Cory and Vi joined them. Elena found that she loved these small gatherings with Cat and whoever decided to join them. But she enjoyed it even more when it was just her and Cat.

"Have you been hanging out at The Bottom Shelf?" Elena asked with an amused look.

Cat chuckled. "Wouldn't you like to know."

Elena raised her brows and dipped her chin. "Do I want to know?"

"I've been making sure the shelves are stocked."

"Have you found a new little friend?"

Cat shook her head. "No, but I'd be glad to help you choose a friend to go with Aqua."

Elena put her arm through Cat's and led them to the reading nook. "Aqua and I are doing just fine, thanks."

Cat giggled. "I have something new to show you." She pulled Elena behind a shelf that hid them from the rest of the store. "I have a new color." Cat pulled her shirt away from her chest so Elena could peek at her new bra.

Elena's eyes widened.

"What does this color remind you of?"

It was Elena's turn to giggle. "Aqua," she said quietly.

Cat laughed and rearranged her shirt. "Yep. I thought of you when I bought it."

A flutter awakened in Elena's stomach. It seemed that Cat said or did something nearly every day to make those little flutters a common occurrence.

Cat walked over to her chair and sat down. "I've been thinking," she began.

"About?" Elena said, joining her.

"I think we should go shopping."

"Shopping?"

"Yeah. I've told you how indulging in my sexy underthings makes me feel."

"Underthings?" Elena chuckled.

"Yes. Maybe they'd give you a little lift the way they do me," Cat explained.

"Lift?" Elena snickered, looking down at her chest.

"I swear, Elena Burkett. Sometimes you are too much."

Elena laughed. "That's why you love me."

Cat joined her laughter. "It's true."

"I think Cory and Vi enjoyed hanging out with us last night," Elena said.

"Ah, changing the subject. Okay." Cat grinned. "Cory came by this morning and asked if we could all do it again. She wants to take us to The Neon Rose."

"I'm not sure I know it." Elena furrowed her brow.

"It's a favorite LGTBQ hangout. Cory and the owner dated briefly," Cat explained.

"Oh?"

"They were better as friends."

Elena nodded. "I'd love to go."

"Okay. I'll tell her."

"I still can't get over their 'I love you' story."

Cat laughed. "You should've been there."

"Tell me again. I love it."

"They were going on this big date and CeCe was doing Vi's hair. They still hadn't said I love you yet, but you've seen them. You can tell they're head over heels for each other. Anyway," she continued, "CeCe and I thought we'd have a little fun, so I went over while Vi was getting her hair styled. We both crossed our arms and looked at her in the mirror."

"What did she do?"

Cat chuckled. "She thought we were ganging up on her. As her hair fell over her eyes she proceeded to tell us how amazing our big sister is and how much she loves her."

Elena laughed. "Is that when CeCe moved the hair from her eyes?"

"Yep and there stood Cory with her mouth hanging open, looking at her in the mirror. It was so cute! They were both shocked, but it didn't take them long to declare their love. Then they shared the sweetest kiss."

"Aww, what a moment."

Cat nodded. "CeCe had to run Cory off so she could finish Vi's hair."

"What a story," Elena said.

"I know. That reminds me, Vi's parents are coming in this weekend and Mom wants to have Sunday lunch for them. Would you like to come with me?"

"Are you sure?"

"Of course I'm sure. You've been to these Sunday things with me before. CeCe and Alexis are hosting."

"I'd love to," Elena said. "What can we bring?"

Cat shook her head. "CeCe said she and Alexis have it covered, so just us."

"Is Cory nervous to meet Vi's parents?"

"I think she's more excited than nervous."

"They'll love her. How can anyone not love the Sloan sisters?" Elena grinned.

Cat smirked. "I can give you a list, starting with—"

"Nope. Don't say her name. She doesn't deserve even one thought from us."

Cat chuckled. "Yes ma'am."

Elena gasped when she noticed two women walking through the entrance from CeCe's salon. "Is that Krista Kyle?" she asked excitedly.

Cat looked over and smiled. "Want to meet her?"

"Yes! Oh my God, is that Tara Holloway with her?"

"Come on," Cat said, walking towards Krista.

"Hey, there she is," Krista said, giving Cat a hug. "Cat, I'd like you to meet Tara Holloway."

"How have we not met before?" Tara said, extending her hand. "I want to thank you for the little toys you left with Melanie. We've been having fun with those."

Cat chuckled. "That's what they're for." Cat turned to Elena and reached for her arm, bringing her closer. "I'd like you both to meet my good friend, Elena Burkett."

"It's so nice to meet you," Krista said with a friendly smile.

"I'm such a fan of both of your work," Elena gushed. "I'll try not to embarrass any of us."

Tara laughed. "Thank you. I love meeting fans. It's because of you that I get to make movies."

Elena grinned and shook her hand. She knew Cat was friends with Krista, but couldn't believe she was actually meeting two of her favorite actresses.

"Our wives are getting pedicures and Tara has a business proposition for you," Krista said.

"My wife has convinced me to write a memoir and I've been working with an author," Tara said.

"Melanie has been after me forever to write a memoir," Krista said.

"You should. We've both got interesting stories to tell," Tara said.

"Let's see how yours does then I might be convinced."

"I'd love to be the first to sell it," Cat said excitedly.

"I don't only want you to sell it. I want to do a book signing."

Cat gasped. "Here?"

"Yes!"

"I'd love that," Cat said.

"Lauren has some ideas on the book signing," Tara said.

"Why don't y'all come out to Lovers Landing and we can

have a planning session," Krista said. "You know, it's a magical place. Just look what it did for your sisters."

"Oh, come on," Tara said, turning to Krista. "You think everyone falls in love at your lake resort. Don't you think they were already on their way when they came to see you?"

"It is magical," Krista said defensively. "You fell in love with Lauren there."

Tara scoffed. "We can meet at our home. It's on the lake and has a much better view."

Elena couldn't believe this back and forth between these two women. She stole a look at Cat and could see her delight as well.

"Uh, well," Cat stammered.

Tara and Krista turned to them and grinned.

"We do this all the time," Krista explained. "She knows if it wasn't for me she wouldn't be living her happily ever after."

"And she likes to take credit for every couple falling in love," Tara deadpanned.

"It's what I do." Krista shrugged.

Elena and Cat both chuckled.

"Don't scare them," Tara said. "Please, I'd love for you to come to the lake and meet with Lauren. She has some good ideas."

Cat smiled. "I'd be glad to. Thank you for the opportunity."

"Elena, I hope you'll join us," Tara said.

"Are you sure?" Elena asked, looking at Cat.

Cat nodded. "Yes, you know this bookstore as well as I do."

"Great. I'll get your contact info from Krista and we'll text you," Tara said to Cat.

"Okay."

"We're going to look around and see if we can surprise our wives with new books," Krista said.

"Let me know if you need any help."

Krista and Tara walked further into the store and began to browse the shelves.

"Can you believe this? You're going to be hosting Tara Holloway's book signing! I'm so proud of you!" Elena said, squeezing Cat's hand.

Cat's face was lit with excitement. "You've got to help me."

"Me?"

"Yes, I don't want to freak out. You keep me calm, Elena."

Elena smiled. "I'll be right beside you."

18

A few days later Cat was checking an inventory report on the computer at the register when Elena walked up beside her.

"Did you find it?"

"It says there are two copies," Cat said, pointing to the screen. "They should be with the sapphic thrillers."

"I didn't see them. Do you think someone put them with the mainstream thrillers near the front?" Elena asked.

Cat narrowed her eyes and stared at Elena for a moment. "I've started putting sapphic romances in with the general romance shelves and vaguely remember doing the same with a few other books."

Elena smiled. "You can't possibly remember where every book is on every shelf. I'll go look."

"Thanks, El, but I can do it," Cat said.

"Nope, I promised to take Vi's dad a sapphic thriller and I will find it."

Cat smiled as Elena walked towards the front of the store. Cory had come to the bookstore with Vi's dad this morning while Vi and her mother were shopping.

"Found it!" Elena yelled, holding the book over her head.

Just then Jessica walked in the front door. "What did you lose?"

"It wasn't actually lost," Elena explained as she walked to the register and joined Cat.

"Thanks for letting me come in late today," Jessica said.

"No problem. I need you to close tonight because Elena and I are going to CeCe's for dinner with Vi's parents."

Jessica furrowed her brow. "Say what?"

Cat chuckled. "Vi's parents are in town and it's a family dinner. It's the parents meeting the parents, or in our case, parent."

"Oh, now I get it."

"Vi's dad and I were talking about books this morning and I promised to bring him a sapphic thriller," Elena said, holding up the book.

"You know Vi's dad?"

"No. He came in with Cory this morning and we like the same books." Elena shrugged.

"So a big meet the parents weekend for Cory," Jessica commented then chuckled. "Once they solved their liquor sales dilemma, those two fell hard and fast."

"That's probably how the sales dilemma was solved," Cat said, turning back to the inventory report.

"Uh, I don't really know how to tell you this."

"Tell me what?"

"Hattie's back in town."

Cat looked up and met Jessica's eyes. "Oh?"

"Yeah. Do you think she'll come to the bookstore?"

"Why would she?"

"Because you're here," Jessica said bluntly.

Cat scoffed. "It's been over a year, Jessica. I doubt she wants to see me."

"You know, I never told you this, but I'm proud of you."

"Why?'

"I can't imagine how hard it must have been when she walked out, and then you started a new business."

"She left before you decided to open the bookstore?" Elena asked.

Cat nodded. "It was a couple of months before Cory spotted this building and came up with the idea for us to open the shopping center. This opportunity came around at just the right time. I needed to start new and look at what I have now."

Elena smiled. "Jessica's right. You should be proud."

"What if she's come back for you?" Jessica asked tentatively.

"It's been over a year. I haven't heard from her. Why would she all of a sudden come back to town for me?"

"She's had time to find out what a big mistake she's made."

"I don't think so, Jess. She had a new girlfriend less than a month after she moved out."

"She what?" Elena exclaimed.

"I told you that. She was dating and had a girlfriend before I knew what hit me."

"I didn't realize it was so fast," Elena mumbled.

"Yeah, it didn't take her long to find someone new," Cat said. She could still feel the pain in her chest from when a friend had told her about seeing Hattie with someone.

"She doesn't any longer."

Cat raised her brows then looked back at the computer. "It doesn't matter whether she has a girlfriend or not. She probably came back because she wants her half of the house."

"The house isn't yours?" Elena asked.

Cat shook her head. "We bought it together. Of course, when she left she didn't bother to keep paying her part of the mortgage."

"I can't believe that. She just left you with it?"

"Yeah and she wouldn't discuss what to do about it." Cat sighed. "I admit, I didn't push it at first because I hoped we could work things out. As time went on, I texted her, I called her, but nothing." Cat threw up her hands. "What was I supposed to do?"

"Wow, what a bitch," Jessica said, shaking her head. "I had no idea. Do you have other things together?"

"No. Well, I guess some of the furniture could be considered hers. We bought a few things together."

"What will you do if she's come back for her part of the house?" Elena asked.

"I don't know. I'm not able to buy her out right now. Most of my money is tied up in the bookstore. I guess we'll sell it and I'll find another place."

"Don't worry, Cat. We'll find you an even better place. The best part is she'll be gone and out of your life," Jessica said.

Cat nodded but didn't say anything. She wished she could get Hattie out of her life, but just when she felt like herself again, here she comes right back in to mess it all up.

"I'm going to hang my coat up in the back," Jessica said.

"There's a box of books I've already tagged into inventory. Would you put them on the shelves, please?"

"Sure thing," Jessica said as she walked away.

Elena walked around the counter and gently put her hand on Cat's shoulder. "I'm really sorry."

Cat Sloan is Swirling

Cat sighed, but didn't look up. She was afraid if she looked at Elena she wouldn't be able to hold back the tears that suddenly stung the back of her eyes.

"I'm here," Elena said softly.

It was all too much. She knew Hattie would come back someday, but instead of being angry, she was filled with sadness. Cat turned and Elena immediately put her arms around her and hugged her close. It felt like she was protected and surrounded by warmth. Yeah, that's what she felt. Protected.

Cat pulled away and looked into Elena's eyes. She saw concern, affection, and perhaps a little flash of anger. "I'm not sad because Hattie left. I'm sad because I failed at our relationship."

"Oh, no," Elena said, shaking her head. "You didn't fail. You didn't do this all by yourself."

"I know that, but it doesn't make it any easier."

"What do you need from me right now?" Elena asked.

Cat was almost surprised, but not really. Elena had proven over and over that she would always be nearby to help Cat in whatever way.

"I need you to go home then come back and pick me up for our family dinner tonight," Cat said.

"Are you sure? I can stay."

"You came in this morning and spent time with me. Cory and Vi's dad hung around to have lunch with us. Go home and come back this evening."

"I enjoy being here with you. I always do."

"I know, but I'll finish with the inventory and be right here waiting when you come back," Cat said, dropping her arms.

Elena didn't move.

"Don't worry. I'm not going to be thinking about Hattie. She's taken up enough of my life."

Elena nodded. "Okay, but if you change your mind I can be here in minutes."

Cat chuckled. "I know you will. Thanks, El. I'm so thankful you walked into my bookstore."

"Me too." Elena put her hands on Cat's shoulders and squeezed. "I'll see you later."

Cat nodded and watched her walk away. She took a deep breath and let it out. It was time she did something about the house.

"I almost hope you will come here so we can finish this, Hattie," she whispered to herself.

A few hours later, Jessica was at the register finishing up a sale while Cat walked around the store, tidying the shelves. She didn't usually wear jeans to work, so she'd decided to run home and change her clothes before Elena came by to get her. The soft flannel shirt she wore over a T-shirt felt warm and cozy. It reminded her of Elena's hug from earlier that day. She smiled, closed her eyes, and imagined Elena's arms around her once again.

The ringing of the bell over the door brought her back to her task. She looked towards the register and saw Jessica finishing a sale, so she stepped out from behind the bookcase and walked towards the front of the store.

Cat rounded the corner of another bookcase and stopped. She stared into the once familiar eyes of the woman she thought she'd spend her life with.

"Hattie?"

"Hey, Cat." She looked around the store and smiled. "I heard you opened a bookstore. This is great."

"Yeah, thanks. What are you doing here?"

"Is there someplace we could talk?"

Cat released a shaky breath and walked over to the reading nook. She started to sit down in the chair she always sat in with Elena, but then stopped and went to Elena's chair instead.

Hattie followed her and sat in the other chair. She smiled and gazed at Cat. "You look great, but then again, you always do."

Cat sighed and folded her hands in her lap. She had imagined the moment she would see Hattie again and had played out several different scenarios in her head, but instead of saying anything, she waited.

"Uh, I'm sure you're angry with me and I don't blame you," Hattie began.

"I'm no longer angry," Cat said evenly.

"I'm sorry I didn't return your calls or respond to your texts, but you know me, talking about my feelings or important things is hard."

"Important things? Is that what our relationship was, Hattie? A thing?"

"No, of course it wasn't." Hattie closed her eyes and took a deep breath. "I'm sorry."

"Sorry?" Cat asked as she raised her brows. She thought when she saw Hattie again all her feelings would come back, but there was nothing. However, she didn't intend to make this easy for Hattie. Whenever they had an important conversation, Cat usually ended up doing all the talking. Not this time. It was Hattie's turn.

Cat looked on as she saw Hattie take a deep breath and slowly let it out. "I'm sorry for the way I left." Hattie looked into her eyes. "I'm sorry for leaving. I made the biggest mistake of my life and I'm here to make it right."

Cat hadn't seen that coming. She once thought if Hattie came back and apologized then maybe they could work things out. But not now. Cat didn't feel any kind of affection and certainly not love for the woman sitting in front of her. "And how are you going to do that?"

"By first apologizing then showing you how much I love you and how much I want to make this work."

"Show me?" Movement over by the register caught Cat's eye and she saw Elena walk in from the entrance to CeCe's store. When their eyes met, her heart sped up and butterflies erupted in her stomach. Suddenly she didn't care what Hattie had to say.

19

Elena had walked into CeCe's salon to pick up a new product CeCe wanted her to try. When she glanced over at the bookstore she saw Cat talking to someone in the reading nook. It was odd to see Cat sitting in her chair.

"Here you go," Ryan said to Elena as he walked towards her from his station. "CeCe left early to get things ready for the big family dinner. She said to try this and she'd settle up with you later."

"Thanks, Ryan." Elena smiled and took the sack from him.

"Y'all have fun tonight."

"I'm sure we will," Elena said.

She walked into the bookstore and over to the register. "Who's that with Cat?" she asked Jessica. But something inside her began to smolder. "Wait. Don't tell me..."

"Yep," Jessica said. "That's Hattie."

Elena wanted to march over there and smack the woman that had caused her Cat so much pain. *Her* Cat? But when her eyes met Cat's, the anger lifted and suddenly the plan came back to her. She knew exactly what to do.

Elena saw Cat stand and smile at her. That's all she needed to see. Elena started walking towards Cat and without a glance at Hattie said, "Hey, babe." Then she reached for Cat's hand and softly pressed her lips to Cat's. She didn't expect all the air to leave her body and be replaced with warm flutters that buzzed through her veins. The kiss didn't last a moment, but what a moment it was. Elena knew she would never forget the feel of Cat's lips pressed to hers. They were perfectly soft and full as Cat kissed her back.

She intertwined their fingers and inched her lips away and gave Cat a soft smile. Elena couldn't quite read the expression in Cat's eyes. It wasn't surprise, it was more like awareness or recognition.

Cat returned her smile and held their hands together tightly. "Hattie, this is Elena Burkett, my girlfriend," she stated with confidence.

Elena turned to the woman and didn't offer her hand. She simply nodded once. "Hello."

Hattie cleared her throat with obvious shock on her face. "Uh, hi," she said quietly.

"We have plans, so..." Cat shrugged.

"Right. Um, I'll come back another time," Hattie said. She stood and pulled her shoulders back, seeming to regain her composure. "We still have things to talk about." She walked past them and turned just before she opened the front door. "This isn't over, Cat." Then she walked out the door.

Cat released a dramatic breath and looked into Elena's eyes. "That was so much better than a throat punch."

Elena nearly doubled over with laughter.

"That was the best thing I've seen in a long time. You should've seen her face," Jessica said, walking up next to them. "Of course you couldn't see because you were kissing!"

Cat chuckled. "Elena said if she ever saw Hattie she was going to throat punch her."

"What!" Jessica looked at Elena and shook her head. "No way. That's not you."

"That's what I said!" Cat exclaimed. "Instead, she said she was going to kiss me to show Hattie she'd missed out and to move on."

Jessica laughed. "What a plan. I thought it had worked, but..."

"I know she'll be back, but that's okay. We can get this business with the house decided and Hattie will be gone for good," Cat said.

"We'd better get going," Elena said, looking at her watch. She realized she was still holding Cat's hand and slipped her fingers away. She missed the soft touch and warmth of Cat's hand as soon as she pulled hers away.

Once they were in the car, Elena looked over at Cat. "Are you okay?"

"Yep. You know, I thought when I saw Hattie again all these feelings would come rushing back, but there was nothing. I didn't hate her. I wasn't angry with her. I certainly didn't feel love. There was nothing."

Elena pulled onto the street and they were quiet for a moment.

"But I am going to need you to be my girlfriend a little longer," Cat added.

"I can do that." What Elena would give to actually be Cat's girlfriend.

"She'll be back."

"I'll be right beside you," Elena said then added, "Babe."

Cat smiled, reached over and squeezed Elena's knee. "That was a nice touch."

"It seemed appropriate." Elena smirked.

Cat chuckled and looked out the window. "I'll tell Cory and CeCe that Hattie is back, but I don't want my mom to know. There will be too many questions and tonight is about Vi and her parents."

Elena smiled. "I understand. I can imagine Christine would have a lot to say."

"That's an understatement." Cat reached over and pulled Elena's hand into her lap. Elena felt Cat intertwine their fingers once again as she continued to stare out the window.

The rest of the ride to CeCe's was quiet as Elena contemplated what took place at the bookstore. Elena could still feel Cat's lips on hers and it just verified what she already knew. She was falling in love with Cat Sloan. But did Cat feel the same way? Ah, that's what Elena wanted to find out, but how? With Hattie back in town, Cat's heart was vulnerable. She may not have felt anything when she saw Hattie, but this wasn't the right time to explore their feelings. Elena would be there for Cat in any way she needed her. That was one thing Elena knew for sure.

* * *

Cat sighed and gently stroked the back of Elena's hand. So much had happened today that she didn't know where to start. Once again thoughts swirled through her head. *I should be dizzy.* But the thing that stood out above everything was that kiss and Elena's hand in hers. She closed her eyes for a moment to stop everything. It was time to focus on this dinner and supporting Cory and Vi.

As Elena pulled into CeCe's driveway Cat smiled over at her. "Well, babe. Here we go."

Elena chuckled and eased her hand from Cat's. She reached into the back seat for the book she planned to give to Vi's dad.

"Alberto is going to love that," Cat said. "I'm glad you remembered to bring it."

Elena gently laid her hand on Cat's shoulder. "Let's have a good time and try not to think about you-know-who."

Cat smiled. "I can't imagine who you mean."

Elena nodded and they got out of the car. Once inside Cat watched as Elena presented Alberto with the book. She smiled while Elena gave him a brief summary.

"Your friend knows a lot about books. Does she work with you?" Vi's mom, Josie, asked.

"No, but she may as well. She has come into the bookstore nearly every day since we've opened."

"Alberto couldn't stop talking about her at lunch, and you as well. You both made quite an impression on him," Josie said.

"You've made quite an impression on us," Cat countered. "We love Vi, especially how she puts Cory in her place. Now we know how she became such an incredible woman."

"Thank you, Cat, but you give us too much credit. Vi has always been independent and focused on her goals, but Cory has given her more than goals to think about and we're very happy about that."

"I want to hear about your grandchildren," Christine said, joining their little circle.

"Oh!" Alberto exclaimed. "They're the reason we have to

go back early tomorrow. Their parents are going out of town and of course they want to stay with us."

Cat discretely backed away from the conversation before her mom started in on her to have kids. She made eye contact with Elena and nodded slightly towards the kitchen.

"I did not want to hear my mom start in about not having grandkids," Cat said quietly to Elena.

"I hear you," Elena said.

"Hey," Cat said as she and Elena walked up to CeCe, Alexis, Cory, and Vi where they stood around the island. "Elena came along because..."

"Because she's more than welcome to be here," Alexis said.

"Thanks, Alexis." Elena smiled.

"There's been a development that I'll tell you all about later. I don't want a bunch of questions from Mom," Cat said tentatively.

"What kind of development?" Cory asked.

Cat sighed. "Hattie is back in town."

"What!" CeCe exclaimed.

"Shhh!" Cat shushed her. "What part of I'll tell you later did you not understand?" She was afraid her sisters would overreact and that's the last thing she needed today.

"Un uh," Cory said, shaking her head. "She does not get to come back to town and upset you all over again."

Cat knew her sisters would fiercely defend her against anything, but she didn't need that right now.

"It's okay," Elena said, giving Cat a sweet smile. "I'm helping Cat with it."

"Is this the ex whose name we don't speak aloud?" Vi asked quietly.

Cat chuckled. "That's Cory's rule, not mine, Vi. But yes, Hattie's my ex and she came waltzing into the store proclaiming her love for me, saying how she made a huge mistake."

"She did make a mistake, but fuck her!" CeCe said.

"Sisters!" Cat whispered. "Later!"

Cat glanced over at Elena and widened her eyes. She really didn't want to tell her mom she'd seen Hattie today and wanted this dinner to be about Vi and her parents.

"Cory and I are going to teach CeCe and Alexis how to salsa," Vi said, trying to steer the conversation away from Cat's ex. "Would you and Elena like to learn, too?"

Cat gave Vi a grateful smile then looked at Elena. "That sounds like fun."

Elena nodded. "It does."

"Sure, count us in," Cat said.

"What are y'all scheming about over there?" Christine asked from the kitchen table. "When those three girls get together I have to keep a close eye on them," she said to Vi's parents.

"We're not scheming, Mom. What would you like to drink? My beautiful partner has requested mocktails and I'm happy to be your bartender for the evening," Cory said.

"Partner? That's so formal. What happened to girlfriend?" Christine said in an amused voice.

"It's simply the truth." Cory smiled at Vi. "We're in this together."

"Then why don't you live together?" Christine asked.

"Whoa!" Cory exclaimed.

"Told ya so," CeCe teased. "Cory's on the hotseat."

"We are acting like bougie people who have more than one home," Vi explained. "I think CeCe and Alexis did the same thing." Vi winked at them.

"Nice try," Alexis said. "But we are now living in this sweet little bungalow together."

"Oh, this is fun," Elena commented quietly to Cat.

"Isn't it though," Cat said, grateful the conversation had moved on from her and Hattie.

"For everyone's information, our friend Ella is keeping an eye out for a house for us," Cory explained. "Now, how about those drink orders?"

The rest of the evening was spent in lively banter between the sisters as the parents told stories of when their kids were younger.

As they said their goodbyes and walked to the car, Elena turned to Cat. "That was fun. What a great family."

"It was nice to have everyone together."

"Vi's parents are so much like your mom and they had such joyful looks on their faces telling embarrassing stories about you all."

"They did seem to enjoy that, didn't they?" Cat chuckled.

Once they were in the car and Elena had them on the road back to the bookstore, Cat turned to her. "Thank you for tonight."

"Me? It was your family," Elena replied with confusion in her voice.

"I know, but it felt good to have you there with me," Cat said. "I know you've been to family dinners with my mom and sisters before, but tonight I needed my friend, not my nosy family."

Elena chuckled. "They're nosy because they love you."

"I know that, but I didn't want that tonight. I'm glad Cory and Vi were the center of attention."

"You don't like to be the center of attention, do you?"

Cat could feel Elena glance over at her. "Not really."

"Do you want to come to my place or would you like me to come to yours?" Elena asked as she pulled up next to Cat's car in the mostly empty parking lot of the shopping center.

Cat sighed. "I think I just want to go home and process this day."

Elena nodded. "I'm here if you want to talk."

Cat smiled. "I know you are." She leaned over and kissed Elena's cheek then opened the car door. "I'll see you tomorrow."

"You can count on it."

Cat unlocked her car and waved at Elena as she drove away. "I'm so glad you're in my life," she whispered.

20

When Cat got home she walked straight to her bedroom, undressed down to her bra and panties, then fell onto the bed. She looked down at the red lingerie she was wearing and realized she didn't get the chance to share it with Elena. Was it strange that they played this little game? The red set was Elena's favorite and Cat reached for her phone to text her.

In all the excitement today I forgot to show you what I was wearing underneath. It's your favorite.

It didn't take long before her phone dinged with Elena's response.

I forgot to tell you how cute you looked in flannel.

Cat smiled. She didn't know how she'd gotten so lucky to have a friend like Elena, but her head couldn't possibly think about that now.

Her thoughts drifted to Elena's lips and how they felt pressed against hers. They were soft but firm and Cat couldn't stop herself from kissing Elena back. That wasn't the biggest shock though. When Elena interlaced their fingers, Cat was immediately reminded of the dream she'd had months ago. For weeks she'd hoped to have the dream again so she could see the woman's face.

When Elena pulled away and smiled, Cat realized Elena was the woman in her dream. They were walking along the lake and when she looked at the woman in the dream it was Elena giving her the most contented smile.

Could Elena not only be the woman in her dreams, but also be the woman who would make her dreams come true? Was that just a fake kiss for Hattie's benefit or was it real?

Cat touched her lips and could almost feel the heat from Elena's lips. Since they had to keep up this charade there was a very good chance another kiss would happen. If and when it did, Cat hoped it wouldn't lead to more confusion for her, but maybe give her answers.

Was she ready to move on from Hattie? More importantly, was she ready to trust her heart? And what about Elena, was she ready to explore her sexuality? What would they discover?

"Enough." Cat sighed. "I've got to get some sleep."

* * *

The next morning Cat walked into the living room to answer the front door and expected to find Elena standing there with a soft smile.

"Hey, little sister," CeCe smiled, holding a drink carrier with three coffee cups.

"What's all this?"

"Can't I bring my little sister breakfast on Sunday morning?"

"You can," Cat said, stepping aside so she and Alexis could walk into the house. "But I don't remember you ever doing it."

"Donuts." Alexis grinned, holding up the box as she followed CeCe inside.

"You looked like you were expecting someone else," CeCe commented, carefully lifting the cups from the carrier. She handed one to Cat then to Alexis.

"I did?"

"Mmhmm." Alexis nodded. "That bright smile wasn't for us."

"Why wouldn't it be?" Cat replied. "I'm happy to see you."

"Right." Alexis smirked. She opened the donut box while Cat took three plates out of a cabinet.

Once they all had a donut and were sipping their coffee, CeCe looked at Cat. "After what you told us last night about Hattie being back in town, we wanted to make sure you're okay."

"And we want to know how Elena is helping you," Alexis added.

Cat grinned. "We're pretending."

"Pretending?" CeCe raised her eyebrows.

Cat nodded and took a bite of her donut. She could see the confusion and anticipation on their faces as she swallowed. "Elena came by to pick me up from the bookstore and Hattie was still there. She walked over and kissed me."

"She what!" CeCe exclaimed.

"I love it," Alexis said with a wide smile.

"She once asked me what I would do if Hattie came into the bookstore and we had this plan. Elena kisses me, showing Hattie that I've moved on and she's missed out."

"Did it work?"

Cat shrugged. "Sort of. Hattie said she'd be back, but Jessica said she could tell Hattie was totally surprised and it rattled her."

"Was it pretending?" Alexis asked.

Cat looked from Alexis to CeCe and sighed. "I'm sure you share everything."

"Of course we do, especially when it's about my sister. Alexis didn't have to tell me you have feelings for Elena. it's obvious in the way you look at each other."

"It is?"

"Duh," CeCe said.

"Hattie will be back. There's still the issue of the house to resolve. She owns half."

"Bullshit!" CeCe yelled, slamming her hand on the table. "She left you with the mortgage payment when she walked out and hasn't helped with one single penny."

"I know, but she did before then." Cat sighed. "I can't afford to buy her out right now."

"I have money," Alexis stated. "How much do you need? It's yours."

Tears immediately sprang to Cat's eyes. "Alexis, that is so kind."

Alexis shook her head. "It's not kind. I love you, Cat. You're family."

Cat reached over and squeezed Alexis's arm. "Thank you, but I want to sell the house. It's time to find something new."

"And someone," CeCe said.

Cat shrugged.

"What did Hattie say before Elena came in?" Alexis asked.

"She said she made the biggest mistake of her life," Cat said dramatically. "The funny thing is that it didn't matter. I don't love her anymore. There was no spark, no nothing."

"She'll try to win you back," CeCe said flatly. "You had a good relationship for a time."

Cat nodded. "But when it started to fall apart, she wouldn't talk to me. Why would I want to go through that again?"

"You don't," Alexis said.

CeCe reached over and took Cat's hand. "I was worried about you at first, but since we've opened our stores you have become my little sister again. I can see happiness on your face and it's real. I remember how you would force a smile when we were at Mom's or Cory's and I tried to get you out of this house. But your beautiful smile is back, Cat."

That made Cat smile. "I am happy."

"I know Elena has become a close friend," CeCe said. "But don't forget, we're here for you, too. I remember how mad I was when Hattie left and I'm sure that made you not really want to confide in me. I'm sorry about that."

"CeCe has told me about that time in your life," Alexis said. "She was angry because you were hurting and she couldn't do anything to help you."

"But I tried, which was a big mistake," CeCe said. "You were hurt and here I was trying to make you smile or ask you over and over again to go out with me. I understand now that was the last thing you needed or wanted to do."

"I wasn't upset with you. I knew you were trying to help," Cat said. "Then there's Cory."

CeCe chuckled. "It's a good thing Hattie left town. Cory was after her!" CeCe leaned in a little. "You know, it may have been fun if she'd found her."

Cat shook her head. "No, that would've been bad for Cory."

"But you and Elena have found each other," Alexis said gently.

Cat nodded. "I can't tell you how happy I am that she walked into the bookstore the day we opened."

"I've gotten to know Elena, too," CeCe said. "There are no secrets between a hairstylist and client." CeCe once again reached for Cat's hand. "She needed you, too."

"I know. We've talked about it."

"So is this fake relationship going to continue?" Alexis asked.

"It will until Hattie gets the message. The next time I see her I'll tell her we need to sell the house," Cat said.

"And then?"

Cat looked at CeCe and Alexis and decided that maybe they could help her make sense of the thoughts swirling in her head. She sighed. "A few months ago, I had this dream. I was walking along the lake near Lovers Landing. I was holding a woman's hand and as we walked I could feel the happiness in my heart. It was because I was with this woman. Somehow in my dream, I knew it was because of her."

Cat paused and CeCe and Alexis waited patiently.

"When I turned to look at her face it was a blur and then I woke up. All this time I've been trying to figure out who the woman was. I knew it wasn't Hattie, but whoever it was, she was so familiar."

Cat took a deep breath and slowly let it out. "Yesterday, when Elena kissed me, she also slipped her hand into mine and interlaced our fingers. The dream flashed through my head, only this time I could see the woman's face."

"It was Elena," Alexis whispered.

Cat nodded. "It was Elena."

"Holy shit, Cat! If that isn't a sign!" CeCe exclaimed.

"Easy, babe," Alexis said, putting her hand on CeCe's arm.

"I don't know if Elena feels the same way," Cat stated, taking another sip of her coffee.

"Ask her!"

"Really, CeCe?" Cat said. "Did you tell Alexis you were in love with her? No, you waited until she was ready to hear it."

CeCe snorted. "Okay, okay. You're right."

"Besides, I need to end this with Hattie before I do anything. And what if Elena doesn't feel the same way? How awkward is that going to make our friendship? It's so risky! I don't want to lose her."

"You won't lose her," Alexis said firmly. She smiled at Cat then eased the tone of her voice. "You told me once that you had a front row seat to watch CeCe and me fall in love. Remember?"

Cat nodded.

"That's what we're seeing between you and Elena. If you would've told me that's what CeCe and I were doing, I wouldn't have believed you. When you're in it sometimes your vision gets a little blurry."

"There's nothing wrong with taking your time," CeCe said. "Just don't waste it."

"I won't," Cat said.

"I think you do need to settle this with Hattie, but don't be afraid to tell Elena how you feel. You tell her everything anyway, don't you?" Alexis grinned.

"Yeah. I haven't shared what happened yesterday when she kissed me and took my hand."

"You will and it's going to be beautiful," CeCe said.

Cat smiled and was suddenly very grateful her big sister and Alexis had brought her breakfast.

They were having second helpings of the donuts when Cat's phone began to vibrate on the living room table.

"Good morning," Cat said cheerily with a big smile on her face.

"Wonder who that is," CeCe said with a wink.

Cat gave her a menacing look.

Alexis chuckled. "With that kind of smile, you know it's Elena."

"Sorry about that," Cat said as she walked down the hall to her bedroom. "CeCe and Alexis brought donuts over this morning. Why don't you come join us?"

"Are you sure?" Elena asked.

"Of course I'm sure."

"I got to thinking that Hattie might show up at your house."

"Hmm, I hadn't thought of that," Cat said. "I guess you'd better get over here and plan on spending the day with me. If you don't have anything else to do, that is."

Elena's laughter coming through the phone made butterflies erupt in Cat's stomach. It seemed that nearly every time Elena walked into the bookstore lately those butterflies came out to play.

"You know I don't have anything else to do on a Sunday. Besides, we've got Hattie where we want her. We can't back down now."

It was Cat's turn to laugh. "Get over here. We'll binge watch something this afternoon or find a couple of movies. Your choice."

"I'm on my way. Save me a donut."

Cat laughed and disconnected the call. She didn't know how long they'd have to keep up this little act, but she hoped to figure out if Elena felt the same way she did.

"I wonder who that was," CeCe yelled from the kitchen.

"Ha ha," Cat said, sitting back down at the table. "Elena's on her way over. Why don't we all watch a movie?"

"I'm in," Alexis said.

CeCe chuckled. "My fiancée has turned into a movie buff."

"Cuddling under a blanket with you makes me want to watch movies every night," Alexis replied.

Cat grinned at them both. She'd always wanted a love like they shared, but now she knew exactly who could make that possible.

21

The next day Cat was at the register getting things ready for the day's business when Cory walked in.

"Hey," Cat said.

"I talked to CeCe and she told me about your plan with Elena. I'm here for you and I will control my animosity towards Hattie. Let me know what you need."

Cat smiled. "Thank you. You can be mad at Hattie. I'm over it."

Elena walked into the store and gave them both a big smile. "How are the Sloan sisters this morning?"

"I was just telling Cat that I think your plan with Hattie is brilliant," Cory said.

"Mmm, we'll see. I hope it doesn't backfire," Elena said.

"Why would it?" Cory asked.

"It may make things worse. Don't you think your sister is worth fighting for?"

Cory smiled and put her arm around Cat. "Hattie missed her chance. Cat is the best of us."

Cat chuckled. "CeCe might have something to say about that."

"Nope, she'll agree," Cory said.

"My oh my," Cat said. "This is getting a little sappy."

"No it's not. We know who you are and we love you," Elena said.

Cat smiled at her and tilted her head.

"Okay. I know you two probably have a book date and I have deliveries to make," Cory said. She hugged Cat. "Oh, I almost forgot. Vi and I want you to go to Talia's with us for a drink."

"Is that The Neon Rose you were telling me about?" Elena asked.

"Yep," Cat replied.

"We had fun at Betty's and wanted to take y'all to the Rose. What do you say?"

"I'm in, it sounds like fun," Elena said, looking at Cat.

"Me too. Just let us know when."

"How about tonight? We have some news on the housing front," Cory said.

"Did Ella find you something?" Cat asked excitedly.

"Come have drinks and we'll tell you all about it." Cory grinned.

Cat chuckled. "Okay."

"I'll text you both later," Cory said and left the store.

"It's quiet in here this morning," Elena said, looking around the store.

"Shall we?" Cat nodded towards the reading nook.

"Is that what we do? Are these book dates?" Elena asked, sitting in her favorite chair.

"Hmm, I guess so, but it's more than books," Cat replied.

Elena smiled and nodded at her. "I had fun yesterday."

"I did too. CeCe and Alexis live just around the corner. Maybe we should make it a regular thing. We'll take turns choosing the movie."

"I'd love that," Elena said.

"I'll tell CeCe."

"I'm getting my hair highlighted this morning. I can tell her."

"Okay. This will be fun."

"Are you doing okay? Really?" Elena asked. "You know Hattie will be back and that has to give you anxiety."

"Not really. There's nothing she can say that would make a difference. I've decided I want to sell the house and go from there."

Elena nodded. "Ella works with Victoria at Make It Easy Designs, right?"

"Yes."

"Maybe they could help you find something. Didn't Marina help you with the shopping center and CeCe's house?"

Cat nodded. "They are all so helpful. I won't qualify for their program, but that doesn't mean they can't help me find something."

"Moving can be fun. I'll help you."

"I know you will." Cat smiled then studied Elena for a moment. "So you're afraid our plan might backfire?"

Elena sighed. "It's the way she said 'this isn't over.'"

"We're about to find out because she just walked in," Cat said, getting up from her chair.

"What do you want me to do?" Elena asked, her eyes widening.

Cat reached out her hand and pulled Elena up. "You go get your hair done and come back when you're finished." She reached up and gently kissed Elena, knowing Hattie would see. The look in Elena's eyes caused the butterflies to stir in Cat's stomach. It wasn't lost on Cat that kissing Elena felt like the most natural thing in the world. Their lips fit perfectly together. *Pretending is kind of fun*, she thought as she gazed at Elena.

Elena glanced over at Hattie and nodded then walked towards the entrance to CeCe's salon.

"Does she work here?" Hattie asked.

"Nope. She just likes to be with me."

"I can't blame her," Hattie said quietly.

Cat raised one eyebrow and smirked.

"I've been doing a lot of thinking," Hattie began. "I remember how you said we were right for each other."

"We were then, but we grew, just not in the same way or the same direction."

Hattie sighed. "Come on, we were Cat and the Hat. We go together."

Cat shook her head and remembered how cute Hattie had thought that moniker was. "Not anymore."

Hattie looked down and shuffled her feet. "I should've been more open, but you know how hard it is for me to talk about my feelings."

"Yeah, I do, but that doesn't give you a pass, Hattie. Maybe we could've figured out what was happening and spared each other a lot of pain," Cat said. "Well, I was hurt. I don't know about you."

Hattie's head snapped up and she stared at Cat. "Of course I was hurt. You have no idea how hard it was for me to make the decision to leave."

"That's just it. *You* made the decision. Don't you think we should've talked about it instead of you walking in one day and saying you were leaving?"

"I'm sorry, Cat. I really messed up."

"I knew you weren't happy. I wasn't either, but you chose to end it instead of trying." Cat sighed. "We've been through this. There's no need to rehash everything."

Hattie plopped down in Cat's chair. She blew out a big breath then looked up at Cat.

"How *old* is your girlfriend?" Hattie asked with a haughty tone to her voice.

Cat shook her head. "You ask about Elena, but you haven't asked about me. That's what I'm talking about, Hattie. You don't know who I am. I know who Elena is and she knows me. She loves me for me."

"But if you grow," Hattie said, making air quotes, "then you'll keep growing. What happens if you don't grow with her?"

"That's just it, we know we're growing and we're doing it together. We don't hide our problems from each other. We *talk* to each other."

"You said we grew apart and in different directions. If it's about sex, Cat, we were going through—"

"A rough patch," Cat said, interrupting Hattie. "No we weren't. We were growing apart and I saw it and I felt it, but you didn't believe me."

Cat sat down and gentled her voice. "You felt it too, but wouldn't admit it. You were too afraid to try. Elena and I aren't afraid." When Cat heard those words tumble from her mouth she realized everything she'd said was true. They had both changed for the better since the day Elena walked into the bookstore. She couldn't be afraid to tell Elena her true feelings. Elena had encouraged her and Cat trusted her, so she should trust if Elena didn't feel the same way they could still figure it out. Together.

"I want you to be happy," Hattie said, looking down at her hands. "I know you probably don't believe that, but it's true. I can still make you happy."

Cat pulled her focus back to Hattie. "What would make me happy is to sell the house."

Hattie looked up in surprise. "Sell the house?"

Cat nodded.

"Let me think about it."

"What's there to think about?"

"I don't know. That's a big step."

Cat closed her eyes, trying not to scream or laugh. "Moving out was a big step, Hattie. We'll sell the house, split the proceeds, and move on."

Hattie narrowed her eyes. "Move on? Is that what you've done?"

Cat sighed. "That's what you did when you moved out. You wouldn't answer my calls or texts and had a girlfriend two weeks later." Cat was through being nice. "You moved on. It took me a while, but so have I. The best thing to do would be to sell the house and end this once and for all."

Hattie huffed. "Oh, so now you're making the decisions."

"Fuck," Cat whispered.

The bell over the door rang and a customer walked in. *Thank goodness*, Cat thought. "I have to wait on this customer."

Hattie stood up and looked back at the front door. "I'll get back with you on the house...and everything."

"You do that," Cat said softly as Hattie walked away. *How was I ever in love with this person?*

* * *

Elena sat down in CeCe's chair and met her gaze in the mirror. "Cat is talking to Hattie."

"Right now?"

Elena nodded. "She came into the bookstore."

"Do we..." CeCe trailed off and pointed to the door.

"No. Cat told me to come back after you finish with my hair."

CeCe separated a few strands of Elena's hair and applied color to it then wrapped it in foil. She continued the process while Elena watched in the mirror.

"Cat and I were talking and we really enjoyed yesterday."

CeCe smiled. "We did, too."

"Cat thought it would be fun to make it a regular thing and take turns choosing the movie."

"What a great idea. I'll tell Alexis." CeCe sighed as she highlighted then wrapped another strand of Elena's hair.

"She'll be fine," Elena said.

CeCe smiled. "I know she will. I was just thinking about her and Hattie. People don't realize how great my little sister is. Just because she's quiet doesn't mean she's not fun. There were certain times during the year when Cat's workload caused her to have to be at the office late. I think sometimes she didn't want to go home to an empty house because Hattie wasn't there. Cat was lonely."

Elena felt her heart clinch in her chest.

"Hattie was in corporate sales. She met with clients oftentimes in the evenings. I guess she was wining and dining them. These meetings turned into parties and led to many late nights. What she didn't realize is she could've taken Cat along with her and she would've helped her close the accounts."

"Maybe she didn't want her there."

"Exactly," CeCe said. "Hattie was too busy trying to impress clients instead of being with Cat. I know Cat tried to talk to her about it, but Hattie always said they would be all right."

"That makes my heart hurt."

"I know. Mine too."

"I don't get it," Elena said. "Cat is such a good person. Did you see how cute she looked the other night in her jeans and that flannel shirt?"

CeCe's eye brows rose on her forehead.

"Have you set your sights on my sister?" CeCe asked with a grin.

Elena laughed nervously.

"You know, this idea you came up with is brave. I would've loved to see you walk up to Cat and kiss her right in front of Hattie."

"I didn't think twice about it. I just did it. I could feel my hands shaking, so I grabbed one of Cat's," Elena said.

"And?"

"Do you want me to kiss and tell?" Elena asked, raising her brows.

"I certainly do."

Elena laughed then narrowed her gaze. "I'm not sure I should tell you this."

"Come on, now. If you can't talk to your stylist, who can you talk to?" CeCe said.

"But she's your sister," Elena said.

"Spill it."

Elena sighed. "It may not have been a fake kiss on my end."

"Noted."

"And when Hattie walked into the bookstore just now, we kissed again."

CeCe smiled. "And who initiated this kiss?"

"Cat did."

CeCe nodded. She leaned close to Elena's ear and quietly said, "Fake it till you make it."

Elena stiffened. Was CeCe telling her to go for it with

Cat? "Uh, Cat wants to sell the house," she said, changing the subject away from kisses.

"Yeah, she told me and Alexis before you came over yesterday. I think it's a good idea."

"What do you think she'll do? Where will she go?" A hint of an idea began to take shape in the back of Elena's mind.

"She'll figure it out. Cat's the planner in our family. She gets that from my dad. I'm a little surprised she hasn't done something with the house before now. It's been over a year."

"Do you think it's because she's ready to move on now?"

"Mmm, she moved on a long time ago. I think Cat had to get her sparkle back."

"Sparkle?" Elena repeated, raising her brows.

CeCe chuckled. "Yeah, I guess sparkle would describe me more than Cat, but you know what I mean."

"Yeah, I do. I think Cat has a sparkle beneath that librarian demeanor. You just have to know where to look."

"Librarian." CeCe giggled. "Oh, she sells books. I guess so." CeCe stopped and stared at Elena. "And you know where to look."

Elena shrugged.

"Okay." CeCe nodded.

22

Cat and Elena walked into The Neon Rose and saw Cory and Vi already seated at a table.

"Hold it!" a woman said, coming around the bar. "I get a hug before you get a drink."

Cat grinned and held out her arms. "Hi, Talia."

"It's so good to see you. It's been a while," Talia said.

"Too long," Cat replied. "Talia, this is Elena Burkett."

"It's nice to meet you," Elena said with a smile.

"Welcome to the Neon Rose," Talia said. "What are you drinking? I'll bring them to your table."

"Uh, I think I'll have a beer. You know, Vi says you have the coldest beer in town," Cat said.

Talia smirked. "Just between you and me, Vi seems to be perfect for Cory."

Cat chuckled. "She is."

"What can I bring you, Elena?"

"I'll try one of your cold beers, too," Elena replied.

"Coming right up." Talia turned to Cat. "We've missed you around here."

"I needed a break, but I'm back now," Cat said with a smile.

Talia went back behind the bar to get their drinks.

"So she and Cory dated?" Elena asked.

"Yep. It was brief. They figured out they were better friends than girlfriends."

Elena nodded. "You're wearing flannel again."

"I am. Someone commented that I looked cute in flannel, so I thought, why not?"

Elena raised her brows and smiled. "Is that right?"

Cat giggled and turned to walk over to the table.

"You know, you look cute in your dresses too," Elena said, leaning in near Cat's ear. A curl tickled Elena's nose and she felt warmth spread through her body.

Cat stopped and turned her head towards Elena. "Is Hattie around here somewhere?" she teased.

Elena chuckled. "It's a real compliment. Own it."

A shy smile crossed Cat's face. "Thank you, I'm glad you noticed."

Elena smiled and wondered if Cat had any idea of the things she'd noticed. She wanted to hear that little giggle again because it was such a sweet sound that went straight to Elena's heart.

"By the way, the color is lavender today," Cat said quietly.

"Oh, will I get a peek later?"

Cat winked and walked to the table.

"Hey," Cory said. "Glad y'all could make it."

"Thanks for asking us," Cat said, sitting across from Cory.

Elena took the seat next to Cat and tried to calm her rapidly beating heart.

"Tell me about this book signing you're having at Your

Next Great Read," Vi said. "I love the name of your bookstore."

Cat grinned. "Tara Holloway wants to start her book tour in our little establishment."

"Our?" Vi asked.

Cat gave Elena a quick glance. "I feel like the bookstore belongs to all of us. We are still in the planning stages for the book signing. Tara and Lauren invited us out to their lake home."

"Oh!" Cory exclaimed. "I made deliveries to them. It's beautiful. I hope you can take in the sunset from their dock while you're there."

Vi looked over at her. "Who are you watching the sun set with on the lake?"

Cory chuckled. "Jealous? For your information, I was making a delivery and Tara invited me down to the dock where Lauren was waiting for her."

"I'm not jealous because you're all mine now." Vi draped her arm across Cory's shoulder and kissed her on the cheek.

"We're supposed to go one evening later this week," Elena said. "They were nice enough to invite me along as well."

"It makes sense. You have to keep this fake relationship going. You never know who is around and word might get back to Hattie," Cory said.

"We have that under control, don't we?" Cat said, looping her arm through Elena's where it rested on the table.

"Yeah, we do."

"Here you go," Talia said, setting their beers on the table. "Let me know when you need something else."

"Thanks," Cory said.

They all took generous drinks of their beers and Cat said, "Mmm, you're right Vi. That's a cold beer."

"One thing I do know is where to get the best drinks," Vi said.

"And what else?" Cory asked with a frown.

"That I love Cory Sloan." Vi grinned.

Cat chuckled. "Okay, lovebirds. Tell us about this house news."

"We were planning to have a relaxing day at Vi's yesterday when Ella called."

"By relaxing, do you mean making out or what?"

Cory nearly choked on her beer.

"I may have mentioned what we were doing yesterday when Cat called to invite us to watch movies," Vi said sheepishly.

"Anyway," Elena encouraged them.

"Ella showed us a house that we could see ourselves in," Cory said.

"Yeah, after talking to Alexis, I was all for selling my townhome and redoing a few things at Cory's place, but this home..."

"It feels like it was built for us," Cory said, finishing Vi's thought.

"Where is it?"

"Not far from the shopping center," Vi said. "It has a big backyard my nephews can play in when they come to visit."

"Or we can play in when they aren't there." Cory chuckled. "I can see us having family get-togethers and parties there."

"That sounds wonderful," Cat said. "I guess I need to talk to them about finding me a place."

"What?" Cory asked.

Cat nodded. "Yeah, I've decided to sell the house."

"Have you told Hattie?"

"I told her today."

"Today?" Cory asked, looking confused.

"Yeah, she came in this morning not long after you left."

"How did that go? Were you still there, Elena?" Vi asked.

"Yes, but Cat needed to talk with Hattie alone so I left," Elena explained.

"I meant to tell you earlier," Cat said, turning to Elena. "Your hair looks beautiful."

"Thank you." Elena smiled.

"Did CeCe do it?" Vi asked.

"Yes, I've been getting it highlighted for a while now. There's a little gray and I wasn't ready for that."

"Your hair is beautiful whether you get it highlighted or not," Cat said.

The sparkle in Cat's eyes once again caused warmth to course through Elena's body. She pulled her gaze away and looked over at Cory and Vi. "When can we see this house?"

"Soon. We have to make an offer, but I'm sure Ella wouldn't mind showing it again," Cory said.

"We'd love to see it," Cat said.

Elena took a moment to gaze around the bar and noticed it was mostly women occupying the tables and bar. The vibe was casual and friendly.

"Is this the first time you've been here?" Cory asked.

"Yes," Elena said. "I love it. Everyone seems so friendly."

Cory chuckled. "It's a Monday night. On Friday and Saturday it gets rather lively."

"And loud," Vi added. "They turn the music up and you have to shout to be heard."

"Is that a dance floor?" Elena asked, indicating a small area towards the back of the bar.

"Yeah," Cory said.

"Do you want to dance?" Cat asked Elena.

"Maybe after a few more beers," Elena replied.

Cat chuckled. "I hear you."

"Uh oh," Cory said, looking towards the door. "I think Hattie just walked in."

"Oh, great," Cat groaned.

"Don't turn around. I don't think she saw you," Cory said.

Elena immediately put her arm around Cat and scooted her chair a little closer. "Too much?"

"Perfect," Cory replied, keeping her eyes towards the door.

"I don't care if she sees us. I'm out having drinks with my sister, her girlfriend, and *my* girlfriend," Cat said.

Elena squeezed Cat's shoulder and smiled.

"She came in with a couple of women. I recognize one of them. She's come into the liquor store a few times," Cory said.

"Don't let her spoil our evening. I'm not," Cat said.

"That's right," Vi agreed.

"Is she back for good or just visiting?" Cory asked.

"I have no idea. She didn't say and I didn't ask. I really have nothing left to talk to her about besides selling the house," Cat said.

Cory nodded. "It still makes me mad. It's one thing to break up and move out, but to leave you with the financial responsibilities... That's low."

"It's okay, Cory. I've made it work and it'll be fine once the house is sold," Cat said.

"I'm so excited about our new house," Vi said. "I'd be happy to help you look."

"Thanks, Vi," Cat said, taking a sip of her beer. She turned to Elena. "Let's dance."

Before Elena knew what was happening, Cat grabbed her hand, pulled her out of her seat, and led them to the dance floor.

The music changed to a slow song and Cat took Elena's hands and placed them on her hips then wrapped her arms around Elena's neck.

"Does this remind you of your library crush?" Cat asked.

"Is that what we're calling her?" Elena chuckled. She relaxed into this intimate embrace as they began to move to the music. Cat's fingers were playing with the hair at the nape of Elena's neck and she intended to enjoy every moment.

"I know I'm not your first dance with a woman," Cat said.

Elena could feel Cat's warm breath on her neck as the scent of Cat's shampoo wafted through her nose. She could lose herself in those curls. She pulled Cat a little closer, nuzzling her neck, and imagined the possibilities of firsts with Cat. This may not be real, but it certainly felt real to Elena.

"This is perfect," Cat whispered.

"It is," Elena mumbled, not trusting her voice to say more. She closed her eyes and wanted to commit to memory every spot Cat's body was touching hers.

The music waned and a more upbeat tune began to play.

Cat pulled away and smiled at Elena. "More beer?"

"Definitely, if you want me to dance to that."

Cat led them back to the table and as they sat down Hattie appeared.

"I didn't think you liked this place," she said to Cat.

"What? I've always loved Talia's bar. You should know that."

Hattie grimaced.

"Hey, Hattie," Cory said with a bite to her voice.

Elena saw Vi gently place her hand on Cory's arm and she immediately calmed. They definitely had a connection. Elena remembered times like that with Dean and suddenly realized she had those moments with Cat as well. Theirs might be a look or a hint of a smile, but the connection was there.

"Hattie, this is Vi Valdez," Cat said.

"Hello," Vi said with no emotion.

Hattie smiled at Vi and turned back to Cat. "I'd be happy to buy you a drink and talk about the house."

Cat shook her head. "No thanks. We're out having fun." She smiled at Elena and squeezed her hand.

Hattie smirked and walked away.

"Well played, sister," Cory said with a big grin.

"I'm not playing. We're having fun and I want to dance again."

Elena could see Hattie staring at them out of the corner of her eye and leaned over and gently kissed Cat. "Me, too."

These soft kisses were turning into something Elena wanted every day. She could get used to this.

* * *

When Elena leaned in and kissed Cat with those soft lips she couldn't help but think this was real. Or were they still pretending? They danced to several more slow songs and Cat even got Elena to stay on the dance floor for a faster song.

But it was the slow dances that had Cat's heart pounding. She marveled at how their bodies melded together and there was never an awkward step. There were times when she had danced with other women and there was always a step the wrong way or a bump here and there. Once Cat placed her arms around Elena's neck, if felt like they were in sync. She didn't think about where to step or how to move, she simply let her body flow with Elena's.

Cat liked to play with the hair at the nape of Elena's neck and felt Elena nuzzle her hair more than once. The touch was intimate in a way that felt like anything but pretend. Cat had to stop herself from kissing Elena's neck several times and longed to nibble her ear lobe. She sighed in Elena's arms and held her a little closer.

"Is everything all right?" Elena asked softly.

"Mmm." That's all Cat dared to say.

When the song ended they leaned back and stared into each other's eyes. Cat couldn't stop herself. She leaned up and softly pressed her lips to Elena's. Elena's fingers dug into her hips and her lips slightly parted. Cat ran her tongue over Elena's bottom lip and when their tongues touched Cat felt a rush of heat melt her body. She moaned and tightened her fingers in Elena's hair. Cat didn't want the kiss to end, but she suddenly realized they were on the dance floor in the middle of Talia's bar. The kiss had taken her away from everything. It was only her and Elena.

This time when they pulled away, Cat saw a darkness in Elena's eyes she'd never seen before. Elena took a shaky breath and Cat wondered if Elena had felt the same thing she had.

Without a word Cat took Elena's hand and led them back to the table. Cory and Vi gave them a questioning look but didn't say anything.

"Uh, I just realized Hattie is gone," Cat said, looking around the bar.

"Yeah, she left a while ago," Cory said.

Cat looked at Elena and then to Cory and Vi. "Thank

you for this evening. I'm having such a good time I didn't even notice she left."

Elena smiled. "That's a good thing."

Cat nodded. *She has no idea how good this evening has been*, Cat thought.

23

A few days later Cat saw Hattie walk into the bookstore.

"Where's your girlfriend?" Hattie asked, standing at the other side of the counter. "I thought she was here all the time."

"Ah, you just missed her," Cat said flatly.

Hattie smirked. "I heard you're having a book signing here for Tara Holloway."

"We are."

"You know how much I like her movies."

"I remember," Cat said.

"I had no idea you knew her. I always hoped I'd run into her someday since she moved out to the lake."

"Elena and I have been invited to her lake home this evening to discuss the preparations for the book event," Cat said. She couldn't resist being petty since she knew how much Hattie loved Tara Holloway.

"Wow, do you think you could introduce me to her?" Hattie asked excitedly.

Cat just stared at her. That was how it had always been: What could Cat do for Hattie? She'd helped her several times with clients by showing them the tax advantages to teaming up with Hattie's company, but whenever Cat asked for something it was always such a production.

"Oh, okay." Hattie huffed.

"Look, Elena will be here any minute to pick me up. Do you want to talk about the house?" Cat was ready to put the house on the market, but she would rather Hattie agree to it before she took that step.

"Um, I'm still thinking about it. There's a lot to consider."

As if on cue, Elena walked into the bookstore from CeCe's salon.

"Hey, babe," Elena said, putting her arm around Cat's waist.

Cat turned to her and smiled. She gave her a quick kiss then looked back at Hattie. "We've got to go."

"Right," Hattie said dejectedly. "See ya later."

"I just have to get my purse, it's in the back," Cat said, looking at Elena hesitantly.

"It's okay." Elena glanced at Hattie. "We'll be all right."

Cat nodded and walked to the back of the store.

Hattie watched her go, then turned to Elena. "So, how did you meet Cat?" Hattie asked.

"Here," Elena said. "We both love books."

Hattie smiled. "She always loved to read."

Elena nodded and raised her eyebrows.

"So, just like that then," Hattie said.

"No, it took us a while. She was very hurt when we first met."

Hattie nodded. "I never liked to read much."

Elena smiled. "There's a lot more to Cat than books. I know you saw how much fun we were having the other night at the bar."

"I noticed. You'll never find a better person than Cat."

"I know."

Hattie gave her a sad smile. "It took me too long to figure that out."

Elena shrugged.

"I can see you make her happy."

"That's all I want to do," Elena said.

Hattie nodded and studied Elena for a moment. Then she turned and left the store.

"Is everything okay?" Cat said, walking up beside Elena.

"Yep." Elena kissed Cat softly.

"What was that for?"

"For being you. Ready to go?"

Cat nodded and wondered what Elena and Hattie had talked about. She was sure that kiss was real.

"Are you excited to see Tara's home?" Elena asked as she drove them to the lake.

"I've heard it's incredible."

"I can't wait to see it. So you'd never met Tara before that day she came into the store with Krista, but you know her wife?" Elena asked.

"Yes, Lauren is a realtor and my firm helped her with some of the more expensive properties around the lake." She glanced over at Elena before continuing. "Hattie heard about the book event with Tara. I kind of rubbed it in her face because I know she's such a fan," Cat said.

Elena chuckled. "Who can blame you?"

Cat glanced over at her again and grinned.

"Did you talk about the house?"

"She's still thinking about it," Cat said. "I'm losing my patience."

"Hang in there, *babe*," Elena said, giving Cat a grin.

Cat chuckled. "She wasn't an asshole to you, was she? I didn't want to leave you with her."

"No. Is this where I turn?" Elena asked.

"Yeah, it's not far now." The last thing Cat wanted to do was think or talk about Hattie. Tara had given her bookstore quite the opportunity and she wanted the event to be a success.

"Wow," Elena said as she pulled into Tara and Lauren's driveway.

"Ditto," Cat said. She smiled at Elena and raised her brows. "I'm glad you're here with me."

"There's no place I'd rather be."

They walked up to the front door, but before they could ring the bell Lauren opened the door.

"Hi!" she said with a friendly smile.

"Hi, Lauren. It's so good to see you," Cat said.

"You, too. I miss your tax help with my clients. It gave us a reason to catch up."

Cat smiled. "Lauren, I'd like you to meet Elena Burkett."

Lauren extended her hand and Elena shook it. "You have a beautiful home," Elena said.

"Thank you. Come in and I'll show you around. Tara is—"

"Right here, darlin'." Tara met them in the foyer with a big smile. "Thanks for coming out."

Lauren and Tara gave them a tour of their impressive home and Cat enjoyed the playful yet loving banter between them. It sounded a lot like she and Elena when they discussed different sections of books they were reading.

After Tara poured a glass of wine for each of them, they settled in the great room.

"Cory mentioned the beautiful views, but this is amazing," Cat said.

"Thank you," Tara said. "That's what sold me on the place." She looked over at Lauren, who sat in a chair next to her, and smiled. "That and the realtor."

Lauren chuckled. "I'm glad you could come out early. We hope to get the business part of this meeting done so we can take in the sunset."

"We've heard the sunset is quite a show from your dock," Elena said.

"It is. We're lucky it isn't too cold today, so we should be able to enjoy it."

"I wanted to thank you again for letting Your Next Great Read host your book signing," Cat began. "We expect there will be a large crowd."

"I've thought about that. We were wondering if there's a way to keep everyone happy while they wait in line," Lauren said.

"Cory and Vi have offered to provide some kind of refreshment while people wait," Elena said.

"We've met Vi. Is she working with Cory?" Tara asked.

Cat and Elena exchanged a look. "She may as well be." Cat chuckled. "She spends all her free time there." As the words left her mouth she realized Elena did much the same with Cat at the bookstore.

Elena gave her a knowing smile. "When you find a place that makes you happy, you want to be there."

"A place or someone?" Lauren asked.

"Both," Cat and Elena said in unison.

Tara and Lauren laughed. They discussed the other details of the event while Elena and Lauren took notes.

"Oh, I almost forgot," Tara said, getting up and walking over to the large island that separated the kitchen from the great room. She came back and handed each of them a copy of her memoir.

"I can't wait to read this!" Cat said.

"Do you have a favorite part?" Elena asked, studying the table of contents.

"Meeting and falling in love with Lauren is always the best part to me," Tara said.

"I kind of like that part, too." Lauren grinned.

Tara and Lauren took turns giving them the highlights of the stories that made up the book.

"I knew that you and Krista started in Hollywood around the same time," Cat said. "Times are different now and there's not as much of a risk to coming out."

"No, but it still can be risky," Tara said.

"I wondered..." Elena trailed off.

"Go ahead," Tara encouraged her. "You can ask me anything."

"Do you think you and Krista would have stayed together if things were different back then?"

Tara smiled. "Nope. Krista was in love with Melanie and has been since they first met. If times were different they would've been together from the time Krista came to Hollywood."

Tara paused and sipped her wine.

"I don't know that I believe in destiny," Tara continued. "But I think we have to go through the times in our lives to make our way to who we're supposed to be with. I had to go through the—shall I say, casual—hook-ups to find myself and be the woman Lauren fell in love with. I had to be who her heart was looking for. All the other women led me to Lauren and she made me want to have a love and the life that I do now."

"I don't think I'll be thanking all of them," Lauren said with a smirk.

Tara chuckled. "I never thought this life, this love was possible for me. I didn't think that was who I was, but when I stopped and took a look at myself, I found I wanted that love, but more importantly, I *was* that woman. I never imagined this much happiness, but it's mine now and I'm never letting it go. I get up every morning excited and looking forward to how I get to love Lauren every day. I love who I am and the life I have with Lauren. It wasn't just my journey, though. It took us both a while to get here. We had to be ready at that moment in time and here we are."

"It was different for me," Lauren said. "This is like another life or another chapter, since we're talking about books."

Cat and Elena chuckled.

"I had a good life with my husband, but when my kids grew up we found out they were our only real connection. For me, there had to be more. I've found an everlasting love with Tara and my past and present intersect with our children."

"She calls them our children, but Lauren is their mother. I think they like having me around, though."

Lauren laughed. "They love you and you know it."

"And I love them." Tara turned back to Cat and Elena. "I talk about the fun and partying in the book, but back then, I was afraid to be still. I was afraid to look at myself. When I found Lauren, all of that changed. It isn't about fun all the time; it's about living. I love being with Lauren and living in those quiet moments. It's the easy moments like right now, sitting and talking and just being, that mean the most."

Cat thought about Tara and Lauren's words and looked over at Elena. What Tara described was what she and Elena did most evenings. They sat in the sapphic study and simply loved being together. Cat's heart began to pound in her chest. She had to tell Elena how she felt. There was nothing fake or pretend about her feelings and Elena should know.

"That was a lot more than you asked for," Tara said. "I'm not sure where all that came from."

"It was beautiful," Elena said. "I think my life might be similar to yours, Lauren. I was married for almost twenty-five years and my husband died last year. I feel like I'm starting the next chapter or the next life I'm supposed to live."

"I'm sorry for your loss," Lauren said. "It seems you've found a good place to start with Cat and the bookstore."

Cat and Elena shared a look.

"Can I top off your wine? It won't be long until the sun goes down, so we'd better make our way outside," Tara said.

After another splash of wine, they followed Tara out the back door and onto a patio that overlooked the lake.

"The view is great here, but this time of year is special. When you stand on the dock, the sun looks like it's setting right into the water."

"Honey, Justin and Ruby are on the phone. I'll be out in a minute," Lauren said from the back door.

"Justin is our son and Ruby is his daughter. I understand about every other word, but she's the cutest thing you ever did see." Tara beamed with pride. "Y'all follow the steps down to the dock. I'll wait on Lauren and we'll see the sunset from up here."

"Are you sure?" Cat asked.

Tara nodded. "Go on, enjoy the show."

As they began to follow the path down to the steps which led to the dock, Cat slipped her hand into Elena's and intertwined their fingers, just like in her dream. "I need to tell you something while we watch the sunset."

Elena smiled at her and nodded.

24

They stepped onto the dock and walked around the area where the boat was kept.

"This looks like a good spot," Cat said, sitting down where they could gaze across the lake.

Elena sat down next to her and dangled her feet over the edge. "Are you cold?"

Cat shook her head and once again took Elena's hand. Elena hadn't realized how much she loved holding hands until she and Cat began this charade. Dean was never one for public displays of affection. She would feel his hand on her back when they walked into a restaurant, but they never held hands. Elena almost looked forward to when they knew Hattie would be around so she'd have an excuse to slip her hand into Cat's.

"Do you see that span of beach right over there?" Cat pointed to an area on the other side of the cove.

"Is that Lovers Landing?"

"Mmhmm, you can just see the restaurant up from the beach. The cabins are sprinkled through those trees."

"Is that the beach you were walking on in your dream?" Elena could feel her heart thumping in her chest.

"You remember that?"

"Of course I do." The way Cat's voice sounded when she was telling Elena about the dream was still in her head. There was such longing and Elena wanted to hold her. She wanted to tell her everything would be all right.

"I was walking along the beach hand in hand with another woman and I felt such happiness. I knew it was all because of her."

"But you couldn't see her face."

"Do you remember the first time Hattie walked into the bookstore and you walked over and kissed me?"

Elena nodded, scared to utter a word.

"When you kissed me, you put your hand in mine and interlaced our fingers. Just like this," Cat said, holding their hands where they both gazed down at them.

"I remember. My hands were shaking and all I knew to do was grab yours to steady it."

"When you kissed me and our hands came together, the dream flashed through my head."

"It did?"

Cat nodded. "It was your face, Elena. You're the woman in my dream."

"I hoped," Elena said so quietly she wasn't sure she spoke aloud.

"None of our kisses have been fake for me," Cat said.

"Me neither," Elena whispered.

Cat let out a relieved breath.

Elena tilted her head. "What is it?"

"I wasn't sure. I've been so confused and afraid to trust my heart, but today, after Hattie left the bookstore and you kissed me… I knew that was real."

"Oh, Cat. They've all been real."

Cat smiled and shook her head. "I guess we have to thank Hattie for making us do something we were both afraid to do, but wanted for a long time."

Tara's words from earlier rang through Elena's head. "Maybe you had to go through that pain with Hattie to get to me."

"Maybe I'm who you are without Dean," Cat replied. "Maybe I'm your next chapter, your next life."

"We're missing the sunset," Elena said.

"Nothing could be more beautiful than what my eyes see right in front of me," Cat said.

Elena reached up with her other hand and cupped the side of Cat's face. She stared into those bright blue eyes she'd come to love. Her eyelids fluttered closed and she pressed her lips to Cat's. The softest moan escaped Cat's throat and Elena parted her lips. Their tongues touched, softly at first, but now that Elena knew this was real for both of them she couldn't hold back.

Her hand slid into Cat's curls while she freed her other hand to wrap it around Cat's back and pull her closer. The moan that came from deep inside Elena's heart was one of complete bliss. It was as if her heart was saying: *Finally, what took you so long!*

They explored while their tongues did the dance of wonder and delight accompanied by the sweet music of their breaths mixed with moans and groans.

Elena remembered the soft lips of her library crush, but this kiss was so luxurious and Cat's lips were so perfect she couldn't think of anything except Cat. She never wanted this kiss to end and wondered if all their kisses would be like this. Because one thing she knew for sure was that she was going to be kissing Cat Sloan from now on.

Cat pulled her lips away and took a deep breath. She stared into Elena's eyes and said, "I want to keep kissing you."

A small smile played at the corner of Elena's mouth. "I want you to, but..." Elena still held Cat close and she tore her eyes away to quickly look around.

Cat giggled. "Oh, yeah. We're supposed to be watching the sunset, not making out on the dock of a very famous actress who is letting me host her book signing."

"Bringing a lot of business to the bookstore," Elena added with a giggle of her own.

She pressed her forehead to Cat's and smiled. "I've had feelings for you for quite some time. I knew you didn't trust your heart, so I kept them inside. I don't want to do that any longer."

"Thoughts have been swirling around my head and I've been so confused, but they keep leading me to you. When I'm with you, the confusion clears and I can breathe."

"Will you be my next life?" Elena asked softly.

A loving smile crossed Cat's face. "I think we're living your next life."

Elena grinned and pressed her lips to Cat's once again. Before she could deepen the kiss, she pulled away and glanced over the lake. "Babe, look!"

The sun had changed into a deep orange ball that looked as if it was about to touch the water.

Cat gasped. "It looks like the lake is on fire."

"Kind of like my heart," Elena said, putting her arm around Cat's shoulder.

Cat rested her head on Elena's shoulder while they watched the sun put on a show. "I think my whole body is on fire from that kiss."

"No more pretending," Elena said quietly as she watched the sun slowly fall into the water.

"It never was. Now we know."

"Now we know," Elena whispered. "What do we do?"

"Well, *babe*," Cat said, raising her head and smiling at Elena. "We're going to go back inside and enjoy dinner with our new friends." She chuckled.

"What's so funny?"

"I feel like I can breathe again, but then again I can't," Cat said with a giggle.

"I'm confused," Elena said, shaking her head as if to rid the bewilderment.

"I can breathe because now I know you feel the same way. But you take my breath away with a look, a touch, or especially a kiss."

A big smile grew on Elena's face. "Now you know how I feel."

"We'd better go back up, but first I'm going to kiss you and you're going to know how I feel," Cat said.

The way Cat looked at her lit a fire inside Elena to rival the sunset they'd just witnessed.

Cat gently took Elena's face between her hands and pressed their lips together. Elena's hands squeezed Cat's wrists and when Cat deepened the kiss, Elena thought her heart would race right out of her chest. Her arms went around Cat, mainly to hold on. Elena could feel Cat's passion and desire with every stroke of her tongue and touch of her fingers on her cheeks.

Their kisses before were of wonder and affection. This kiss was filled with want, hunger, and lust. Elena couldn't wait to find out where this kiss would lead them. *Later*.

Cat began to pull away, but Elena had to have just one

more. When their lips separated, Elena pressed hers to Cat's one more time.

"Mmm," Cat moaned.

"Exactly," Elena said, begrudgingly pulling away.

Cat smiled and stood up. She reached her hands out to Elena to pull her up.

"You expect me to walk after kissing me like that?"

"You'll get used to it." Cat chuckled.

Elena let Cat pull her up to her full height and she looked down at Cat. "I'll never get used to that. I'll always want more."

"I have plenty of kisses for you, El," Cat said as she began to lead them off the dock and up the steps.

"Wasn't that beautiful?" Tara said from her chair on the patio.

"So much so I didn't want to come back up," Cat said, squeezing Elena's hand.

"I know what you mean," Lauren said. "Sometimes we sit down there until it's dark."

"Let's go inside. I'm getting hungry," Tara said, getting up and opening the back door.

"You can tell us about your kids and Ruby," Elena said.

"I'm not sure you want to get me started on her. I'm a smitten grandmother, that's for sure."

"We'd love to hear about them," Cat assured her.

They went inside and had a casual dinner around the table at the end of the kitchen.

"My daughter, Emily, is a chef and with a few lessons from her, Tara now fancies herself a budding culinary artist," Lauren said.

Tara chuckled. "You seem to like every creation so far."

"You know I do," Lauren said, kissing her on the cheek

and setting a large salad on the table. "Plus, I don't have to cook."

"One of Cat's favorite meals is creating sandwiches," Elena said. "I will add that she's quite good at it."

"It all began because some places make them so thick you can't get your mouth around them," Cat said.

"Oh, I hate that," Lauren agreed.

"This is a casserole Emily and I have been working on as a main dish," Tara explained, setting the dish on the table. "It's kind of like throwing everything in and hoping it tastes good."

"You and Emily are working on, huh," Lauren said with an amused grin as she served Cat and Elena each a big helping.

Tara shrugged. "You never know. It could become restaurant worthy."

Elena chuckled. She loved the playful barbs Tara and Lauren tossed at one another, always delivered with a loving smile.

"I hope this is the first meal between new friends and many will follow," Tara said, raising her glass when everyone had been served.

"We'll have you over for sandwiches," Cat said, touching her glass to the others.

"Can't wait," Lauren said.

Elena gave Cat a quick glance, loving how Cat had said *we*. The idea that had been patiently building in the back of her head became a little more urgent. She hoped Hattie would agree to sell the house and soon.

* * *

Once they'd said their goodbyes to Tara and Lauren and promised to have them over for sandwiches soon, Elena drove them back to town.

Cat reached for Elena's hand and pulled it into her lap. She didn't want to let Elena go or the night to end. Telling Elena she was the woman in the dream had opened her heart and all she could feel was love. It was as if the love in her heart that had grown every day since Elena walked into the bookstore could finally be free. She could feel it all and she wanted Elena to feel it too.

"When we get back to town, I don't want you to take me home," Cat said.

"Okay. Where do you want to go?"

"I want you to take us to your house, but I don't want to sit in the sapphic study with you."

Cat saw Elena glance over at her and nod. "I want that, too."

Cat smiled and the nervousness that was coursing through her body changed to excitement. She couldn't wait to show Elena how much she loved her.

25

They didn't say much on the ride home. Elena could feel her heart pounding and tried to take a deep breath to steady the jitters that had taken up residence in her body since Cat had asked to go home with her. *This is Cat*, she told herself. *She is the person you have fallen in love with. Of course you're nervous, but it's Cat. Your Cat.*

Elena pulled into the garage and they both got out of the car. Cat waited for Elena to open the door to the kitchen then took her hand once they were inside.

Elena led them through the kitchen, but Cat stopped them outside the sapphic study. She reached up and gently stroked Elena's face. Her fingers felt so good and her touch somewhat calmed the nervousness running through Elena's body. Elena looked into Cat's now dark blue eyes.

"I know how important this is to you, El, but I want you to know it's just as important to me," Cat said. "This is your first time, but it's my first time with you. It's just as special to me." She pulled them into the sapphic study.

"I didn't think you wanted to sit in here," Elena said with confusion on her face.

"We're not going to sit. In a way, this room brought us together," Cat said. "And in this room is where I want to tell you for the first of many times that I'm in love with you, Elena. I think from the first day you walked into my life and our eyes met, I started to fall in love with you."

"Oh, Cat," Elena said, her voice full of emotion. "I've fallen in love with you, too." Being able to tell Cat this made Elena's heart beat with joy. Cat loved her and she loved Cat. In some ways it was so simple. Their hearts helped them through the confused thoughts so they could be in this moment together.

Elena smiled at Cat and softly kissed those perfect lips. She led them down the hall to her bedroom and stopped at the foot of the bed. She turned to face Cat and they simply stared into each other's eyes for a moment.

Cat slowly unbuttoned her shirt and Elena could see the deep red bra underneath.

Elena gasped and Cat grinned. "I wear this one when I want to feel you near me and I need a little extra confidence. I knew tonight would be special because I had to tell you about the dream. I had to tell you that you're the woman my heart knew would make me happy before my mind was ready to grasp it."

Elena pushed the shirt from Cat's shoulders and let it fall to the floor. Then she pulled her own shirt over her head and tossed it aside.

Cat reached for the front of Elena's jeans and raised her eyebrows as she looked into her eyes. She unbuttoned them then slid the zipper down.

The corner of Elena's mouth twitched into a smile as Cat

pushed the jeans down her legs and waited for her to step out of them.

Once again Elena followed Cat's lead and slid the jeans down Cat's legs to reveal the matching red undies.

"You are beautiful," Cat whispered as she reached around and unclasped Elena's bra.

"I'm older than you and my body—"

Cat silenced Elena with a soft kiss then placed her hand over Elena's heart. "This is what is beautiful and makes all of you beautiful to me."

Cat guided Elena's bra strap slowly down her arms and Elena could see the desire in Cat's eyes. It looked like an inviting pool of lust and love that she wanted to immerse herself in and never come up.

Cat reached up and cradled Elena's face and stared into her eyes. "I love you," she whispered and brought their lips together in a long, soulful kiss. When she pulled away Cat said, "Look into my eyes. You'll see the wonder and love as I discover all of you."

Her fingers began to slowly trace down from Elena's cheeks and outlined her collar bones then whispered over her chest until Cat cupped both of Elena's breasts.

Elena could hear her own shaky breaths, but when Cat cupped her breasts she closed her eyes and savored the feel of Cat holding her so intimately. *If this feels* this *good, how will I survive the night*, she wondered.

Cat ran her thumbs over Elena's nipples that were already hardened pebbles. Elena heard Cat take a deep breath and moan. "So beautiful."

Elena couldn't wait any longer and wanted to be naked with Cat. "As much as I love this lingerie I want to feel your skin pressed to mine."

Cat smiled. "Then take it off."

Elena gave her a shy grin and reached around and unfastened the red bra. She let it fall to the floor with their other clothes then slid Cat's panties down her legs. She marveled at Cat's beautiful body and couldn't wait to touch every inch. Elena took a deep breath to slow her eagerness. There was no way she was rushing through this.

At one time she may have dreamed of touching and having sex with another woman, but this was Cat. This was so much more than sex and climax and orgasm. This was sharing their love in the most intimate way.

"You okay?" Cat asked softly.

Elena nodded. "I can't believe I get to discover and touch every inch of your body."

"I want you to," Cat whispered. "So desperately."

Elena's eyes snapped back up to meet Cat's and she crashed her lips to Cat's. She wrapped her arms around Cat's back and felt their breasts press together as she pulled her closer. Their moans echoed around the room and Elena deepened the kiss. She poured all her anticipation and anxiety into that kiss and when she pulled her lips from Cat's she felt emboldened. Elena may have never had sex with a woman, but she was confident Cat's body would lead her where she needed to be.

Elena quickly removed her own panties and took another deep breath. They stretched out on the bed side by side, face to face. Cat reached over, pulled Elena's lips to hers for another passionate kiss, and gently pushed Elena onto her back. Elena felt Cat's fingers trail down between her breasts until she cupped one then gently squeezed her nipple between her finger and thumb. She gasped and moaned with pleasure.

"That feels so good," Elena whispered.

"Mmm." Cat moaned then began to trail kisses down Elena's neck and over her chest. Her tongue swirled around Elena's other nipple and she whispered, "Breathe."

Elena took a deep breath then lost it as Cat took her nipple into her mouth. "Oh, God," she moaned and buried her hands in Cat's curls. She'd imagined what it would feel like to have those curls wrapped around her fingers, but this was so much better.

Cat gave Elena's other breast the same attention and she couldn't stop her hurried breaths. "So good," she mumbled. Elena could feel Cat smile against her skin as her hand began to slide over her body, across her stomach to the outside of her thigh. Cat's fingers trailed back up her inner thigh and Elena spread her legs a little wider.

Cat began to kiss a path down Elena's body and swirled her tongue around Elena's belly button as she reached under Elena's leg, pushing it to bend at the knee. She looked up at Elena and whispered, "I love you. Let me show you."

Elena traced her fingers over Cat's cheek. "Show me."

She saw Cat take a deep breath and her lips were everywhere. Cat kissed across Elena's stomach and she felt such a want deep inside. Then Cat's magical tongue slid through her folds and Elena's hips bucked off the bed. "Oh, God!"

"Breathe, babe," Cat said softly.

Elena's hands slammed down on the bed and fisted the sheets then once again ran her fingers through Cat's hair. She could feel Cat's love in every touch, every lick, and every moan. Cat's tongue explored and swirled until Elena thought she might explode. When Cat sucked Elena into her mouth, a loud groan flew from her chest and Elena's hips once again raised into the air. But Cat held her down as a powerful orgasm flowed through her body.

Elena had never felt anything like it. The waves crashed

and zipped through her body as her muscles tensed, wanting to hold on to this ultimate climax. When her hips fell back to the bed she realized she was tightly holding Cat's curls and loosened her grip.

"Catarina," she gasped.

Cat laid her head on Elena's stomach for a moment then began to kiss back up her body.

When their lips met Elena could taste their love and she wrapped her arms around Cat, pulling her as close as she possibly could.

She felt Cat's hand begin to trail down her body again and tickle over her inner thigh. Her finger began to slide through her wetness and Elena said, "Oh!"

Cat pulled her face away so Elena could see into her eyes. "We're just beginning," Cat said with a sexy grin.

Dear God! Elena was surprised she didn't come again right then.

"Look at me, babe," Cat said. "I want to watch you go over the edge and I want you to see how that makes me feel."

Elena locked her eyes on Cat's and could feel her finger circle and then push inside her. The groan that came from Elena surprised her, but she could tell Cat loved it.

Cat added another finger and began to slowly push in and out as Elena's hips matched her rhythm. The heat that began to build inside Elena's body was glorious. She could feel every place that Cat's body touched hers: their breasts, where Cat's hip brushed along Elena's middle, and especially where Cat's fingers moved inside her.

Cat's fingers thrust inside Elena one more time and she ran her fingers over the velvety spot Elena had only read about in books. The power of the orgasm that built and exploded inside her was all consuming. She stared into Cat's eyes and hoped she could see what was happening inside her body. Cat's eyes were the darkest blue Elena had seen them, but she didn't see the color, she saw love. Were those stars she saw in Cat's eyes, too? Because she was sure the world had just exploded around them.

Elena took Cat's face into her hands and said, "I love you." She then pressed their lips together in a kiss she hoped bonded them for life.

Cat pulled away and said, "I love you, too." Then she laid her head on Elena's shoulder and neither said anything while their breathing slowed.

Elena was pretty sure no words needed to be said. Their hearts had taken over and they basked in the euphoria.

Elena ran her hand up and down Cat's back and loved the weight of Cat's body resting on hers. "You're not falling asleep are you?" Elena asked suddenly, trying to look down to see Cat's face.

Cat chuckled. "It's okay."

"Oh, no it's not," Elena said, squirming under Cat and pushing her over on her back. "I want all of you. I want to touch you. I want to taste you. I want to hear your every moan and every groan. I want to hear you call out my name."

"Make me yours," Cat said in a low voice.

Elena smiled and crawled on top of Cat. "You sexy woman," she moaned and began to kiss Cat's neck then nibbled her earlobe.

Cat groaned and Elena whispered, "When we were dancing I wanted to do this so badly."

She stopped and looked into Cat's eyes. "I don't know what I'm doing."

"My body will tell you," Cat said.

Elena saw such desire in Cat's eyes, but she also saw love. She couldn't believe this amazing woman was in love with her. Maybe she did know what she was doing after all. Their love would lead her.

26

"Good God, El," Cat said, trying to catch her breath. "I thought you didn't know what you were doing?"

Elena giggled. "I read a lot."

Cat chuckled. "Come up here. I need a kiss."

Elena raised her head from where it rested on Cat's stomach and when their lips met Cat could feel the desire begin to build all over again. What was Elena doing to her? She'd always loved having sex, but this was world class. Cat chuckled as Elena pulled her lips away.

"What's funny?" Elena asked, narrowing her gaze.

"Okay, look," she began. "I've had sex with several women, but El, I'm chuckling at myself because this is above amazing. You make me feel—God, I can't even put it into words."

Elena smiled. "I think I know what you mean. Sex is one thing, but this seems way better, way bigger than just sex."

"Exactly," Cat said, widening her eyes.

"Maybe it's because we've both admitted our feelings

and don't have to wonder or hide them any longer," Elena said.

Cat nodded and gazed into Elena's eyes. "Your eyes are so dark brown. The color reminds me of the expensive liquor Cory sells. I could melt right into your eyes and never come back."

"Funny," Elena said. "That's what I thought about your eyes earlier."

Cat smiled. "I'm sure about this, Elena. I know I can trust my heart when it comes to you. I've been able to trust it for a while now. That's because you showed me I could."

Elena smiled. "I could see and feel your pain, babe. I wanted to take it away and all I knew to do was love you. Actually, it was you that convinced me."

Cat furrowed her brow as she ran her hand up and down Elena's arm. "What do you mean?"

"You told me Alexis showed CeCe they were right for each other every day. She gave CeCe time to wrap her heart around it. Nicolas—"

"You talked to Nicolas about us?" Cat asked, surprised.

Elena chuckled. "I talked to Nicolas about the feelings I have for you. Can't you just hear him?" Elena snapped her fingers and imitated Nicolas's high energy voice. "Girl, you know you're falling in love with Cat!"

Their laughter echoed around the bedroom. "I can hear him saying that!" Cat exclaimed.

"I told him about what Alexis did and he said, 'there's your answer,'" Elena explained. "So I simply tried to show you that I loved you and no matter what, I was here for you."

"I felt it," Cat said, kissing Elena tenderly. "You know, Alexis and I talked about the risk of letting you know how I feel. I was afraid to lose our friendship, but later when I thought about it, I knew I could trust you with anything. If you didn't feel the same way I knew we could find our way to remain friends. I knew you would make that happen."

"And here I was loving you right back and just as afraid. But I knew you'd figure it out, that *we'd* figure it out. These feelings, this love is too big to hold back." Elena kissed Cat and sighed. "I love you so much."

"We keep saying that." Cat giggled. "I hope you don't get tired of it."

"I'll never get tired of saying it or hearing it," Elena said. "But you have to go to work tomorrow, so snuggle up here beside me and let me hold you."

Cat did as Elena said and put her arms around Elena. "I'll never get tired of this."

"I know The Bottom Shelf isn't really a secret, but you said it surprised your sisters. It makes me wonder what other secrets you have," Elena said.

Cat yawned. "You know my sexy lingerie secret, but I might have a few more."

"Mmm, I love that secret," Elena whispered as she snuggled closer.

"Thank you for making my heart happy again," Cat murmured into Elena's neck. She could feel the rhythmic rise and fall of Elena's chest and knew she'd fallen asleep.

Cat closed her eyes and relaxed into the embrace of the woman in her dreams.

* * *

Cat's eyes fluttered open as she felt Elena's arm around her middle. She could feel Elena's breasts pressed into her back and closed her eyes again, sinking into all the sensations swirling around her. They'd made love several times and couldn't get enough of each other. Cat smiled at Elena's exuberance and lack of fear to ask questions. She was never tentative and only wanted to give Cat the utmost pleasure. Elena didn't realize it wasn't so much the physical act, but rather the love Cat felt from her that made every time incredible.

Cat smiled as she began to feel little kisses on her shoulder. She rolled over and looked into Elena's sleepy eyes.

Elena didn't say a word but kissed her lips then her neck and across her chest.

"Good morning," Cat moaned.

"It is," Elena said between kisses. "I know you have to go to work, but I can't get enough."

"Jessica offered to open up this morning," Cat said.

"She did?" Elena's head popped up from between Cat's breasts. "But I thought she closed last night so you could leave early."

Cat nodded. "She knew we were going to the lake and might be out late."

A sexy smile grew on Elena's face. "We weren't out late, but we were up late."

Cat ran her fingers through Elena's hair and smiled.

"Does that mean I don't have to stop what I was doing?" Elena asked.

Cat raised her eyebrows. "I don't want you to stop."

Elena leaned up and brought their lips together in a kiss which Cat quickly deepened. Elena wasn't the only one who couldn't get enough. Cat loved their kisses. Some were playful, some were full of lust, and others said *I love you* without the words.

"Mmm," Cat murmured as Elena began an assault down her body with kisses, nips, and touches.

Elena swirled her tongue around Cat's nipple then gave it a gentle bite before sucking it into her mouth. Cat gasped and arched her back, pushing her nipple further into Elena's mouth. "You have a magical tongue," she moaned.

Elena nibbled that nipple once again then swept her tongue over to Cat's other breast. Cat's fingers were buried in Elena's hair as she closed her eyes and gave way to the glorious waves of pleasure surging through her body.

"So good," Cat whispered, then gasped again.

Elena kissed down Cat's stomach as her fingers replaced her mouth on Cat's breasts. *This just gets better and better,* Cat thought as she spread her legs to give Elena more room. One lick from her entrance up and around her clit almost made Cat come undone, but she held on because there was more to come.

"Oh, baby," Cat whispered over and over.

Elena sucked Cat into her mouth and Cat couldn't hold on any longer. Her hips bucked and she held Elena's head in place as wave after wave of pleasure once again flowed through her body. She dropped her bottom back on the bed and relaxed her grip on Elena as she said between heaving breaths, "I could start every day like this."

"Look at me, babe," Elena said.

Cat opened her eyes to Elena's beatific face hovering over her. She could see the love and wonder in Elena's eyes.

"I swear, I came with you," Elena said with surprise in her eyes. "I could feel your orgasm in my mouth and that was it. I was in it with you."

Cat smiled and put her hand on the side of Elena's face. "That's why it was so powerful then, because, babe..." Cat trailed off.

"I know!"

Cat pulled Elena's face down so she could give her a kiss full of love.

"It's our love," Elena said, pulling away. "It's only going to grow. Can you imagine—"

Elena had a gleam in her eyes Cat hadn't seen before.

"We're going to explode one day in ecstasy," Elena finished, flopping down on the bed next to Cat. "I can see the headline. 'Couple ignites into flames from hot love that couldn't be contained.'"

Cat laughed. "Oh, this is going to be fun." She rolled onto her side and gave Elena a menacing look. "Don't you dare go without me."

Elena began to laugh. "Oh, Cat. I don't want to go anywhere without you."

"Good," Cat said, raising up. "I am going to have to go to work soon, but first, let's be sure you felt what I felt."

Cat claimed Elena's lips in a kiss that left no doubts about what was about to happen.

* * *

Elena was trying to take a deep breath and said, "One of these days, I want to spend the entire day in bed with you."

Cat chuckled. "That sounds like fun, but right now you've got to take me home so I can get ready for work."

"Do you promise?"

"Promise what?"

"That you'll spend a day in bed with me," Elena clarified.

Cat smiled as she rested her head on her hand. "Let's do it this weekend."

"Okay." Elena smiled. "You know, you could shower here."

"Yes, but I didn't bring any other clothes. You're not

going to make me do the walk of shame into my bookstore, are you?"

Elena narrowed her gaze then her eyes widened. "You could wear your jeans from last night and one of my shirts."

"Hmm, I guess I could go commando and wear my bra another day."

"That way," Elena said, brushing a curl from Cat's face, "we could have breakfast together."

"You're going to feed me?"

Elena chuckled. "I'm sure I can find something you'd like."

Cat gave her one of those sexy grins that Elena couldn't resist.

"God, I love you," Elena said.

"I love you, too." Cat said, sitting up on the side of the bed and slapping Elena on the butt. "You've got a deal, ma'am. I'm getting in the shower while you find me a shirt."

* * *

Elena watched Cat walk naked to the shower and couldn't quite believe she'd spent most of the night making love to this incredible woman. The best part was that she knew Cat loved her back.

She looked through her closet and found a shirt she hoped Cat would like. Elena left it on the bed and went to start the coffee. They hadn't slept much last night, but she felt more rested than she had in a long time.

Elena busied herself making coffee and was toasting them both an English muffin when Cat walked into the kitchen.

"Do I smell coffee?" Cat said, inhaling deeply.

Elena chuckled. "Here you go," she said, handing Cat a mug. "Are you going to be tired all day from lack of sleep?"

Cat took a sip and closed her eyes. "Mmm, this is so good. Almost as good as..." she trailed off and winked at Elena.

Elena giggled and took a sip from her mug.

"We may not have slept much last night, but I feel great," Cat said. "Happy."

"I do, too."

"How do I look?" Cat asked, smoothing her hands over her shirt. "Do I look like you?"

Elena laughed. "No, but you look like the woman I'm in love with."

"Right back at you," Cat said, leaning over and kissing Elena on the lips.

As Elena put their muffins on a plate, the doorbell rang.

"Are you expecting someone?" Cat asked with raised eyebrows. "It'd better not be your girlfriend."

27

"Haha," Elena said, opening the door.

"Good morning, Ms. E!" Nicolas exclaimed, rushing inside the house. "You'll never be—" Nicolas stopped mid-word and stared at Cat. "Well, good morning, Cat."

"Hi Nicolas," Cat said, taking another sip of her coffee.

Elena walked around to the other side of the island and poured Nicolas a cup of coffee. She slid it over to him and smiled.

"Uh, is there something you girls need to tell me?" he asked, pointing from one to the other.

Cat and Elena exchanged a look then looked back at him. "I don't think so," Cat said with a grin.

"Uh huh. Well," he began, "I think you do. I didn't see Cat's car outside. You look like you've just come from the shower and you both look freshly fu—um, I mean, you're wearing one of Ms. E's shirts, which is one of my favorites, by the way."

"It is a nice shirt," Cat said, smiling at Elena.

"It's one of my favorites, too." Elena returned Cat's smile.

"Come on! Don't make me say it. Spill the tea!" Nicolas exclaimed.

Elena and Cat both laughed.

"I hope you don't mind, Nicolas, but I'm madly in love with your bestie here," Cat said, putting her arm around Elena. "And I spent the night."

Nicolas gasped and grabbed his chest. The excitement on his face was brighter than the sunshine coming in through the front window.

"I couldn't let my love take the walk of shame so I lent her my shirt," Elena said, wiggling her eyebrows at Nicolas.

He screamed and excitedly jumped around the island and hugged them both. "This makes me so happy!"

Cat giggled. "It makes me very happy, too."

"What? When? I need every detail," Nicolas said, reaching for his cup of coffee and sitting at the table.

Elena brought their plates to the table while Cat sat next to Nicolas.

"You know, you played a part in this," Cat said, spreading jelly on her muffin. "Your craftsmanship is how Elena lured me over here."

"Lured?" Elena laughed. "Yeah, I don't quite remember it that way."

"I remember it perfectly," Cat said. "You told me you'd redone a room and I had to see it." She turned to Nicolas. "Of course I had no idea how beautiful your work was and pretty much fell in love on the spot."

"With the room or Ms. E?" Nicolas asked, narrowing his gaze.

"Both!" Cat chuckled and took a bite of her muffin.

A proud smile crossed Nicolas's face. "I was happy to do my part."

Elena laughed at them both and sipped her coffee. *How*

can I be this happy? She loved listening to her two favorite people laugh and exclaim at their new love. *It doesn't get better than this.*

"I hate to rush this wonderful breakfast, but I do need to take you to work," Elena reminded Cat.

"Are you trying to get rid of her? That's not how this works, Ms. E," Nicolas teased. "You see, now that Cat's spent the night you need to get a U-haul so we can start loading it while she's at work. That way she can be all moved in by tonight."

Elena nearly choked on her coffee while Cat laughed.

"He's just teasing, babe," Cat said, reaching for Elena's hand and giving it a squeeze.

These two had no idea that Cat moving in was exactly what Elena wanted.

Elena cleared her throat and smiled. "I know he's teasing. Trust me, Nicolas. I know how this works."

"Ohhhhhh, did you just school me, Ms. E?" he exclaimed.

"I'd say she did." Cat laughed and held her hand up for a high five.

Elena slapped Cat's hand and joined their laughter.

"However, my babe here is right. I do need to get to work," Cat said.

"OMG, listen to y'all calling each other babe. I love it!" Nicolas said with a big grin.

"And I love her," Cat said, leaning over and kissing Elena's lips.

"I'll be your best man," Nicolas quipped.

"Whoa!" Elena exclaimed. "You're going to scare her away!"

Cat laughed. "You're moving me in today and are we getting married tomorrow?"

"Why wait? Haven't you waited long enough?" he said in all seriousness.

Cat and Elena stared at each other.

"Too much, too fast," Nicolas said. "Take a breath, we'll get there." He reached over and covered their hands with his.

"We?" Elena said, raising her brows.

"We're in this together, Ms. E. We have been since I was six. I'm not about to leave you now. Don't worry, Cat loves me," he said, giving Cat a wink.

Cat chuckled. "He's not wrong."

"Okay, Nicolas. You'll be the first to know when we make any major changes or decisions. How's that?" Elena said.

"I can live with that," he said. "But don't expect me to wait for long."

* * *

They waved to Nicolas from the front door.

"Oh my God, that boy!" Elena exclaimed.

"He's not a boy," Cat said.

"I know, but he's always saying this boy, that girl and it's rubbed off on me," Elena explained.

Elena closed the door and Cat wrapped her arms around her neck. "As much as I'd like to stay here with you all day"—she wrinkled her nose—"I really need to get to work."

"Okay." Elena sighed.

Cat reached up and kissed her softly then deepened the kiss until they were both clinging to each other for air. "Come by this afternoon," Cat said. "I'll need another kiss."

"What if I can't wait that long?"

"Then stay there with me."

"People will start to talk," Elena said with an amused look.

Cat chuckled. "Oh my God, imagine what my sisters are going to say!"

Elena gasped. "I hadn't thought about that."

"Let them think this is fake, it'll be fun to mess with them," Cat said.

"I want them to like me," Elena said.

Cat furrowed her brow. "What? They love you!"

"As your best friend. This is different."

"No, it's not. They'll be happy for us just as we're happy for them."

Elena leaned down and kissed Cat. "I love you, you know."

"Hmm, I couldn't tell from all the sex we had last night and the declarations of love in between."

Elena smirked.

"I love you, too." Cat kissed Elena again and let her go. "Now, please take me to the bookstore."

Elena drove Cat to the bookstore and promised to come by later that afternoon. Cat leaned over and kissed her goodbye before she got out of the car. "Love you," she said.

"Love you, too," Elena replied.

Cat watched her drive off and walked into the bookstore with a big smile on her face.

"Someone looks happy this morning," Jessica said.

"It's a beautiful day," Cat replied, holding out her arms.

"I guess everything went well last night?" Jessica asked.

"You wouldn't believe me," Cat mumbled.

"What?"

"It went great. We have the book signing all figured out, now we just have to get things ready," Cat said.

"Oh good. This is going to be fun."

"You have no idea, Jess."

Jessica gave Cat a confused look. "Are you sure you're all right?"

"I'm more than all right," Cat replied. "Thanks again for closing last night and opening this morning."

"I was glad to do it." Jessica smiled.

"There you are," Vi said, hurrying into the bookstore.

"Hey," Cat said. "Aren't you moving today?"

"Yes. Cory is at the house directing the movers, but I need some help from you and CeCe." Vi tilted her head and gave Cat a look. "Something's different about you."

"She went to Tara Holloway's lake house last night," Jessica said.

"Oh, that's right. Cory and I are ready to help with the event."

"Thanks, I told Tara and Lauren," Cat said.

"I know what it is," Vi said with a smile. "You look happy."

Cat chuckled. "Well, I guess because I am."

CeCe walked up to the counter in a huff. "Sorry about that. That particular client likes to talk."

"It's okay. I just found Cat," Vi said to CeCe.

"I didn't know I was lost," Cat teased.

Vi chuckled. "I don't know what happened at the lake, but I like the change in you."

"The lake?" CeCe said, confused.

"It's nothing," Cat said. "What do you need our help with?"

"I've talked Cory into staying at her house tonight because when we spend our first night in our new home, I want her to be my fiancée."

Cat and CeCe gasped. "You're going to propose!"

"I want to propose in The Liquor Box at the exact spot

where we first looked into each other's eyes," Vi said dreamily.

"How romantic," CeCe said. "That's kind of what I did with Alexis."

"I remember. I was there," Jessica said. "It was amazing."

"Hopefully this will be, too," Vi said. "Cat, I need you and Elena to pick up the food at Betty's and CeCe, I'll have the champagne ready for you and Alexis."

"When are we doing this?"

"Tomorrow night at closing. Once she says yes," Vi said, holding up crossed fingers.

"Oh, come on, you know she will," Cat said.

"When she says yes, y'all come in through the front door and we'll party," Vi said.

"Are we supposed to stay hidden?" CeCe asked.

"No, I'm going to tell her I'll lock the front door and y'all can look in the windows. We're going to salsa before I get down on one knee," Vi explained.

"Oh my God. Cory will love this!" CeCe exclaimed.

"I hope so." Vi grinned.

"CeCe's right. She'll love it," Cat agreed.

"Okay, I can count on you, right?"

"Of course you can!" Cat and CeCe said in unison. "Anything for our big sister," Cat added.

"I'd better get back to the house. You're welcome to come help us start unpacking," Vi said, walking towards the front door. She waved and then she was gone.

Cat wanted to tell them why she was happy, but decided to wait. This was Cory and Vi's moment and she wanted them to have all the attention.

Later on that afternoon Elena came walking into the bookstore with a big smile on her face.

Cat watched as Elena's eyes scanned the bookstore to

find her. Once their eyes met, the smile on Elena's face got even bigger.

"Hi," Elena said.

"Hi yourself," Cat replied, reaching for her hand. "Jessica, we'll be in the back."

"Okay," Jessica replied, not looking up from where she was shelving books.

"Where are we going?" Elena giggled.

"Where do you think we're going?" Cat replied, wiggling her eyebrows.

Cat led them into the toy room, then closed the door and locked it. She pushed Elena against the door. "I've got big news, but first." Cat claimed Elena's lips and kissed her like they'd been separated for days instead of a few hours. She held Elena's hands against the door and pressed her leg between Elena's to the echo of both their moans.

Cat ran her hand down Elena's side and to the front of her pants.

"What are you doing?" Elena panted.

"Those leggings you're wearing are screaming for me to put my hand down them."

Elena giggled then pressed her lips to Cat's in reply.

Cat pushed her hand past Elena's waistband and into her wetness. "Mmm, babe."

"That's what you do to me," Elena said, spreading her legs a little wider.

"I love you so much," Cat whispered as she stared into Elena's eyes and circled her clit. She pressed one finger then another inside and saw Elena's eyes close momentarily.

"Oh, babe," Elena gasped with a heavy breath.

Cat's hand started to move and she increased her rhythm as Elena's hands tightened on her shoulders.

"Oh, Cat!"

Cat could feel Elena clench around her fingers and held them still. She could see the orgasm flash in her eyes and quickly kissed her in hopes of smothering her louder groans.

Elena dropped her head onto Cat's shoulder. "Good God, woman."

Cat smiled and gently removed her hand. "Cory and CeCe have both asked me if anyone's gotten busy in The Bottom Shelf. Why not us?"

Elena chuckled. "That was intense."

"I had no idea how much I missed you until you walked in the door. I mean, I was looking forward to you coming in, but as soon as I saw you I had to kiss you."

"Uh, that was a little more than kissing," Elena said, narrowing her gaze.

"That's what you do to me," Cat said, using Elena's words from earlier.

Elena softly kissed Cat and smiled.

28

"Maybe I'll wear these leggings more often."

Cat chuckled. "Oh! I almost forgot, Vi is proposing to Cory!"

"That is big news. When?"

"Tomorrow night and we're going to help," Cat said. She explained Vi's plan and what their jobs were in the surprise.

"Cory is going to be over the moon," Elena said.

"I know!" Cat grinned. "I wanted to tell them about us, but I didn't because this needs to be about Cory and Vi."

Elena shrugged. "Do they need to know? Let's just be ourselves, which means kissing and holding hands in public, and see if they notice Hattie isn't around."

"Oh that could be fun," Cat said.

Elena straightened her pants and shirt then kissed Cat on the lips. "Just wait until you get home after work."

Cat furrowed her brow. "I just remembered my car isn't here."

"I'll come back and get you," Elena said.

"How about you take me home, I pack a bag, and stay with you again tonight?"

"Or I can stay with you," Elena suggested.

"Let's stay at your place. There aren't any exes roaming around who could pop in on us," Cat said.

"Has Hattie been by your house?"

Cat shook her head. "Not yet, but I wouldn't be surprised if she shows up some evening."

"Okay." Elena pulled Cat close and kissed her.

"Mmm," Cat said. "We could've been doing this all along."

"You'd never sell any books or toys, you'd be in here with me all the time," Elena said.

"That's true," Cat said, unlocking the door and leading them back into the bookstore.

"I'll come back and get you at closing," Elena said, walking beside Cat.

Cat stopped and turned to her. "What? You're not staying? You always stay for a while."

"Don't you have to work?"

"Yes, but we do this every day. Do you not want to stay?"

Elena smiled. "Of course I do. I wasn't sure…"

Cat reached up and gently ran her fingers along Elena's cheek. "Our time together each day is how we fell in love. Why would that change now?"

"Okay," Elena said softly.

They walked back to the reading nook and Elena stayed for a visit just as she'd always done.

* * *

Elena backed out of Cat's driveway and began to drive the short distance to her house.

"Are you sure you don't mind bringing me to work in the morning?" Cat asked. "I could've followed you home."

"I don't mind. We won't need both cars tomorrow for the engagement party," Elena said.

"Okay. I guess it's a good thing I packed for several days."

Elena glanced over at her and smiled. "We can stay at your house, too."

"Maybe sometime. I love your home," Cat said. "You know that."

"I do. Hey, what do you want to do tonight?"

"You're not going to take me to bed and have your way with me when we get home?" Cat said.

Elena chuckled. "Yes, but not as soon as we get there. I got something together for dinner and I want to dance."

"Dance? Do you want to go out?"

"No, I want to dance with you in the sapphic study. There are a few songs I want to play for you," Elena said.

"Did you make us a playlist?" Cat asked with excitement.

"Maybe... Is that dumb?"

"No," Cat said. "I think it's romantic. When did you make it?"

"I loved dancing with you at The Neon Rose, so I started to make a playlist then and added to it," Elena said.

"Is that why you've mentioned going back there several times?"

Elena chuckled. "Yep."

"Why didn't you just ask me?"

"We were dancing because Hattie was there," Elena reminded her.

"I asked you to dance with me because I wanted to. Honestly, once we put our arms around each other I forgot Hattie was even there."

"Oh, she was watching," Elena said.

"You never did tell me what y'all talked about in the bookstore that day," Cat said.

"She said you were the best and I agreed."

"Really?" Cat said skeptically.

Elena nodded. "She said it took her too long to realize it. But I knew the minute I walked into Your Next Great Read."

"Did you really? Because I remember how easily we fell into conversation and before you left that first day I knew we were going to be friends."

"I was nervous when I walked in, but there was something about you that calmed me. I could see in those sparkling blue eyes—you have the most beautiful eyes, you know," Elena said, glancing over at Cat.

"Thank you, but you were nervous?"

"Yeah, I knew the books I was looking for and planned to browse around the store until I found them. But you walked up and shook my hand, and when I looked into your eyes I thought, this woman would understand."

"When you left that day I hoped you would come back. I wanted to sit in the reading nook with you."

"I think it's working out for both of us." Elena grinned and squeezed Cat's hand.

"Yeah, it is," Cat said as Elena pulled into her driveway. "Is Nicolas coming back by this evening?"

"Nope. He texted and said he would not be showing up unannounced for a while," Elena said. She hit the button to close the garage door and walked into the house with Cat right behind her.

"What did you plan for dinner?"

Elena giggled and turned around. "Sandwiches."

Cat's face lit up. "You are romancing me, El."

Elena took Cat's bag and set it on the island then put her hands on Cat's hips. "I love you and I want to show you."

"Oh, you're showing me," Cat said.

Elena kissed Cat softly. "Wanna dance?"

Cat nodded.

They walked into the sapphic study and Elena got her phone out to pull up the playlist. "I have a sound system in here that connects to wifi," Elena explained. She looked up at Cat and grinned. "Some of these songs I heard with Nicolas."

"That means they'll be fast with a beat." Cat laughed.

"Yes, but some of the words remind me of us," Elena said.

Cat pushed the end table to one side of the room then did the same with the coffee table in front of the loveseat where they usually sat. "Wait a minute, you don't need a couple of beers to do this?"

"Not this time. I want to remember every moment," Elena said. "I want to start with a sort of slow song by Harry Styles. It's called 'Satellite' and it's how I felt when I started to fall in love with you."

"We sang to it that day we went to Betty's," Cat said as soft notes began to fill the room.

Elena took Cat into her arms. "I was spinning out, 'round and round' like a satellite, just like the song says."

"And you were right here waiting for me to pull you in," Cat sang softly.

They held each other close and moved to the music.

Once the song was over Cat asked, "Can you put that on repeat?"

Elena nodded and felt Cat push her down on the loveseat. "Do you know how many times I imagined us together right here?" she said as the music played quietly.

"Catarina," Elena whispered. She sat on the couch with Cat between her legs. Her arms were pulling Cat closer as they shared a passionate kiss.

"Mmm," Cat moaned. "I don't want to listen to the other songs right now."

Elena smiled and caressed her cheek. She watched Cat reach for the waistband of her leggings and slide them down her legs.

"These leggings," Cat said with a sexy smile.

Once they were off, Cat leaned up and Elena stared into her eyes. She could see love and desire.

Cat kissed her again and said, "Lie back."

When Cat kissed her again right below her navel Elena sucked in a ragged breath. She reached for Cat's curls and buried her fingers in her hair.

Elena felt Cat's tongue slide through her folds, lapping up her wetness. Their moans accompanied the soft music still playing around the room. Cat circled Elena's clit and sucked it into her mouth gently at first then harder.

Elena had to grab the edge of the loveseat to steady herself. The orgasm built quickly and Elena's thighs tensed. Cat reached for her other hand and intertwined their fingers as Elena flew over the edge.

"Oh, Cat," Elena gasped. "Cat! Oh my God!"

While Elena caught her breath Cat contentedly sighed.

"Catarina fucking Sloan, what are you doing to me?" Elena panted.

Cat giggled. "My girl is vocal."

Elena opened her eyes and looked down at Cat. "Am I your girl?"

"Mmhmm, you are."

"I like being your girl."

"I like it, too."

"Want to see if you can make me scream louder?"

Cat giggled again. "Are you challenging me?"

"If it'll make you do that to me again." Elena moaned.

Cat stood up and reached for Elena's hands.

"What about dinner?" Elena said.

"That's the good thing about sandwiches. They'll keep," she replied with a wink.

* * *

They contentedly sighed with their arms around each other where they sprawled on the bed.

"Does my vocalness bother you?" Elena asked.

"Vocalness? Do you mean singing or..." Cat looked over at her and grinned.

Elena smacked Cat on the arm in reply.

"I love your singing and I love your moans, groans, and loudness. It tells me I'm making you feel good," Cat said.

"Feel good? Are you kidding me? This is so much more than good."

Cat giggled. "Yeah, it is. I've noticed you like to call me Catarina when you're..."

Elena chuckled. "When I'm about to explode with love."

"You could call it that."

"Hey," Elena said, brushing a curl from Cat's eyes. "Does Vi's proposal put pressure on you?"

"No," Cat said. "But just imagine how much my mom is going to be talking about it now." She chuckled. "Cory, CeCe, and I talked right after Mom won it and agreed not to ever let that wedding influence our decisions when it came to love."

"At CeCe's engagement party, you did say you'll never get married," Elena said.

"I know." Cat nodded. "Then I turned around and looked straight into your eyes and something happened."

"Happened?"

"Yeah, I had a jolt of hope run through me." Cat raised up and looked into Elena's eyes. "Did you ever think about getting married again, after Dean?"

Elena shook her head. "Not to a man. When Dean told me to find out who I was without him I think he knew." She frowned. "I miss him so much."

Cat nodded.

"But it's the friendship and companionship I miss. Intimacy with him was different," Elena said. "I love being like this with you. Simply holding each other and lazily running my hand along your skin."

Cat smiled and let her continue.

"I want to know every inch of you, inside and out," Elena continued. "When I would read that in books, I thought it was kind of hyperbole, but baby, I get it now."

Cat kissed Elena on the cheek. "Me too."

"Please don't misunderstand. I was very happy with Dean."

"I know that. There was a time when I was once happy with Hattie, but not like this."

Elena furrowed her brow.

"I know we are just at the beginning and all we can think about is making love," Cat said.

"Yeah, I can't seem to keep my hands off of you."

"That usually slows after a while, but I can tell it won't with us. Don't ask me how I know. I can just feel it."

Elena raised up to look into Cat's eyes. "I can't imagine not kissing you, not touching you. It's become a part of my being." She fell back on the bed and groaned. "I can hear how that sounded."

Cat looked over at her. "It sounded like we're in love and intend on keeping it that way. We're in this together, El.

That's where it went wrong with me and Hattie. We both have to keep at it."

"There's nothing more important to me than loving you," Elena said, pushing Cat down and showing her how much she loved her.

29

The next evening Elena and Cat waited outside The Liquor Box. They had picked up several platters of food for the party after Vi's proposal.

"There she is," Cat said with a grin.

"Let's go."

They got out of the car and joined CeCe, Alexis, Christine, and the rest of their friends outside the store and watched through the windows.

"Look at Cory's face," Cat said.

"Oh, there they go," Alexis said as Cory and Vi began to dance.

"I can't wait until they teach us how to do that," Cat said, putting her arm around Elena's waist.

"Me, too. Dance party at Cory's this weekend," CeCe said.

"They may be a little busy," Christine commented.

"Mom!" CeCe exclaimed.

Christine chuckled and looked over at Cat and Elena. She nudged CeCe with her elbow and nodded towards them.

"It's supposed to be fake, but I've got to find out what's going on with them," CeCe said quietly.

"Leave them alone," Christine said. "They'll figure it out."

Cat gasped. "Vi's on one knee."

"Aww, I can see Cory tearing up from here," CeCe said sweetly.

Elena leaned into Cat and sighed. "Just look at them," she whispered.

Cat pulled her a little closer and put her head on Elena's shoulder. "I love you, babe."

Elena looked over at her with widened eyes.

Cat grinned. "It's okay. Everyone's watching Cory."

Elena leaned near Cat's ear. "I love you, too."

After Cory did say yes, everyone streamed into the store and the party began. Cory's friends from the various bars around town where she'd worked at one time or another along with Vi's friends from work all congratulated the happy couple.

As the party grew a few people spilled over into the beauty salon to make more room and find a place to sit.

"Here you go, Christine," Elena said, pulling a chair over from CeCe's waiting area.

"Join me," Christine said.

Elena found another chair and set it next to Christine. "There's a lot of happiness bubbling out of the liquor store," Elena said.

"Isn't it great," Christine said, watching Cory show her ring to her friends. She turned towards Elena and smiled. "Seeing my girls like this makes me wish their daddy could be here."

"I can imagine," Elena said.

"If I remember correctly we've been widows about the

same amount of time, but it happened to me much later in life."

Elena nodded. "It's been almost two years."

"I knew when I lost the girls' father that I would find my happiness by watching them find theirs," Christine explained.

"You must be very proud of them, especially with the shopping center and what they've created here," Elena said.

"I am, but what I like the most is the happiness they've found doing it. I don't think any of them expected to love being together every day and working side by side like this."

Elena smiled and looked over where Cat stood with her sisters, talking and laughing.

"You know, the funny thing about happiness is that sometimes you find it and sometimes it finds you," Christine said. She looked into Elena's eyes. "And sometimes you have to pursue it."

Elena stared at Christine and her heart started to pound in her chest. *Does she know what's going on with me and Cat?*

"I hope you'll pursue yours," Christine said with a soft smile and a wink.

Elena didn't know what to say and hoped her mouth wasn't wide open in surprise. She had been to several family dinners and always enjoyed talking with Christine. Elena knew she was direct, but this truly astonished her.

"Cat's my baby girl. I can see when she's happy and I know who makes her feel that way."

Elena smiled and nodded. "Can you tell who's made me happy?"

Christine chuckled. "Cat!" She called to her daughter. "Elena and I need a refill."

Cat hurried over with a bottle of champagne and refilled their glasses.

"Thanks, hon," Christine said.

"You're welcome, Mom." Cat turned to refill Elena's glass.

"Thanks, ba—" Elena stopped and looked at Cat wide-eyed. She heard Cat giggle.

"Are you happy, Mom?" Cat asked, covering Elena's embarrassment.

"I am. Elena and I have found a good spot to watch all the action."

"Cory loves showing off her ring," Elena commented.

Cat chuckled. "That's another surprise in all this. She's not much on jewelry, but just look at her."

"You know what surprises me?" Christine said.

"What's that, Mom?"

"Your daddy wanted you girls to do something together, so you opened this shopping center. Look what happened with CeCe and now Cory. They're getting married."

"Easy, Mom," Cat said.

"I'm not talking about the big wedding, Cat. What I mean is that maybe your dad is with us and knows about our happiness."

Elena gasped. "Now that's a thought."

"You never know," Christine said, looking at Elena. "I wouldn't be surprised if your Dean knows about your happiness as well."

Elena had never thought about that. Christine was full of wisdom or something tonight. Elena wasn't sure which. She looked up to find Cat staring at her.

"I hope he knows," Cat said, smiling at Elena.

"Well, I think the crowd has died down and I can go congratulate the happy couple," Christine said, getting up. "Cat, you can have my chair."

Cat sat down and looked at Elena. "Are you okay?"

"I'm not sure. Your mom knows about us and I think she may be right. Your dad and Dean probably do, too."

Cat gave her a confused look. "Yes, she knows we're in a fake relationship. But what are you talking about?"

"You heard her. Maybe your dad and Dean helped us find each other so we could find happiness again."

Elena watched Cat blink several times and tilt her head.

"It's okay, babe," Elena said with a smile. *Thanks, Dean.*

* * *

It had been a week since Cory and Vi's engagement party and Cat had been busy getting ready for Tara's book signing.

"We're checking things off this list like we've done this dozens of times before," Jessica said, looking over Cat's shoulder.

"I know," Cat said.

"Elena has been so helpful with promoting the event," Jessica said.

"She has," Cat said, putting the notebook on the counter. "And she loves it. I think she's found her next career."

"Did her husband really leave her set so she doesn't have to work?"

Cat raised her brows. "It wasn't just him. They made some good investments and they've paid off."

"Hey, Cat," Cory said from the entrance to CeCe's salon. "Do you have a minute?"

"Go ahead. I can take care of the store," Jessica assured her.

"What's up?" Cat said, walking with Cory to the back of CeCe's salon.

"Sisters meeting," Cory said, opening the door to CeCe's break room.

"Hey," CeCe said when they walked through the door.

"Is something wrong?" Cat asked, eyeing her sisters.

"No," CeCe said, patting the couch next to her.

Cat sat down and waited, wondering what her sisters were up to.

"We wanted to talk to you about the wedding," Cory said tentatively.

"Okay," Cat said, her voice trailing off.

"But first, have you heard from Hattie?" CeCe asked.

"She hasn't been in the bookstore, but she's texted me a couple of times." Cat noticed the usual dread that accompanied talking about Hattie was gone. Elena had given her more than something to look forward to. She felt like she was living again, not just trying to get through the day.

"What about the house?"

"She's thinking about it. I hope she decides to sell, but I've decided after the book signing I'm putting it on the market. I'd rather her agree to it, but it's not going to change things between us."

"So she believes the fake relationship thing with Elena?" Cory asked.

"Yep. It helps that nearly every time she's come into the store Elena has been there." Just thinking about Elena made Cat smile.

Cory nodded and furrowed her brow. "You two are believable. If I didn't know what was going on I'd think y'all were together."

"That's the way it's supposed to look," Cat said with a grin.

"Uh, we wanted to reassure you that our agreement still holds on the big wedding Mom won," CeCe said.

"Yeah, we're in no hurry to get married and we were afraid Mom might say something to you," Cory added.

Cat smiled. "I love you both very much. But there's no way I'm going to get married just so we can have this big wedding for Mom."

"We know that!" CeCe exclaimed. "We just didn't want you to feel any pressure or feel bad because now we are both engaged."

"I still can't believe it!" Cory exclaimed.

Cat chuckled. "It is a bit surreal. Mom thinks Dad had something to do with it."

"Wait, what?" Cory said.

"The night of your party she told me and Elena that she thinks Dad is with us and knows we're happy."

"Hmm, that's interesting," CeCe murmured.

"I didn't think there was any way Mom would get her wish, but here we are—CeCe and I both engaged within a few months of each other."

"Maybe she could talk them into doing it for the two of you. That's still a pretty big deal," Cat said.

"She could talk anyone into doing just about anything." CeCe laughed.

"It's okay, y'all," Cat said. "I'm happy for you both, but if you want me to be your maid of honor maybe we could do it at the same time."

"We haven't even talked about the wedding yet," CeCe said. "Alexis and I are enjoying being engaged."

"Us, too," Cory said. "We've been so busy unpacking and getting the house the way we want it, the wedding is the last thing on our minds."

CeCe reached over and took Cat's hand. "I don't think any of us expected to be in this position. I certainly didn't. I figured we'd be helping one another plan our weddings one at a time."

"I'm happy to help with whatever you need, but can you

wait until I get Tara's book signing done? That's all I've been thinking about and working on," Cat said.

"It's going to be so much fun and good for the bookstore," CeCe said. "I'll be right there helping to keep the folks in line entertained."

"I know you will and I appreciate it," Cat said.

"Vi and I have the drinks ready. All we have to do is mix everything up on that day," Cory said.

"Alexis is even taking the afternoon off to help," CeCe added.

"She is? She doesn't have to do that. I mean, she's a friggin doctor. I'm sure she has more important things to be doing, like saving lives," Cat said.

"Oh, no. She's the one who suggested it. You are her family and she is here to help. Those are her words." CeCe grinned.

"Y'all are the best," Cat said, leaning back on the couch. She looked at CeCe and narrowed her gaze. "Hey, isn't Elena coming in this afternoon to get her hair done?"

"Yep," CeCe replied.

"Could I ask for a favor?"

"Sure. What do you need?"

"Could you keep her here just a little longer, and Cory could you send her home with a bottle of wine?" Cat asked.

"What are you up to?" CeCe asked.

"It's a little surprise. When Elena comes into the bookstore today, I'll tell her I'll meet her at her house after her appointment," Cat said. She'd had a romantic idea brewing in her head since they'd danced in the sapphic study. "If you could keep her here, I'd have time to go to her place and get things set up."

"Do you have a specific bottle of wine in mind?" Cory asked.

"Yeah, I'll have to come to the liquor store and show you. I can't remember the name, but I know where it is because Elena told me," Cat said with a chuckle.

Cat could see CeCe and Cory trying to figure out what was going on. She and Elena hadn't told them that there was nothing fake about their relationship and Cat didn't want to explain it to them right then.

"I can't tell you how much Elena has helped me and Jessica prepare for the book signing. I want to surprise her with something nice, but it's hard to catch her away from her house unless she's at the bookstore. This would be the perfect opportunity," Cat explained.

"Okay," CeCe said. "I'll text you when she's leaving the salon."

"Perfect," Cat said with a big smile.

"Come on. Show me which wine and I'll make sure she has it when she leaves the salon," Cory said.

"When I see her come in, I'll have just enough time to get to her house and set it up before she's done. Thanks y'all," Cat said, getting up from the couch.

"So we're okay with this wedding thing?" CeCe asked.

Cat nodded. "Of course."

"Let's surprise Elena then," Cory said as she and Cat left the back room.

30

Cat had tried to think of something special and romantic to do for Elena. She knew what she wanted to do, but hadn't quite worked out how to make it happen. Cory and CeCe had given her the perfect opportunity today and she couldn't wait to see the look on Elena's face when she walked into her house after her hair appointment. The surprise had nothing to do with the book signing, even though she'd told her sisters it did.

To be honest, Cat was enjoying her and Elena's little secret. They made it look real because it was, but her sisters and the others didn't have to know that.

Since admitting their feelings for each other on Tara's dock, they hadn't spent a night apart. Cat had always been one who needed her alone time, but with Elena she got what she needed. They could sit in the sapphic study, read a book, and not say a word to each other and be perfectly content. They'd been doing that for months now.

Other times they would watch TV together or prepare dinner and Cat loved their new routine. One thing she did know for sure was that she wanted to keep falling asleep at night with Elena next to her and waking up the same way. Cat had worked late a few nights in preparation for the book signing and it was nice to fall asleep in Elena's arms after a sweet goodnight kiss.

Nicolas had been by a couple of times and entertained them with his latest romantic antics or watched a movie with them. They'd asked him not to say anything to CeCe or Cory about their relationship when he came into their stores. Nicolas loved knowing a secret. Cat chuckled at the image of him zipping his mouth shut with his fingers.

No one seemed to notice or didn't realize Cat had been living at Elena's for over two weeks now and she was fine with that. Cat did go by and check the mail every day and grab more clothes when she needed them. She wondered if Alexis had driven by and wanted to stop, but kept going when she didn't see Cat's car.

She didn't have time to wonder about that right now. Cat had to change before Elena got home.

"Oh, baby. I can't wait," Cat said softly as she walked to the bedroom.

* * *

"Hey, Elena," CeCe said. "Did you go by to see my little sister?"

Elena smiled warily at CeCe's tone of voice as she sat down in her chair. "I did. Are you ready for the big book signing next week?"

"I am. Your ideas to keep the folks in line happy while they wait will be fun. I'm glad I get to help," CeCe said, wrapping the cape around her.

As CeCe began the process of highlighting her hair, Elena could see Cory approaching them in the mirror.

"Hi," Cory said with a smile. "Cat asked me to give you this bottle of wine to take home."

"Oh," Elena said. "I wonder what she's making for dinner."

"Alexis mentioned she hasn't seen Cat's car at home lately," CeCe said.

"She's been spending the evenings with me," Elena said, then quickly added, "In case Hattie comes by their house."

"Y'all are really making this fake relationship thing look real," Cory said, raising her eyebrows.

"If it helps Hattie figure out she doesn't have a chance with Cat and agrees to sell the house then it's worth it. Don't you agree?"

"Yeah," Cory said. "I can't believe she left in the first place, but now she's just drawing it out. It's inevitable."

"Yep," Elena agreed.

"So," CeCe began, "has it been weird kissing my sister?"

"Oh, no you don't," Elena said, raising her brows. "I'm not talking about that."

Cory chuckled. "Okay, okay. It's just that when we've seen you together doing your little act, you both seem to be enjoying it."

"Cat's my friend and I love her," Elena stated. "I want her to be happy and getting closure with Hattie is what she wants so that's what I want."

"You're a good friend," CeCe said.

"Wouldn't you do the same for your friends?" Elena asked.

"I would, but I'm not sure about kissing them," CeCe said.

"You wouldn't now," Cory said. "You're engaged."

"So are you," Elena pointed out.

"I know." Cory held out her hand and stared at the engagement ring on her finger.

Elena chuckled. "It's a beautiful ring."

"It is," Cory said, "but not as beautiful as my fiancée."

"I seem to remember Cat and CeCe doing the sisters thing with Vi when she was getting her hair done," Elena said. "If that's what this is, you can relax."

"Oh we can?" CeCe said. "Does that mean you're not attracted to our little sister?"

Elena cleared her throat, trying to think of the best way to answer that question, especially since CeCe knew Elena was exploring her sexuality.

"Hey girls," Christine said, walking up.

"Hi, Mom," Cory said.

"What's going on here? Are they grilling you, Elena?" Christine asked.

"No!" CeCe exclaimed.

"It kind of feels that way, Christine," Elena said. Thank goodness Christine walked up when she did.

"I've told them to leave you and Cat alone, and that y'all are taking care of things," Christine said

"We are," Elena said.

"That's what we're trying to find out, Mom," Cory said. "Just what things are they taking care of?"

"I'd say it's none of your business," Christine said. "Don't you have a liquor store to be running? I came to pick up wine."

"Yes ma'am," Cory said.

Christine put her hand on CeCe's shoulder. "Leave her alone."

"Yes ma'am," CeCe replied.

As Christine and Cory walked away, CeCe made eye contact with Elena in the mirror. She gave her a smile and said, "You know, you could be more than friends with Cat. I think she would be open to it."

Elena stared at CeCe. *If she only knew.*

"That's all I'll say. I didn't mean to make you uncomfortable."

Elena raised her brows and chuckled. "Sure you didn't."

CeCe laughed and shrugged.

* * *

"Hi honey, I'm home," Elena said, walking in the front door. "That's kind of fun."

She walked into the sapphic study and stopped. "Oh my God," she whispered.

Cat was sitting in one of the chairs wearing an unbuttoned flannel shirt, revealing a black bra made of see-through lace and matching panties. A pair of black high heels completed her outfit. She had her legs crossed, gently moving her foot up and down.

"It's my turn to bring the romance tonight," Cat said with a sexy smile. She could see and feel Elena's eyes as they roamed over her body. *I don't think I've ever felt so wanted.*

"If you expect us to drink this wine before I touch you then you're mistaken," Elena said, setting the bottle of wine Cory had given her on the table.

"Slow down, baby," Cat said from where she sat. "I have something for you." She reached for a box that sat on the table next to her and held it out to Elena. Cat took a deep breath, wanting to settle her excitement so she could remember every moment.

"For me?"

Cat nodded.

Elena took the box and set it in the other chair. She held

out her hands to Cat and smiled. Cat put her hands in Elena's and stood.

"You are the most beautiful woman I've ever seen," Elena said, taking in Cat's outfit from head to toe.

"Open it," Cat instructed her.

"Can I have a kiss first?" Elena asked.

Cat nodded slightly and pulled Elena's lips to hers. In heels, Cat was almost as tall as Elena. She felt Elena's hands slide under her shirt and wrap around her back. Their soft lips melded together and Cat could feel the fire rush through her. She pulled away and took a breath. "Open the box."

Elena stared into her eyes and Cat could see she didn't want to let her go.

"I promise you'll like it," Cat added.

"I like what's in my hands right now," Elena said.

Cat giggled. "We'll get to all of that. Please, open the box." She reached behind her and took Elena's hands from her body.

"You are so fucking sexy," Elena said.

Cat smiled, raised her eyebrows, and nodded towards the box.

Elena dropped Cat's hands and turned towards the box. She took the top off and underneath several layers of tissue paper she discovered a matching bra and panties that looked like the ones Cat had on, only they were red.

"I want to see you in red and find out if it does the same thing to me as it does to you when I wear your favorite bra."

Elena held up the bra and looked into Cat's eyes. "I've never worn anything like this."

"I'm hoping you'll feel special just as I do when I put on my sexy lingerie because you, Elena Burkett, are an incredible woman."

Elena smiled at her.

"I laid a shirt on the bed you can wear over them. Go change, please," Cat said. "I'll be there in a minute."

"I can't believe this," Elena said.

"Believe it," Cat replied. "You are the most amazing woman I've ever met and I want to show you what you mean to me."

Elena put the bra back in the box and picked it up. "Don't take too long."

Cat smiled, leaned over and softly pressed her lips to Elena's. "I'll be right there."

When Elena left the room, Cat took another deep breath. Desire was running through her like never before and her heart was pounding. She wanted to give Elena a special night and planned to take her time, but it was proving to be harder than she'd thought.

Cat grabbed the bottle of wine and went into the kitchen to open it. She had already packed a light supper into a basket and placed it in the middle of the bed. After grabbing two glasses, she took one more deep breath and walked down the hall.

Elena was in the bathroom when Cat walked into the bedroom. She poured them both a glass of wine and sat on the foot of the bed.

"I'm waiting," Cat said, "and not so patiently."

She could hear Elena giggle from the bathroom and wasn't ready for what she saw once Elena opened the door. Cat had always thought of Elena as beautiful. She carried her lithe body with a grace that often made Cat pause. And now she stood in the doorway to the bathroom wearing the red lingerie with a crisp white shirt open at the front just like Cat's.

Thank goodness Cat was sitting because just looking at

the woman she loved in that outfit made her weak in the knees. "Oh my God, El. You are even more beautiful than I imagined."

"You're right. I feel special and I love the way you're looking at me," Elena said.

Cat stood up and held out her hand. Elena glided towards her and grasped her hand. Cat looked Elena up and down in awe. "If I know you're wearing this and you come into the bookstore, we will immediately have to go to the back room," she said.

Elena chuckled. "Now you know how I feel when you tell me what color you're wearing under your clothes."

Cat smiled and led Elena around to her side of the bed. She gently pushed her to sit and handed her a glass of wine. Then she went around to her side of the bed and joined Elena. "We're having a picnic in bed. We both knew we were going to end up here."

"This is amazing. You are amazing," Elena whispered as she leaned over and kissed Cat.

"I have a few different nibbles for us," Cat said. She took a grape and held it to Elena's mouth.

"Mmm."

"It's good." Cat nodded, plopping a grape in her mouth as well. She spread out a napkin on the bed between them and laid out two different kinds of cheese with more fruit. "Oh, I almost forgot. I have a few nuts as well."

They sipped their wine and ate the cheese and fruit.

"Your hair looks beautiful," Cat commented.

"Thank you. I had an interesting conversation with your sisters," Elena said, taking a sip of wine.

"Oh?"

"It reminded me of what you and CeCe did when Vi was in CeCe's chair."

Cat swallowed and raised her brows. "What happened?"

"They had questions about our fake relationship, but then your mom showed up and saved me." Elena chuckled. "I'm telling you, babe. Christine knows about us. You're her daughter and she knows I'm the one making you happy, so to speak."

Cat smiled. "I hope I'm making you happy as well."

"You can't tell?"

Cat chuckled. "Yeah, I can."

31

Cat wrapped up the food and put it back in the basket then set it on the dresser. She turned to Elena and took her wine glass, setting it on the bedside table. She went back to her side of the bed and took one more sip of wine. She smiled down at Elena and crawled onto the bed. "Where's Aqua?" she asked.

It was almost comical how Elena's eyebrows shot up her forehead. "Uh, in the bedside table."

Cat reached across Elena and got the little blue vibrator out of the drawer and set it aside. Elena was sitting up and watching every move Cat made.

Cat sat on the bed and faced Elena. She slowly moved the shirt off one of her shoulders and gently kissed the exposed skin. "Let's go slow, baby. I want you to feel every touch, every sensation, and all my love. You can be as loud as you want," she said in between kisses. She could feel and hear Elena's shuddering breath.

"Mmm," Elena moaned. "I don't know how long I can hold out."

"You can do it," Cat assured her as she took the shirt all

the way off and eased Elena back on the pillows. She took her own shirt off and smiled down at Elena. "You are so beautiful."

Elena smiled up at her and Cat could see the love in her eyes. The anticipation was obvious, but she also saw trust. Cat gently trailed her hand over Elena's exposed stomach and watched as goosebumps rose on her skin. She leaned down and softly kissed Elena's eager lips.

Cat cupped Elena's breast and pulled her lips away while she ran her thumb over Elena's hardened nipple. She smiled and took the other nipple into her mouth through the delicate lace. Elena sucked in a breath and Cat could feel Elena's fingers comb through her hair.

Cat slid her hand down Elena's stomach and cupped her sex through the lace panties. She raised her head, looked into Elena's eyes, then slid her hand inside the panties and was greeted with Elena's wetness. "Oh baby, you're so wet."

All Elena could do was nod and Cat gave her a slow, soulful kiss. She pushed the panties down Elena's legs then once again ran her finger through her lover's wetness. Cat reached for the vibrator and saw Elena's eyes widen.

"Do you trust me?"

"With all I am," Elena replied in a hoarse whisper.

Cat turned the vibrator to the first setting and gently touched it below Elena's swollen bud.

Elena moaned loudly and closed her eyes.

"Let it build, baby," Cat whispered. "Feel the love coursing through your body and let it flow." Cat pressed the vibrator a little firmer against Elena then slowly moved it over and around.

"Catarina," Elena moaned.

"Not yet," Cat said. "Will you let me see?"

Elena opened her eyes and stared into Cat's eyes.

"Do you feel it?"

"Mmm," Elena hummed.

"So good," Cat said softly. She could see Elena was getting nearer the edge as Cat moved the vibrator closer to her clit. "Easy, baby. Let it flow."

Elena took a much needed deep breath and her eyes fluttered closed for just a moment.

Cat didn't want to tease Elena so she increased the speed of the vibrator to the next level and slid it up and over Elena's clit.

Elena grabbed Cat's shoulders and Cat could feel her fingers pressing into her muscles.

Cat kissed Elena softly and pulled away. At the same time she pushed the vibrator a little harder against Elena's clit and watched her come undone.

"Catarina!" Elena shouted.

Cat had never felt so much love for one person. She could see the love in Elena's eyes as she turned the vibrator off then rested her fingers on Elena's clit. "I love you," Cat whispered. She was surprised to feel tears sting the back of her eyes.

A small smile grew on Elena's face as she stroked Cat's cheek. "Oh, Cat. I love you."

Cat leaned her head into Elena's hand and returned her smile. "That was incredible. You are incredible."

"I've never felt anything like that," Elena said. "It felt like your love was flowing through me until it exploded into bright lights that surrounded us."

Cat nuzzled Elena's neck and rested her head on Elena's shoulder.

"Move in with me," Elena said, running her hand up and down Cat's back.

Cat raised her head. "What?"

"Sell your house and move in with me. Make this a home, *our* home."

Cat raised her eyebrows. She'd let herself imagine living with Elena, but wasn't sure Elena was ready for that. "Are you sure?"

"I've never been more sure of anything. Let's build a life together like both of us have dreamed, but it'll be even better than that."

Cat smirked. "Will you dance with me in our sexy lingerie?"

Elena chuckled. "Do you really need to ask me that?"

Cat giggled.

Elena pulled Cat to her and kissed her passionately. "Please move in with me, Catarina."

"Oh, El," Cat said. She nodded and grinned. "I'll move in with you."

Elena hugged Cat tightly. "You've made me the happiest person in the world!"

Cat chuckled. "I don't know about that. I may be the happiest."

Elena loosened her grip on Cat and pushed her onto her back. "It's you and me, babe."

"It's you and me," Cat agreed and pulled Elena down for another kiss.

* * *

The day of the book signing had finally arrived. All their preparation and planning were about to pay off, Cat was sure of it. Your Next Great Read had never hosted an event like this, but that didn't mean they couldn't pull it off.

As soon as the event was complete, Cat planned to start moving the rest of her things to Elena's. She needed to go through the house and see what she wanted to keep, but really, there were only a few things besides her clothes that meant much to her. Cat wanted a fresh start.

Elena told Cat she wanted it to be their home, so their next project was furnishing it to fit their blended styles. Cat couldn't wait and neither could Elena.

Things were lively at the bookstore and people were lined up throughout the store and out into the parking lot. Elena had come up with games and giveaways to keep the folks waiting involved until they got their chance to meet Tara.

Prizes included items in the bookstore as well as items from CeCe's salon and Cory's liquor store. They were all excited because Vi had decided to turn down her promotion and was not only going to be Cory's life partner, but also her partner in the liquor store. Things were certainly happening for the Sloan sisters in their businesses and their private lives.

"I need to talk to you about something after this is all over," Elena said, pulling Cat aside and away from all the excitement.

"Is everything okay?"

"Yes, it's more than okay. I've got a great idea going forward," Elena said.

"You mean another great idea," Cat said with a grateful smile. "Look at what you've done." She held her arms out and gazed around the store which was full of people.

"We did this, not me," Elena said.

"Come here." Cat grabbed her hand and led them to the back room out of view of the crowd. "I love you." She pressed her lips to Elena's and pulled her close.

"I love you, too," Elena whispered as their lips pulled away.

Cat's phone beeped in her pocket. She took it out and read the text. "It's go time," she said with a grin. "Tara and Lauren just pulled up to the back door."

They ushered them inside and were about to take them to the table where Tara would sign the books when Tara stopped them.

"There are more people here than I thought," Tara said, sounding a little nervous. "But I'm staying to meet every one of them and signing every book."

"You're going to have fun, babe," Lauren said, kissing her on the cheek. "These are your people."

Cat chuckled. "I'm one of them and I can't thank you enough for doing this in my store."

Tara patted Cat on the cheek. "You're welcome." She looked at Elena then back at Cat. "Let's go back to the house after this is done. We can have a drink and watch the sunset."

"That would be lovely," Elena said.

Lauren laughed. "I know how much work y'all have done and we appreciate it."

Cat nodded. "Let's sign some books. How about it, Tara?"

"Lead the way."

As Tara signed books, Elena orchestrated several different trivia games with CeCe and Alexis's help. Vi and Cory filtered through the line offering refreshments.

There was a party atmosphere in the bookstore. Cat kept moving and mingling through the line to be sure everyone was having a good time. She paused to watch Elena ask another trivia question about Tara's movies and then distribute prizes. Cat couldn't quite believe this amazing woman was in love with her.

Elena must have felt Cat's gaze because she locked eyes

with her and smiled. Cat saw her nod towards the back and wandered through the crowd to meet her.

"Ms. Sloan," Elena said in a low voice. "If these folks knew what you were wearing under that cute dress..."

Cat giggled. "Or you, Ms. Burkett."

"Hey, there are Victoria and Shelby," Elena said, waving to them.

"It's so nice to see you again," Victoria said, joining them.

"And how about this," Shelby said with excitement and her arms raised. "What a great event, Cat."

"Oh, it wasn't me," Cat said. She pointed at Elena. "Elena provided the fun, the promotion, the..." Cat held up a finger for every point she made.

"Stop!" Elena put her hand over Cat's. "We all pitched in."

"I want to know when you're going to start a book club," Victoria said.

Cat and Elena looked at each other and widened their eyes. "I know the perfect person to lead it," Cat said, smiling at Elena.

"That sounds like fun. I know what book we should start with," Elena said, taking a book off the table where Tara was signing.

"Great choice," Shelby said.

"I'll tell the people at my office," Victoria said.

"I know Vi will be interested and there are several women from her and Cory's gym who have come to the bookstore," Elena said.

"We want in," Lauren said, joining them. "Tara will be so honored you chose her book first."

"Oh, wow!" Cat exclaimed. "This is going to be so much fun." She turned to Elena. "Just imagine the books we can share with them."

"There's a list already running through my head."

"I'll let Krista and Melanie know, too," Lauren added.

"Let us know what?" Krista said, walking up to join them.

"They're starting a book club," Victoria said.

"I'd love to join," Melanie said.

A murmur ran through the crowd as people began to recognize Krista.

"Uh oh, I didn't want to cause a stir but I wanted to come support Tara," Krista said.

"It's okay, honey. Just walk through the line and say hello," Melanie suggested.

"This is Tara's big moment," Krista said.

"She was asking about you earlier. She hoped you'd be here," Lauren said. "Come on, let's go see her."

As they walked over to the table, Cat turned to Victoria. "Thank you for this great idea."

"You're very welcome, but it's a purely selfish gesture. I'll get to sit around and talk about books with my friends and maybe this one will see why I love them so much." Victoria put her arm around Shelby and smiled.

"I know why you love them. I'm just not big on the romance ones; give me a little action and I'm happy," Shelby said. "I'm living a beautiful romance every day."

"Oh my God, Victoria," Elena said.

"I know." Victoria chuckled. "I'm one lucky woman."

"Aren't we all," Cat said, smiling at Elena. Movement caught her eye and she turned to see Hattie walk into the bookstore.

32

Cat touched Elena on the arm. "I'll be right back," she said quietly.

"Did you come to get a book?" Cat asked, walking up to Hattie.

"Yeah, but could I talk to you for a minute?" Hattie said.

Cat gazed around the store and could see there were only a few people left in line. "Uh, let's go over here," she said, leading them behind a bookcase away from the table. Cat could feel Elena's eyes on her and looked back to give her a smile. When Elena smiled and nodded, Cat could feel her love.

"I'm ready to sell the house," Hattie stated. "Sorry it took me so long, but I just want to say that I'm glad you're happy. Believe it or not, that's what I want for you. We hadn't been happy for a long time and you've found something and someone you love. It's obvious."

"Thank you for saying that," Cat said. She was surprised, but come to think of it she realized her happiness was obvious. She felt it every day and was sure other people could tell.

"I've come by the house several times, but couldn't catch you at home," Hattie said.

"I stay at Elena's pretty often," Cat replied.

Hattie nodded. "I figured. Listen, I have a realtor friend and if it's okay with you, I'll take care of everything," Hattie said.

"Are you sure?"

"Yes. I know it's hard to trust me to do it, but I won't let you down again," Hattie said. "When it's done, I'll make sure they adjust the payout. I know you paid the mortgage for over a year without my help."

Cat gave her a wary look.

Hattie smiled. "I've played the last few years over in my head and tried to find every way in the world to blame you for our breakup. In all honesty, maybe no one is to blame. I think you're right, we grew apart. However, I handled it terribly. I'm not sure either of us was ready for an honest conversation because in our hearts we knew how it would end. We were together a long time and ending a relationship is hard. You fought for us, but I didn't. It broke both of our hearts, but we'll be okay."

Cat took a deep breath and nodded.

"Don't worry, Cat. I don't want to be your friend or anything like that. It would be too hard. Besides, Cory would kick my ass if given half a chance." Hattie chuckled. "I think she would've when I saw y'all in the Neon Rose if her girlfriend hadn't stopped her."

Cat smiled. "Maybe."

"Uh, I think the line is down and I know you're busy," Hattie said.

"Come on, I'll introduce you to Tara," Cat said. She felt the remaining sadness that was coupled with her feelings for Hattie lift from her heart. There was some truth to

Hattie's words and Cat was glad it was over. Hattie would undoubtedly find someone else if she hadn't already. Cat was reminded of Tara's words from their planning session at the lake, and she realized she had to go through those hard times to get to where she was supposed to be. And Cat was sure Elena was where she was supposed to be.

They walked over to the table that Tara was now standing behind talking to Lauren and Elena.

"Tara, I'd like you to meet Hattie Tucker. She's probably your biggest fan," Cat said with a smile.

"It's nice to meet you," Tara said, holding out her hand.

Cat could see Hattie trying to hold back her exuberance. While Tara signed Hattie's book, Cat walked around to stand by Elena.

"Are you okay?" Elena asked quietly.

Cat nodded. "More than okay. I'll tell you later."

* * *

The book signing was a huge success and even though they were tired when it ended, Cat and Elena couldn't imagine a better way to celebrate than catching another amazing sunset at Tara and Lauren's home on the lake.

"I don't know why y'all are tired," Tara said, topping off their drinks. "I'm the one who had to sign all those books."

"You're kidding, right?" Lauren said with a bite to her voice.

"Of course I'm kidding, honey. I know who did all the work," Tara said. She raised her glass and smiled. "Here's to friends and Your Next Great Read. Y'all put together an amazing event and you should be proud."

They clinked their glasses together and drank. Krista

and Melanie had joined them at Tara's along with Victoria and Shelby.

"I'm excited about this book club," Krista said. "When do you think it will start?"

"Soon," Elena said. "It's all I could think about after Victoria suggested it."

"Hey, we're going to miss the show," Lauren said, opening the door out to the patio.

As they began to walk outside, Tara put her arm around Cat. "I heard the most interesting thing at the bookstore."

"Oh?" Cat said.

"Yeah, I think it was CeCe telling Lauren you and Elena are in a fake relationship to rid you of an ex," Tara explained.

Cat stared at Elena, but neither of them said anything.

"Um, that's what everyone thinks," Cat said.

"But it's obviously not true," Tara said.

"Obviously?" Elena winced.

Tara chuckled. "Yes, to me and Lauren it is. Do you not remember the last time you were here?"

"Of course we do," Cat said, reaching for Elena's hand. "That's when we found out this wasn't fake for either one of us."

Tara gave them a bright smile. "I didn't say anything at the bookstore, and Lauren and I figured we were probably the only ones who knew."

"Thank you. We haven't told the others yet, but we're going to," Elena said.

"There is such a connection between the two of you that it was obvious to us. I'm thinking your sisters and friends believe you because why wouldn't they? We're just getting to know you, so..."

"You knew," Cat said. She looked over at Elena. "We

helped each other through a pretty rough time and as we became friends—"

"You fell in love," Tara said, interrupting her. "I want to hear more about this, but right now you'd better get down on the dock before the sun sets. And by the way, I'm really happy for you both. Once you tell everyone, please let me know because I'm going to tell Krista Lovers Landing isn't the only magical place where people fall in love."

Cat and Elena both chuckled. "You are so right," Cat said.

"Go on," Tara said. "I don't want you to miss it."

Cat and Elena made their way down to the dock while Tara and Lauren entertained the others on the patio.

Once they were settled just as before with their legs dangling over the edge, Cat reached for Elena's hand. "Didn't you want to tell me something after the event?" she asked.

"Oh, yeah. But first, Hattie seemed more relaxed," Elena said.

"She agreed we should sell the house and even offered to take care of it. She happens to have a friend who's a realtor."

"Uh, do you think you can trust her to do that?"

Cat nodded. "We hadn't been happy for a long time and she finally admitted it to herself. She also apologized for the way she handled things. It's over and she gets it."

Elena nodded. "Are we still moving your stuff this weekend?"

Cat smiled. "Yes we are!"

Elena let out a relieved breath. "This is going to be so much fun."

"It already is," Cat said. "Now, what's so important?"

"Well, I've been thinking," Elena began. "I enjoyed

working on the book signing so much and it really brought a lot of traffic to the bookstore. What if we had some kind of event every month? It doesn't have to be a book signing, but something with authors and readers."

"That's a great idea. I love it."

"Also, since I'm at the bookstore all the time anyway, how would you feel about me being your event planner and coordinator?"

Cat gave Elena an appraising look. "Are you asking for a job?"

"I think I am," Elena said with a huge smile. "I don't expect you to pay me or anything like that."

"Since you're there anyway," Cat said with amusement.

"Right." Elena nodded.

Cat turned and pulled Elena into a hug. "You are full of great ideas. We'll arrange some type of adequate payment. I might have something in mind."

Cat looked into Elena's eyes then brought their lips together in a sweet kiss that quickly became heated.

"We're missing the sunset," Elena whispered against Cat's lips.

"Mmm," Cat moaned. "It's okay, this is better."

They shared another passionate kiss then turned towards the lake just in time to see the orange orb sink into the shimmering water.

Cat sighed contentedly. She knew what she wanted to do to announce their relationship to her family and friends. It also solved the question of Elena's form of payment for her work at the bookstore. Cat rested her head on Elena's shoulder and couldn't wait to see this particular dream come true.

* * *

Cat and Elena spent the rest of the week and the weekend moving Cat's things into Elena's house. She had quickly gotten used to the idea of calling it their home. It already felt like Cat had been living there and with some of her things spread throughout the house it really did feel like *their* home.

Elena had started to invite people to the book club and planned to hold their first meeting soon. Since Tara's book was chosen to be their first read, she wanted to host the first meeting and invited everyone to the lake.

Cat had been working on her plan to tell her sisters the truth about her and Elena's relationship and today was the day. She had texted them both and asked them to meet her at her old house. Cat knew they wouldn't be disturbed there. CeCe and Cory were aware the house was on the market, but didn't know she'd moved in with Elena. Cat smiled and chuckled. Sometimes it was so easy to keep things from her sisters because they thought she was the quiet one and always took care of herself.

Cat opened the front door and Cory and CeCe walked in.

"Wow," Cory said. "I knew you'd gotten rid of some stuff for the showings, but it doesn't look like anyone lives here."

"Yeah, what did you do with everything?" CeCe asked.

"I'll tell you about that later. I asked y'all to meet here because I wanted to talk to you about the wedding and I knew no one would bother us here."

Cory and CeCe sat down on the couch and Cat sat across from them in a chair.

"What about the wedding?" Cory asked.

"Wouldn't it be fun to have the big wedding Mom won for us? Don't you think she'd be thrilled?"

"Yeah, but how would we do that?" CeCe said, sounding suspicious.

"Come on," Cat said. "Tell the truth. You'd both love to have that big elaborate wedding."

Cory and CeCe looked at each other.

"Well, yeah. You know I'd love it," CeCe said.

"Me, too, but..." Cory said.

"Let's do it."

"How? You and Elena are doing the fake thing," Cory said. "Who are you going to marry?"

"What if it wasn't fake?" Cat said, raising her eyebrows.

33

"What are you talking about?" CeCe asked, narrowing her eyes at Cat.

She couldn't keep from smiling. "We knew from the first kiss that our feelings were real," Cat began. "We just didn't think the other one felt the same way."

CeCe and Cory gasped. "I knew it!" Cory exclaimed.

Cat laughed. "We've been falling in love since the first time Elena walked into the bookstore. We've spent a lot of time together and become friends, but there was love growing the entire time."

"Oh my God!" CeCe exclaimed. "So you and Elena were falling in love at the same time I was falling for Alexis."

"And I was falling in love with Vi!" Cory added.

Cat nodded. "Grief brought us together in a way. We were two wounded souls trying to find where we belonged. We latched onto each other and found ourselves as well as our love. I'm so in love with her and I want to propose with y'all's help."

"Wait a minute," Cory said. "You two haven't been faking

it. You were dancing together for real at Talia's bar? And you were kissing when Hattie was around, but it wasn't for her benefit?"

"We were afraid to lose our friendship if we crossed that line and we desperately clung to that friendship because we needed it so much. But I finally realized that if Elena didn't feel the same way, we'd figure out how to still be friends."

"When and how did you finally admit your feelings?" CeCe asked.

"We went to Tara's to plan the book signing and went down on the dock to watch the sunset. I told Elena about this dream I had."

"I remember you telling us about that," CeCe said.

Cat nodded. "I told her that I was in love with her and..." Cat's voice broke and she blinked back tears. "She was in love with me, too."

Cory sat back on the couch and Cat could see tears in her eyes as well. "Oh, little sister," she said. "What do you need us to do so you can propose to your love?"

Cat smiled through her tears and told her sisters what she wanted to do.

* * *

"What's this surprise you have for me?" Elena asked as Cat drove them towards the lake.

"You've never been to Lovers Landing and I asked Krista if we could take a walk along the beach," Cat explained. "You can imagine her excitement, especially when I told her you'd never been here."

Elena laughed. "Can't you just hear Tara bragging to Krista that we fell in love at her house and not at Lovers

Landing. Their banter makes me laugh just thinking about it."

"Yeah." Cat chuckled. "It kind of reminds me of my sisters."

Cat drove them down to a cabin next to the water and parked the car. Once they were out of the car she reached for Elena's hand. "Let's walk along the beach."

As they strolled along Elena asked, "Is this like your dream?"

Cat nodded. "You know, I would've never had that dream if you hadn't shown me that I could trust my heart."

"When you told me about it, I was so hoping I was the woman walking along the beach with you," Elena said, squeezing Cat's hand.

"I was looking at you one day in the bookstore when you were sitting in your chair reading and I thought to myself, I want you to find someone who's willing to explore all these discoveries about yourself. I hoped they would embrace them and you for the incredible woman you are."

"Oh, baby," Elena said. "*You* are that person."

Cat stopped, faced Elena, and smiled.

She slowly kneeled in the sand.

Elena gasped and her eyes widened.

"Will you make my dream come true? I will embrace you and our discoveries from now until forever. Will you spend all your days with me, as long as we both live? El, will you marry me?"

"Oh, Catarina," Elena said, falling to her knees. She cradled Cat's face between her hands.

Cat's eyes were swimming in tears as she waited for Elena's reply. She looked into Elena's eyes and saw only love.

"Yes, I will spend all my days with you," Elena said softly.

Cat smiled and touched her lips to Elena's. This had to be the sweetest kiss as tears fell down both their cheeks.

Elena pulled away and ran her thumbs over Cat's cheeks. "These are the only lips I ever want to kiss," she said, pressing her lips to Cat's once again.

Cat chuckled. "To think it all began with a fake kiss."

"There was nothing fake about that kiss and we both know it."

"I love you so much, El," Cat whispered.

"Oh, babe, I love you, too."

Their lips met again in a passionate kiss as their arms tightly wrapped around each other. Time stood still and when they pulled away their smiles could light the evening sky.

Elena furrowed her brow and tilted her head. "At your sisters' proposals, their family and friends were waiting somewhere." She looked around the beach but they were the only ones there.

Cat smiled. "They're all at the restaurant waiting for us."

Elena gasped then narrowed her gaze at Cat. "Wait a minute. You told them about us?"

Cat nodded. "I told Cory and CeCe it would be fun to have the big wedding," Cat explained. "They had the most confused looks on their faces."

"Oh, no. What did you do?"

"CeCe asked how we could pull it off if you and I were in a fake relationship."

"And?" Elena said as a big smile grew on her face.

"I said, maybe it wasn't fake."

"Oh my God! Did they lose it?!"

"Cory said she knew it, but they were both happy for us and then I asked them to help with the proposal. I wanted to tell you how they reacted, but this had to be a surprise. I wasn't so sure you'd say yes," Cat said.

"You weren't sure? Why? I adore you, baby. I'm so in love with you, most of the time I can't think straight."

Cat raised her eyebrows and grinned. "I don't want you to think *straight*."

Elena threw her head back and laughed. "Oh, Cat. I knew your bookstore was going to be special. That's why I couldn't wait to walk in on that first day. Dean told me to go find who I was and I just knew the key was inside those walls. He would be very happy for us. I just know it."

"I hope he knows how much I love you and how much I appreciate him," Cat said.

Elena furrowed her brow. "You do?"

"Yes. I think, in a way, he gave you the courage to walk into the bookstore where you found me. Your heart saw how much I needed you and my heart knew you were the one to show me I could love again."

"Catarina," Elena whispered and kissed her again. "You and your bookstore."

"Oh!" Cat raised her eyebrows. "That reminds me. Since you now work for Your Next Great Read, you're also the co-owner."

"What? No, honey. The bookstore is yours."

Cat shook her head and smiled. "It never has been. You were a part of it from the beginning, just like me. Actually, you're the most important part, in the bookstore and in my heart."

"My lover is a romantic," Elena murmured, grabbing Cat and kissing her with all the love in her heart. "They're going to have to wait a little longer."

Cat deepened the kiss and her heart overflowed with happiness and love.

They heard a noise in the distance and both looked toward the restaurant.

"Well?" Nicolas shouted from the deck of the restaurant, waving his arms over his head.

Elena and Cat both laughed. "I guess we'd better go tell them you said yes."

"Nicolas is going to explode with joy," Elena said.

"So are we," Cat said, pulling Elena up. She intertwined their fingers and held their hands up so Nicolas could see. He began to jump up and down and scream as the others joined him on the deck.

"Oh, wait!" Cat exclaimed. "How could I forget?" She reached into her pocket and pulled out a solitaire diamond engagement ring. She slipped it on Elena's finger and smiled.

"Cat, this is beautiful! And big!" Elena exclaimed.

"It reminded me of you. A single sparkling light that shines in my heart," Cat said. "Our love is big, so your ring should be, too." Cat winked.

"You're going to make me cry again," Elena said.

"I'll kiss away the tears because we're all about joy, babe," Cat said, pressing her lips to Elena's once again.

Nicolas ran down the deck and wrapped his arms around them both before they could pull their lips apart.

Elena chuckled. "I think we made them wait too long."

"My girls!" Nicolas exclaimed. "I'm so happy and proud of you both for figuring this out!"

"We are, too," Cat said.

"It took you long enough," Nicolas deadpanned then kissed them both on the cheek.

They walked onto the deck and Christine was the first to hug them.

"I hope you don't plan on a long engagement," Christine

said. "I thought you two would be the first, but you took your time and had a little fun with it."

"What?" Cat said, giving her mom a confused look.

"I've been watching all three of my girls fall in love since the first day you opened the shopping center. It was obvious you and Elena were perfect for each other, but my quiet, cautious daughter had to think it through." Christine chuckled. "However, Elena brought the fun with this fake relationship thing." Christine grinned at Elena. "You couldn't fool her mama."

Elena laughed. "We couldn't fool our hearts."

Someone turned up the music and the drinks flowed.

A little later, Cat and Elena snuck onto the deck for a quiet moment.

Cat took Elena into her arms and smiled. "For so long all these thoughts swirled around my head, but now the only thing swirling around me is our love."

"Oh, Catarina," Elena whispered.

Cat had come to love the way her name cascaded from Elena's beautiful mouth. Every syllable was laced with love and it sent a jolt of desire straight to her heart. She claimed Elena's lips with her own and this kiss was full of excitement and promise. Their happily-ever-after began now.

TWO MONTHS LATER

"I still can't believe you did all this, Mom," Cat said.

"Why, you know I'm going to take care of my girls," Christine said. "But I didn't do it all by myself."

"Everything is just perfect," Elena said, smiling at Cat.

"I had the best seat in the house." Christine chuckled. "I got to watch all three of my girls fall in love at the same time with women I would want for daughters."

"Aww," Elena said.

"And now you're mine as well," Christine said. "This may not be the wedding of your dreams, but it's the wedding of my dreams for each one of you."

"But you had everything ready and made it easy," Cat said. She gazed around the room at her sisters and their brides. "I mean, look at our outfits. They're perfect."

"While you were falling in love, I also got to know Alexis, Vi, and Elena. I paid attention to your styles and your personality. My girls were easy. I knew what y'all should wear. No one could wear that white suit better than Cory."

"I couldn't agree more," Vi said, kissing Cory on the cheek.

"CeCe had to have a strapless ivory gown." Christine smiled.

"With that flowing red hair and those blue eyes, you are a beauty," Alexis said with a big smile.

"And my little flannel loving baby," Christine said. "I knew you were tired of wearing suits and nice dresses as an accountant all those years. You are a vision in soft lace. I didn't know that they call that a high low hem, but it's beautiful on you."

"I love it, Mom," Cat said.

"I do, too," Elena said, putting her arm around Cat's waist.

"I had a little help with the rest of y'all, but I was confident in the selections you had to choose from," Christine said.

"My mom said the two of you had fun selecting options for me," Vi said. She wore a sleek, elegant, knee-length off the shoulder white dress.

"This suit with the wide pant legs you found for Alexis is perfect. The way it drapes over your body is..." CeCe said, staring Alexis up and down.

"Save that for later," Christine chided her middle daughter.

Elena chuckled. "Nicolas told me how much fun he had with you choosing options for me."

"I'm glad you chose this suit with the sheer jacket. You look stunning," Cat said.

"The two of you look amazing standing next to each other," Alexis said.

"Thanks," Cat said. "I think our outfits complement our

partners. Who knew six brides could look so different and yet go together."

"How did you get Krista involved so we could have our wedding on the beach?" CeCe asked.

"She came to me," Christine said. "She knew the event planner and they went to work."

"Krista knows how special this place is to all of us," Cory said, smiling at Vi.

Christine chuckled. "Tara had something to say about that. She claims her fabulous lake home deserves the credit for Cat and Elena's awakening."

Cat and Elena both laughed. "Her place is rather magical," Cat said.

"I'm glad y'all decided to forego the tradition of not seeing one another before the wedding," Christine said.

"It was nice of Krista and Melanie to give us each a cabin to get ready and see each other in our outfits for the first time," CeCe said.

"Since we're on the beach I didn't have to worry about your shoes," Christine said with a grin.

"Is everyone ready?" Krista asked, coming in from the deck. "Your family and friends are seated and waiting for the brides."

"We're ready," Christine said with a big smile.

"You all look lovely. Absolutely stunning," Krista said. "Take a moment to look out over the beach."

They all walked to the bank of windows that overlooked the deck and the beach.

"Every person down there loves you and can't wait to share this special moment with you," Krista said.

"Our friends from Make It Easy Design are all here," CeCe said. "They helped us start the shopping center."

"I see my colleagues and friends from the practice and the hospital," Alexis said.

"They welcomed me into your world with open arms," CeCe said.

"Look!" Cory said to Vi. "All our friends from Your Way are here."

"I see," Vi replied. "Aww, there's my former boss and assistant."

"They love y'all," Cat said.

"But no one outshines Nicolas," Elena said.

"He kept our secret because he knew we needed time to grow into it," Cat said.

"Okay," Christine said. "Let's get you married."

Krista led them onto the deck and the crowd quieted when she took her seat.

Christine walked down the aisle first then turned and smiled. "I have been entrusted and have the highest honor of officiating this ceremony of love and marriage."

Vi came down the aisle first, followed by Alexis and then Elena.

Everyone turned in expectation to see which Sloan sister would come first.

Cat looked at Cory and CeCe with tears in her eyes. "Krista and Tara may think the lake is special, but I think we created a magical place together," Cat said.

"The Sloan Sisters' Shopping Extravaganza brought us so much more than a business," CeCe said.

Cory returned their smiles then looked up. "Thanks, Dad."

They locked arms and strolled down the aisle together, smiling at their friends then grabbing their partners' hands.

"What a glorious day to share this special time with

friends and family," Christine began. "You won't hear vows from each couple or we'd be here long after the sun sets."

This brought chuckles from the crowd.

"They also exchanged rings privately before the ceremony," Christine added.

They held up their fingers and wiggled them.

"These six wonderful women came together and agreed on these vows. If you'll face your partner and join hands," Christine said.

"Do you vow to always communicate?" Christine said. "That means talking and especially listening to each other."

There were several chuckles from the spectators.

In unison they said, "I do."

"Do you vow to keep surprising each other? Because you have to keep the magic alive," Christine said.

"I do," they once again repeated.

"Do you vow to share your love with each other and help it grow from here on out?" Christine said.

"I do," rang out again.

"Do you take each other to be your partner, your best friend, your wife?" Christine said.

"I do."

"Then by the power vested in me by being your mom and your mother-in-law and of course certification from the internet," Christine said to another round of chuckles, "I pronounce you, Corine and Violet, Cecilia and Alexis, Catarina and Elena, married."

The couples' smiles lit up the dusky evening sky.

"I don't get to use their real names very often unless they've done something wrong. But this, my precious daughters, is the most right thing you've ever done." Christine smiled at the couples. "You may now kiss."

The three couples shared a meaningful kiss full of promise and devotion.

"May I present my married daughters and their beautiful wives," Christine said, holding out her hands.

They all turned towards the crowd as applause and whoops rang out and echoed over the water.

"Let's dance," Christine said.

The music started, the bar opened, and the food was ready on the deck.

Their friends and family congratulated the couples as the party began. Each couple had a special song to dance to, but the crowd went wild when they all began to salsa. Vi and Cory had taught them well. After the salsa dance, everyone joined them on the dance floor.

Christine stood alone at the edge of the group and gazed out at all the happy faces. "Oh, honey," she said quietly. "I know you're here with us; I feel you every day. We did the right thing saving that money so they could do this together. Just look at them: CeCe is swooning, Cory is swearing, and our baby, Cat, is swirling in the love we created."

ABOUT THE AUTHOR

Jamey Moody is a bestselling author of sapphic contemporary romance. Her characters are strong women, living everyday lives with a few bumps in the road, but they get their happily ever afters. Jamey lives in Texas with her adorable terrier Leo.

You can find Jamey's books on Amazon and on her website: jameymoody.com

Join her newsletter for latest book news and other fun. Join here.

Jamey loves to hear from readers. Email her at: jamey moodyauthor@gmail.com

On the next page is a list of Jamey's books with links that will take you to their page.

Jamey has included the first chapter of What Now, her bestselling novel with small town charm and a friends to lovers romance that will make you swoon.

Addison Henry is the new bank president in small-town Brazos Falls, but she's headed to the CEO's office. Then she meets Lissa Morgan. She's never been with a woman. She has no time for love. She's on her way to the top. But her heart has another plan. What now?

ALSO BY JAMEY MOODY

Stand Alones

Live This Love

One Little Yes

Who I Believe

* What Now

The Your Way Series:

* Finding Home

*Finding Family

*Finding Forever

The Lovers Landing Series

*Where Secrets Are Safe

*No More Secrets

*And The Truth Is ...

*Instead Of Happy

The Second Chance Series

*The Woman at the Top of the Stairs

*The Woman Who Climbed A Mountain

*The Woman I Found In Me

Sloan Sisters' Romance Series

CeCe Sloan is Swooning

Cory Sloan is Swearing

Cat Sloan is Swirling

Christmas Novellas

*It Takes A Miracle

The Great Christmas Tree Mystery

With One Look

*Also available as an audiobook

CHAPTER 1

"Man, I wish I had a cigarette," Lissa muttered as she got out of her car and walked across the street. *Where did that come from*, she wondered. She walked into the bank trying to figure out why, all of a sudden, she wanted a cigarette. It had been over twenty-five years since she'd lit her last smoke.

She smiled to herself as the reason why became clear in her mind.

"Can I help you?"

Lissa had stopped in front of a woman's desk that was in an open area of the lobby. The sign in front of her simply read Accounts. "I hope so," Lissa replied with a pleasant smile. She looked down at the nameplate on the woman's desk. "Maise, I need to close an account and open a new account."

The woman returned her smile and looked over her shoulder at the offices that formed an L-shape in her area. Lissa figured Maise was the receptionist/assistant/traffic director for this part of the bank.

There were only two main sections of the bank and they

were separated by the counter where tellers were waiting on customers. In a small town, a bank this size offered customer assistance on one side and the other side usually housed the executives that oversaw operations. It had been so long since Lissa had actually come inside the bank that she began to think she was on the wrong side.

"If you'll have a seat." Maise indicated the couch and chairs immediately behind her which were arranged into a makeshift waiting area. "All our account managers are helping customers at the moment. I'll see if I can find someone else to help you."

"Thanks," Lissa said with another smile. She sat down on the end of the couch and let her gaze wander through the offices. The front wall of each office was glass, so anyone in the bank could see what was happening. Each occupant, whether they were an account specialist or something else, did indeed have a customer sitting across the desk from them.

She sat back and let out a deep breath. It wasn't like she was in a hurry. Her thoughts went back to a few minutes ago. The reason she'd thought about smoking a cigarette was because of her brother. That's the reason she was here in the first place. A sad smile played at the corners of her mouth and she was surprised when tears began to sting the back of her eyes.

"Good morning. How can I help you?"

Lissa sat up and quickly blinked before the tears spilled from her eyes.

"I'm sorry, I didn't mean to startle you," the woman said.

Lissa looked up into warm blue eyes that were full of concern. They belonged to a woman who was obviously younger than Lissa, but she stood with an air of authority about her.

"It's okay." Lissa quickly rose to her feet. "I'm waiting for assistance. They're all busy." She smiled and waved her hand at the offices around them.

"I'm not. Come with me," the woman offered and led them through the lobby, past the tellers and over to the other side of the bank. Her dark brown hair swayed just below her shoulders with each step she took. Lissa fell in step behind her and hurried to keep up.

They walked into the president's office and the woman paused at the chairs in front of the desk. She stuck out her hand and smiled. "I'm Addison Henry. Have a seat."

Lissa took the woman's hand and felt the same warmth from earlier when she'd looked into her eyes. "I'm Lissa Morgan."

Addison nodded and went around the large desk and sat down.

"I can wait for someone else," Lissa explained. "You're the president of the bank. I'm sure you have other things to be doing."

Addison smiled. "Every customer is important. What is it you needed help with? Don't you think the president should be able to handle each job at the bank?"

"Hmm," Lissa mused. "I don't doubt your abilities, but I'm guessing it's been a while since you opened a new account."

"Is that why you're here?" Addison gave Lissa a pleasant look.

"I'm here to close an account *and* open a new one."

"Okay. I think I can handle that," Addison said confidently. She turned to her computer and started tapping the keyboard.

Lissa watched her with an amused smile. For someone who gave off such a commanding vibe, there was also an aura of kindness emanating from Addison Henry. Lissa wanted to concentrate on anything other than the reason she was here and Addison was a welcome distraction.

"Could I have the name or number of the account you want to close?" Addison looked at her with a friendly smile.

"Yes." She recited the account number. "It's my brother's account. He died," Lissa stated.

Addison's gaze immediately found Lissa's eyes. "Oh no." She gave her a compassionate look. "That explains why you had such a sad look on your face. I'm so sorry, Lissa."

Lissa smiled. "Thank you. I was thinking about him when all of a sudden there you were."

"I didn't mean to sneak up on you."

Lissa sighed. "Honestly, I was remembering how much he smoked. It's actually what killed him. But the funny thing is..."

Addison raised her brows and waited.

Lissa looked into her eyes and couldn't believe the bank president was not only helping her manage her accounts, but she was also listening to her.

"The funny thing is that when I stepped into the bank I had such a craving for a cigarette. I couldn't understand it since I gave up smoking more than twenty-five years ago. But while I was waiting, it occurred to me that I was thinking of Peter—that's my brother—and he couldn't give them up, like I did." Lissa shrugged. She wasn't sure why she'd shared that story with this woman whom she'd just met. Surely, it had to be the grief.

Addison smiled. "I'm glad you quit."

Lissa chuckled. "You don't even know me."

"Sure I do. You're one of my bank patrons and I'm guessing you've been with this bank for a long time."

Lissa nodded.

"Then I'd like to get to know you better. You want to close your brother's account and what is it you'd like to open?"

"My sister, younger brother, and I have formed a partnership with our family estate. We want to open a bank account in the partnership's name," Lissa explained.

"Okay. What's the partnership name?"

"Uh, MFP," Lissa mumbled.

"MFP?"

"Yeah." Lissa looked down at her hands. "The P stands for partnership."

Addison tilted her head. "And the MF?"

Lissa shrugged. "It's a m-f-ing partnership."

A burst of laughter passed Addison's lips. "Seriously?"

"Yep. The Morgan Family Partnership, but that's not what we call it," Lissa said with a playful smile.

Addison chuckled. "I think I like your family. I have to admit," Addison said softly as she leaned across the desk, "I've never opened an account for a m-f-ing partnership."

Laughter bubbled out of Lissa and it felt so good. "You asked."

Addison joined her laughter. "Indeed I did." She turned back to her keyboard and began to type. "There is a Calista Morgan who can access your brother's account."

"That would be me."

"Calista," Addison repeated the name. "That's unique and beautiful."

Lissa watched her lips as she said her name and liked the way it sounded. *What are you doing?* She chided herself. *The frigging president of the bank is helping you and you're ogling her lips.*

"Uh, my dad named me. It means most beautiful. He said I was the prettiest little thing he'd ever seen."

"Aw, how nice is that!" Addison stopped typing and met Lissa's eyes.

"I'm not sure he felt that way when I hit my teenage years." Lissa chuckled.

Addison chuckled and looked back at her computer.

"I have the documentation to close the account," Lissa said. She slid the papers across the desk to Addison and she picked them up and studied them for a moment.

"Do you want the remaining money in the account in a check or cash?" Addison asked.

"Can you transfer it into the new account?"

"Sure, we can do that." Addison continued to type. She hit a button and the printer on the table behind her desk began to spit out papers. "I'll need your signature and that will close the account."

Lissa signed the paper that Addison handed her and waited as she went back to her computer.

"I need your sister and brother's names for the new account."

"My sister is Marielle Morgan Cooper and my brother is Ben Morgan. I have copies of their driver's licenses." Lissa gave Addison the papers.

"You are prepared." Addison smiled.

"Oh, I've been trying to get this done for a few weeks. I think I finally have all the documentation the bank needs."

"Your sister uses her maiden name as her middle name?"

"Yeah, my parents thought when my sister and I got married we could use our last name as a maiden name so they didn't give us middle names. It worked for my sister, but I've never been married, so it didn't work out like they planned for me."

"Hmm." Addison furrowed her brow. "I'm not married

either and I haven't ever really thought about it. A lot of women use their maiden names as middle names now." Addison went back to her computer and continued to type. "Almost finished."

Lissa shook her head. "I still can't get over the bank president taking care of this for me."

Addison smiled as she clicked her mouse to print the new account paperwork. She turned to Lissa. "I don't get to interact with customers as much as I'd like, so I'm happy to do it."

"Well, you're very good at it and easy to talk to. I can't believe I've been telling you all this."

Addison tilted her head. "I noticed several accounts with Morgan as the last name. I take it you're from here and your family banks here too."

Lissa nodded. "Our family business is Morgan Milling. I haven't always lived here. I came back a few years ago to help out. I'm kind of stuck here now."

"Morgan Milling, is that livestock feed and such?"

Lissa smiled. "That's right. We actually make some of the feed and wholesale others."

"You make feed?"

Lissa chuckled. "No. I leave that to my brother. I take care of the business end of things."

"How interesting. I'm a city girl. Would you give me a tour sometime?"

"I'd be happy to." Lissa smiled and narrowed her eyes. "I have a question for you. Why would a city girl who's not married come to a small town like Brazos Falls, Texas?"

Addison stared at Lissa.

"The people who move here are usually young families that want a small town vibe to raise their kids or they come here to retire. Oh wait, I know."

Addison's expression brightened. "Go ahead."

Lissa leaned back in her chair and studied Addison. "I think you are a star in the financial world and this is just a stop on your way to the top. Eventually, you'll be the CEO of the holding company that owns not only this bank but many others."

Addison chuckled. "From your mouth to the board of the holding company."

"Well, I have a feeling we're lucky to have you here."

"I hope so."

Lissa stood up. "I've taken up enough of your time. Are we finished?"

"If you'll get your brother and sister to sign these forms, they will be able to sign checks and link the business account to their personal accounts."

"Thank you, Addison. It was a pleasure meeting you."

"Do you come in the bank very often?" Addison asked as they walked to the door.

"I use the drive thru or the mobile banking app, but maybe I'll come in more often."

"You'd better come by and say hello then." Addison gently placed her hand on Lissa's forearm.

"Calista Morgan," a woman said as Lissa and Addison stood outside Addison's doorway. "I haven't seen you in forever."

"Hi Karen."

"I was sorry to hear about Peter," Karen replied, holding a stack of file folders to her chest.

"Thanks. I forgot you don't work in the drive-thru any longer. It's nice to see you." Lissa turned to Addison and smiled. "I'd better get back to the mill. Thank you again for helping me."

"I'll be calling you for that tour." Addison returned her smile.

"I hope you do."

Lissa walked away with a smile on her face. Addison Henry would be an asset to this small town. She had certainly made this day a lot better for Lissa.

Get What Now

Printed in Great Britain
by Amazon